Solarian
Chronicles
One

SOLARIAN

CHRONICLES

ONE

by

Michael Bell

EMPIRE STATE FICTION
Monroe, New York
1989

© Copyright 1989
Michael Bell

Printed in the United States of America

All rights reserved. Permission to reprint
or to reproduce in any form must be obtained
in writing from the publisher.

Library Research Associates Inc.
Empire State Fiction
Dunderberg Road
RD#5 Box 41
Monroe, New York 10950

Library of Congress Cataloging-In-Publication
Bell, Michael, 1922-
  Solarian chronicles one / by Michael Bell
198p.   cm.
  ISBN 0-912526-43-2 : $17.95
I. Title II. Title : Solarian chronicles 1.
PS3552.E52115S6   1989   813'.54--dc19 89-30530 CIP

DEDICATION

This book is dedicated
to my wife, June,
without whose help and understandung,
it could not have been written.

CONTENTS

Prologue
The Dreamers   3
The Library: New York City   9
The Library: The Dark Planet   12
The Key   71
Independence   139

PROLOGUE

There has always existed a division between science and religion, creationism and evolution. Science applies logic and a method to prove or to disprove points. Religion applies faith in the written word of the Bible. Science states that man began as an amoeba and evolved to his present condition; religion states that man was created by a superior being called God.

This book will not add to the controversy but will presume a distinct possibility that both positions are right to a point. To say there is no God, that man began as a molecule floating in the vastness of space raises the question, "Where did the molecule come from ?" The big bang theory exists but with no explanation of cause and effect; yet most scientists agree that space was an empty void.

The religious community has faith that mankind was created by a higher intelligence that abides in an undefinable Paradise or "Heaven" which will become eventually man's final home.

Scientists agree this final place exists and call it a "different" dimension. Both agree there are other dimensions in space. Logical religionists agree that

Earth - Mars

man is evolving.

Think of the crew of the U.S.S. Constitution. The average contemporary man could not fit into the space provided for a sailor of 1700. One does not presume that man's intellectual power has increased, but the measurements recorded indicate that man's physical body has grown.

Civilizations are born, flourish and fade away. Some leave no trace. Others are embedded in eternity and contribute to humanity and the dignity of man by fostering the ideals of liberty and freedom.

Americans have generated and supported these ideals and they long to hear words of assurance that they have not sought in vain, the Liberty and Freedom fashioned from the Almighty's handbook and forever nourished by His spirit. But there comes only faintly the occasional whispers of confirmation which are soon lost in the sounds of discontent.

The ideals of the majority of the American people formed by the Declaration of Independence are often distorted by acts of injustice, unkindness and a lack of charity, although some have recognized the biased wrongs and tried to make them right.

The terrible forces facing Americans in this moment of history are no more terrible than we make them. We have unlocked the power of the atom as the Neanderthal Man unlocked the power of fire; as the Paleolithic Man found the power of the bow and arrow; as the Middle Ages man imposed the power of gun powder.

These powers were faced with the belief and fear that all humanity was to be destroyed by them. Man has not, and will not ever, wrest that power from the hand of the Almighty.

Prologue

Take heart; have courage. Think not of power in the context of what it can destory, but of what it can build. Every generation has witnessed that ultimate weapon of power only to realize that it held an empty shallow threat. That which is sought is locked in the mind. Earth is the cradle of the mind, and one cannot live in the cradle forever.

History has been forged from the sweat and blood of heroes, patriots and the common man to form a strong foundation upon which to build human freedom, dignity and progress. Although the past may be prologue, the past, present and the future merge into one. Live in the present, dream of the future and learn eternal truths from the past.

A pervading illusion remains that freedom is free, a costless benefit guaranteed by history to all the virtuous and respectable populace. But freedom is the exception, not the rule, sought by men. The instinct for self development through free choice has always been rooted deeply in the human condition. Freedom is difficult to achieve and more difficult to maintain.

Freedom requires institutions strong enough to continuously persevere, flexible enough to absorb change, resiliant enough to transmit vitality and challenging enough to stimulate creativity.

It requires a varied and subtle discipline. It also demands individual self discipline for freedom emancipates one from external authority and singly concentrates on an obligation of responsibility.

The strain of freedom can become intolerable. To be free is to choose a continuing battle of thought and deed.

To think effectively is to think honestly, soberly,

Earth - Mars

carefully and informatively. Be aware that thought is one thing, but emotional self indulgence is another. Responsible democracy requires that the two never be confused nor misled in the chaotic din raised by the pervayers of indignant and outraged nationalism; righteousness without responsibility.

It is time to venture into the vast frontier of the Solar System. Everyone, from manufacturers to astronauts, must prepare well not to contaminate, physically or culturally, any outer planet. Earth is daily impaired by pollution. Common sense should rid us of the false assumption that freedomto explore is the sole criteria for space exploration.

Responsibility and intelligent imagination are needed. Scientists have rushed to explore space with careless attitudes and inferior equipment in response to the challenges of this vast unknown.

Tons of space junk have been discarded from inoperative vehicles and satellites. Some burned to ashes and gas in the upper atmosphere.

In the 1980s there were scientists astounded by the discovery of a vast hole in the atmosphere over the Arctic regions. They blamed the spray can industry but never mentioned the daily flights of thousands of aircraft at high altitudes and the pollution from discarded space junk.

We must clean our own house before seriously venturing into space. Earth must be maintained as the "home" base, the place to which we return for rest and sustinance. Recorded history has proved that humanity always needs help to survive on earth. Entities from another "dimension" have provided assistance in times of stress, but humans return inevitably to unnatural attitudes and immoral practices.

Prologue

Once again, entities from another dimension are attempting to help humanity. These Chronicles attest to the actions and the results. We, of the past generations, can rest peacefully in our graves while you, of the present generation, can be confident in the growth of true understanding and can look upon the face of God.

Michael Bell
Summer 1989

SOLARIAN
CHRONICLES
ONE

Earth–Mars

THE DREAMERS

The five sat in a circle on the grassy knoll that was part of the forest on the outskirts of St. Louis. They resembled statues. They had not moved for two hours; slowly breathing, eyes half closed, seemingly oblivious of each other. They were the dreamers.

At birth, they had entered the world with the ability to disassociate themselves from reality, while integrating reality into their dreams. It was not an uncommon group for society had labelled the retarded and sent each one, for his own good, to a state institution. They gravitated toward one another. A casual remark made by one would trigger a response in the other by entering his dream. By means not understood by their guardians, they were drawn to one another throughout the years spent in the institution.

They would sit in a circle when permitted and with half-closed eyes they would dream the same dream. Each one took a part of it and formed a series of events that incorporated the past, present and future of the world. Most of the things they dreamed puzzled them, sometimes making them uneasy, but still, they dreamed together perfecting a hologram invisible to everyone but themselves.

Amos had been the oldest of the six in the group, but he had died that year at the age of ninety-two in the middle of one of their dreams. They felt him fade away. There was no pain, just a lessening of the clarity of the dream. They realized the loss, but they were not sorrowful, nor did they mourn.

Earth - Mars

They carefully picked him up and carried him to the valley where the branches of a huge blue spruce swept the ground. They placed him under the branches, covered him with leaves then returned to the knoll to resume dreaming. This time the dream was different and they were startled subconsciously, but physically, they moved not a muscle.

Aulto, Morrey, Zeke, Otto, Amos and Glorene, the only female, left the institution one night after dreaming about brightly colored schools of fish swimming in a large ocean. A few fish strayed from the school and they were eaten by bigger fish swimming nearby.

When they stopped dreaming, they gathered up their meager belongings, walked unobstrusively out of the institution's back door and traveled intuitively to the dreaming place. They knew that it was there and they knew when they arrived, that it was their place. One week later, Amos died and they were starled by the new dream.

An old shack stood behind the knoll, their dreaming place, and they used it for shelter. The well, twenty feet from the front door, supplied drinking water. The dreamers were retarded to the point of not comprehending the practicalities of life. They took turns walking to the nearby village of Rotoville to beg for food. Hunger and thirst were merely necessary incidentals.

Dreaming together was the important focus of their lives and they spent the days, until they were tired, sitting in the circle. They had put Amos in his resting place, begged some food, drank a little water and had fallen asleep. When they awakened, they returned to the circle and were immediately startled.

Amos appeared in the dream, in the midst of the circle yet apparently facing everyone of them. His outline was clear, his milky blue eyes clearly focussed. They waited silently noting the softening of his glance.

He raised his eyes, looking straight upward through the small opening at the treetops. He fixed his gaze on the single star that was shining brightly overhead. This was not the normal dreaming, but they remained seated, watching.

Amos began to glow, an aura of white light changed into colors, circled his head, then travelled the length of his body. He raised his arm and pointed.

A young man, about eighteen years of age, emerged from the trees behind the circle and walked toward them. As the shining faded from Amos, he smiled. The five made room and as he seated himself, Amos disappeared in a flash, streaking upward through the opening in the treetops toward the bright star in the heavens.

This was Peter, known to them as if he had been with them from the beginning. He was retarded and he had the dreaming gift. They were whole again. The six settled comfortably and they dreamed.

Summer turned into autumn; the rains fell and storms lashed the mountains in the winter. They did not get wet, nor hear the thunder, nor feel the winds. Small animals and birds scampered about them. They were not disturbed by noise or weather.

A few Rotoville residents recalled the beggars and feared for their safety. They searched but found nothing. They placed a bag of food on a flat rock at the edge of the woods by the creek where the retarded ones entered the woods. The food was always gone the next morning and they reasoned it was not taken by animals because there were no scraps or torn bags at the site. A few continued, not knowing why they bothered to do so. The beggars weren't their responsibility, but they did it

Earth - Mars

anyway.

The six dreamed of a world that had three pretty moons, one red, one yellow, and the largest colored like a rainbow. There was a vast expanse of water in this other world and fish that flew through the air, fish that walked on the beaches and fish that climbed trees. Large bowlegged lizards shared the tree trunks with fuzzy tree climbers and swingers. The high mountains spewed forth fire and smoke. The ground shook under the heavy-footed running of huge animals. All living things ate vegetation except the fish that ate each other.

The dreaming usually began where it left off, but once the movement stopped. The picture was frozen in time. They sat in the circle with a still life image for uncountable hours. When movement returned, there were two humans walking naked through the forest petting the small animals. Birds perched fearlessly on their bare shoulders and on the palms of their outstretched hands as they laughed, innocently and happily, unaware of their nakedness. They shared berries and ripe fruits of the forest.

A singular tree, standing alone, bore beautiful fruit. The man led the woman away from it, but she persisted, picked one fruit, stroked its smooth skin. Suddenly, she bit into it, tasting a sweetness she had never known. She coaxed the man, who said no, until he wearied and relented. He bit into the fruit. His eyes first widened with astonishment, then shame. Fatigued from the dreaming, the six rested.

When the dreaming continued, the man and woman wore leaves about their waists. Later, they were clothed in animal skins and were sheltered in a hut constructed of mud and grass. In the distance, other huts were visible with people walking among them.

The Dreamers

The beautiful landscape had changed; the land was harsh and unforgiving. Work overcame obstacles and constant physical dangers. Ignorant and unlearned, man developed survival skills in a hostile world. He developed the use of fire, discovered the wheel, invented explosives, explored the mysteries of propulsion that ultimately led to flight, then to flight into space.

The dreamers watched civilization deteriorate through selfish wars that concentrated power and preached security in all things. The spirit in man dwindled as his possessiveness grew. Through neglectful abuse, the land turned barren, unfruitful. Famine and illness laid waste to the people. The few that remained fled in a spaceship to an unknown destiny, to a new world with one white moon overhead that turned yellow when it set on the new horizon.

The landing was rough, one of desperation more than choice. Damaged in the landing, the spaceship became at first a shelter, then was dismantled by the survivors as they utilized pieces and parts for new means to survive.

The dreamers visualized once again the creation of a civilization through work, struggle and sacrifice. With a shared sense of sadness, the saw the same preparations for the utilization of knowledge, the growth of power, the wars, the violence, the technical advances that led to the "new" discovery of space flight and a landing on the one white moon. It was followed by the eager planning for a journey through space and time to a planet called Mars.

The dreaming vanished. They sat for three days without food, with occasional sips of water. The dreams were gone. On the fourth day, a bright light appeared in the center of their circle. It beamed down from the sky overhead, splayed into rays that touched their froeheads. They were unable to move.

Earth - Mars

They saw the Angel wearing a crown of myrrh. The scent filled their nostrils and peace descended upon them. Their minds grew clear and they became aware of all the events in their dreams. They knew now that their minds had become the receptacles of all the knowledge of the the universe.

They shared a short vision of six chairs about a large table holding computer equipment and a large crystal globe, then the Angel and the vision vanished. Their understanding surpassed that of any human beings and they knew they were to be the Chroniclers of the Human Race.

A small pile of the purest diamonds sparkled in the sunlight where the Angel had appeared. They knew they were to convert them to currency to prepare for the project conveyed by the Angel. No longer retarded, but geniuses for theoretical as well as practical purposes, the six dreamers without any reluctance, left the dreaming place and travelled to New York City.

THE LIBRARY: New York City

Merchants were carefully selected in the diamond district. Each was given a message by Glorene.

"We wish you to bid on our merchandise and we will sell to the highest bidder."

Three hours later, eleven merchants met with the six. A black cloth was spread on a small folding table and one diamond was placed in the center of the cloth. The merchants examined the perfect one-carat jewel.

"Gentlemen," said Glorene, "There are ninety-nine more exactly like this one. The highest bidder must take all of them. We will not sell in lots."

The Jewish mercahnts clustered in groups of two and three. The bidding began and when the last bid of four million dollars was made, three merchants had pooled their bids.

"Before the close of the banking day, you must deliver a certified check for that amount. Two of you may remain to examine the rest of the diamonds," Glorene directed with a smile. Two of the bearded diamond dealers sat close to the table and began a minute inspection of the stones. In three hours, the check was in hand and the exchange was made. The diamonds were flawless, the likes of which had not ever been seen by the three dealers.

The next three days were filled with mundane chores. An account was opened; Otto was to find an apartment and furnish it with the barest necessities; information concerning stockbrokers and corporate reports were

Earth - Mars

gathered and studied. The six decided on an elderly, experienced broker to handle their transactions.

In the apartment, the six chairs and the round table had a familiar look. They seated themselves and concentrated, purging their minds of extraneous thoughts. Collectively, they soared through the solar system, communicating mentally, seeking an outer world in which to establish their new headquarters, The Library.

They found a black shape that reflected no light; an undiscovered planet that travelled on an elliptical orbit between Jupiter and Saturn. The nearest arc of the elliptic was between the two known planets and the farthest one was one light year away from the sun. Thus, the size of the Solar System in their records was changed to one light year across.

They approached the planet and observed with their minds that it was obsidian. The surface was smooth, but broken into planes separated by ridges of mountains and valleys that were glasslike in appearance. Mentally, the six experienced a force tugging at them, a slight pushing and pulling, an external force exerting pressure.

For two days they studied the dark planet then mutually agreed that it was a fitting location. They selected a place to build a structure in an area between two mountains that measured two square miles. When the decision was made, they returned to their physical state and slept from sheer exhaustion.

Weeks stretched into months as the planning was organized into a procedure. Otto worked closely with John Whitcombe, the broker, as they increased their holdings many times over. When the monetary goal of three hundred million dollars was reached, John Whitcombe received his handsome commisiion and retired with no memory of the six as individuals nor of their transactions.

The Library

Aulto and Peter were in charge of engineering the construction and of writing specifications for the materials and tools needed to work on the Dark Planet. Morrey and Zeke became their purchasing agents, often seeking little known equipment or having tools designed and produced by puzzled, but highly paid, manufacturers.

Glorene became coordinator and trouble-shooter; researching companies and materials, finding suppliers and transporters, handling financial arrangements expeditiously and quietly.

A large solar freighter was purchased and docking space rented at the space port. Commercial space contracts were already common and few questions were asked outside of proof of resources. They were accepted as a conglomerate speculating on space trade development.

The space freighter was loaded but they could see that it would demand two trips to deliver the necessary supplies and equipment to last two years in space. Two large antennas and three dome machines were the last items to be stowed within the freighter.

The space pilot was schooled to plot the orbit of the Dark Planet so that at any given time he could locate them. Otto decided to stay behind on the first trip as it was impossible to settle every item until the second trip was at hand. This was their first separation and he was not happy about it.

"Someone has to remain," Glorene told him, "and you are the most knowledgeable about our financial transactions."

"I don't have to like it,: Otto replied. "I'm going to purchase some very expensive transmission equipment so that I can contact the space pilot during the trip. Then, you can use it to contact him when he leaves you."

They nodded in agreement. "Good," said Peter, "If

11

Earth - Mars

we need anything, we can let him know."
   One week later, Otto accompanied them to the Space Port. He felt a great sense of loss as the space freighter lifted off and moved away from him.

THE LIBRARY: The Dark Planet

   The Dark Planet was at the edge of the known Solar System as they made their approach. Completing one orbit around the planet, they found the chosen site and landed without difficulty on the small plane at the foot of the mountain. Donning space suits, the space pilot opened the hatch. They felt a heavy pressure on all sides as Glorene stepped down.
   "Don't come!" she called out. Her feet did not rest on the surface. "Some force is holding me off the obsidian plane." She paced a few steps awkwardly. "Morrey, get me the magnometer."
   He switched it on and handed it to her. "This place is just one big magnet." The needle had snapped to the far positive. She switched it to negative and was immediately pulled over as the magnometer was pulled to the surface. "It must be loaded with black iron oxide or magnetite."
   "I've got an idea," Zeke said. He unpacked space walking boots that every ship carried for making exterior repairs. "See if these work," he told Glorene.
   Glorene changed boots; when she lowered her foot to the planet surface, it stuck just like walking on the hull of a ship. "Good idea. Now, let's get to work."
   The Dark Planet was approximately the same size as

The Library

Mars., so the gravity factor was not a great concern as they unloaded the dome equipment and returned to the ship for tools.

Zeke laughed aloud. "Look at the blasted boxes! They're floating in air. Is this going to work?"

They removed the solar generator from its carton, attached it to the projector and set them both on the flat surface. "How about that? asked Morrey. He activated the projector and they immediately were surrounded by the very large dome. "The molecular structure of the dome has assumed the same magnetic pole as the generator." They placed the remaining dome generators and activated them. "They stick like glue."

Returning from the ship with supplies, they found that nothing would set firmly on the surface, but rather, floated an eighth of an inch above it. They lined up the crates against each other and placed a space boot at each end to block movement. Glorene made a note to have magnets added to the list for the second shuttle trip. With the unloading accomplished, they settled in the domes. The space pilot was given instructions for additional supplies of a high priority. Then, they watched the space ship lift off.

"Look at the bottom of the ship!" Aulto exclaimed. "It's set in angled planes, rather than rounded!"

"You're right," Zeke said thoughtfully. "They are exactly like the surface he set the ship on."

Suddenly, there was a series of snaps that sounded like rifle shots from the dome. As they turned quickly, the domes were no longer rounded, but had become small rectangular planes. They remained the same size, but the exteriors had changed geometrically.

"We shall have to solve problems as they arise," Glorene siad. "Obviously, our studies of this planet did

Earth - Mars

not reveal everything. Let's set up the radio transmitter."

They asembled the component parts and tested it by calling the space ship. Transmission was perfect. They next assembled the powerful laser drilling machine. The plans marked off the mountain, located its center and notched cuts to be made to reach the core.

The laser cut into the obsidian rather easilty, but created considerable smoke. They measured and cut a square entrance and it shifted instantly to a series of small planes. The drilling continued until a ten-foot space was carved and they learned to wait for the resetting of the angles between drillings. The smoke billowed out of the hole.

Standing outside, Aulto observed that the smoke did not rise but rolled along the surface and drifted over the edge of a plane. It disappeared in a downward flow.

"How peculiar," he thought. "I wonder where it is going." He walked to the edge of the plane which was the lip of a cliff. The black smoke was settling at the bottom of the cliff and changing immediately into planed black boulders. He went back to the drilled opening and called to the others who walked with him to the cliff edge to see the transition.

"Let's go back to the dome and take off these suits. I think we should discuss this."

They sat in their circle. "The further we drill into the mountain, the less chance the smoke will have to escape and drift over the cliff. Is this a problem?" Peter asked. "But the smoke does not change until it hits the bottom of the cliff. Is the strata at the bottom affecting the smoke? Or does it take a certain amount of time to change."

"The smoke touches the tunnel roof and does not change. It drifts down the side of the cliff and it doesn't change," said Aulto. "It didn't change color or become thicker or thinner, but it did roll in that direction without any wind."

Zeke stood at the dome entrance looking at the stars. "It can't be sun activated," he said. "The sun is on the other side of the planet."

"I suggest that we get on with our work," Peter said. "We should try to get to the top of the mountain to set up the large antennae so we can receive from all over the solar system. We know we can drill to the center of the mountain without any danger, but we must see if this magnetic giant will interfere with long range radio transmissions. "

"I agree," Glorene said. "We must have full communication with the space ship and we should test our reception capabilities as it gets further away. Let's postpone drilling and get the antennae set up."

Zeke and Aulto each wrapped two thousand feet of thin nylon rope over their shoulders and tied an extra pair of space boots to their waists. It was fairly easy to climb the mountain as the gravity was approximately one third that of earth and the magnets on their boots kept them from slipping. When they reached the summit, they dropped one boot with the nylon rope tied to it and of the four thousand feet of line, about fifty feet was left.

Peter and Morrey had assembled the one hundred fifty foot high antennae made of a very strong aluminum alloy. Zeke and Aulto pulled it slowly up the side of the mountain and raised it on a flat plane, but it would not stand. Zeke muttered in exasperation, "What do we do now? "

Aulto snickered and removed the pair of space boots from his waist. He placed them on the ends of the legs of the antennae and then did the same with the pair that Zeke had. The magnetic soles held firmly.

Earth - Mars

"That will do," he laughed, "until the magnets arrive on the next trip." They uncoiled the antennae wire and lowered it to the three below, then began their descent.

The radio transceiver equipment was a special narrow beam transmitter and resceiver locked on to one very high frequency. The only one that could use it was the space ship locked into the same frequency. Peter, Morrey and Glorene connected the wires and called the space ship. The pilot answered immediately.

"I've been monitoring this frequency for the past two days," he said. "I was afraid something had happened to you. When I landed at the Space Port, the authorities wanted to know what had happened to the ship's hull. I told them I didn't know and that their guess was as good as mine. I didn't hit anything and nothing hit me. We sure have some people confused here. How are thing's going?"

"We have a few problems, but nothing serious," Peter replied. Then he gave a list of supplies to bring on the next trip including a complete laboratory. "And don't forget the magnets!"

"Gotcha. By the way, when I entered the earth's atmosphere, there was a loud boom and a flash of light. I think it was the discharge of the induced magnetism from the Dark Planet. I thought I'd blown up. We have to find a way to discharge it before landing."

"Okay," Peter said, "But right now, we need those supplies as quickly as possible."

On a rest break, Zeke and Aulto had taken the nylon ropes and rappelled down the cliff to investigate the smoke boulders and the strata on the bottom.

"Morrey," Aulto said, "these boulders don't look the same as the rest of the planet. They are black and they are planed but the texture is different." They kept their

The Library

distance. "Let's swing to the other side, but avoid landing on them or too near to them."

Four feet from the smoke boulders, they discussed all the possibilities but came to no conclusion.

"We are working with too many unknowns," Aulto said as he reached forward and rubbed his fingertip on one of the rocks. The instant he touched it, the smoke boulder flashed into a fine line of black powder that disappeared toward the sun. They reared back, astounded and frightened, clambered up the cliff with their ropes and returned to the domes.

Glorene was angry. "That was a foolish thing to do! You might have been hurt! We must do the exploring together."

The six went to the cliff edge. Peter and Glorene rappelled down to the pile of boulders and when Glorene cautiously reached out and touched one rock, it snapped into an ash and disappeared. They could find no cause and no explanation.

Later, seated in their circle, they plumbed the depths of their subconscious knowledge for an explanation, but none came. They only knew that there should be no residue at the site of the library created by their labors. They had only to touch the residue and it would disappear.

As they cut into the obsidian mountain, the smoke billowed out as before, but after a twelve hour shift with the laser, one of them would descend to remove the smoke boulders.

They had cut a large central room ninety feet high and fifty feet square, then they cut smaller rooms at levels of four feet. There were no pressure problems as long as the surfaces were cut in straight lines. Sitting in the center of the great hall at a meal break, Glorene jumped to her feet.

Earth - Mars

"Do you recall the last thing we saw when the angel was last with us?" she exclaimed.

"Of course," Peter answered. "It was a table holding computer terminals with a large crystal ball in the center."

With no clear idea as to why it was necessary, they fashioned an obsidian table from their collective memory. The material seemed to have a mind of its own, for when they shaped one angle, another appeared. They worked and watched in amazement. The finished product was an exact duplicate of the one that had appeared in the dreaming place.

The space ship delivered equipment and supplies, including the computer terminals and the crystal globe for the obsidian table. Arrangements were completed to return every six months with food, water and supplies until their reservoir and storerooms were full.

In the main room, they set up the most sophisticated computer system in the galaxy adding their own innovations.

There was just room enough for six input terminals and six leather chairs. The sixth terminal was reserved for Otto, cut off from the other five. It was utilized for necessary personal arrangements with the earth station. An antenna had been erected on the second mountain. Wires were replaced with solar batteries operated on thin laser beams.

They were ready.

Antennae were turned to the receiving antennae of Moon Central and to Space Coordinating Center. Everything transmitted everywhere within the solar system was recorded in the automated library.

Otto vacated the apartment, packed his few simple belongings and boarded the space ship. His arrival on the Dark Planet completed the circle.

Drilling continued into the obsidian mountain. Cubicles were fashioned to store thousands of computer

18

The Library

tapes: all of the knowledge acquired in the course of human progress.

****

They were awakened late into their sleep time. Their unconscious minds snapped them awake and urged them to the obsidian table. When seated, they turned on the computer and sat waiting. The round crystal began to glow and they fell into the dream state. The Angel appeared. "Record what you see," the Angel instructed, "and make it part of the record." The vision vanished.

The planet Earth came into view then focused on springtime scene. It shifted from various groups of people as flowers bloomed and trees sprouted fresh green leaves. The snow and ice on stream banks melted while squirrels and chipmunks scampered within blossoming meadows. This new season brought a special consciousness; a glad-to-be-alive feeling that pervaded the groups of pro-abortionists, anti-abortionists and pro-choice groups. Letters and telephone calls were exchanged between groups with a peculiar lack of invective. Essentially, they were saying to each other, "Let's talk."

The National Right To Life Committee, the National Pro-Life Action Committee, the Religious Coalition for Abortion Rights, the National Abortion Rights Committee and splinter factions of all degrees joined in the communication, including the respected members of the Supreme Court. It was agreed that a Great Convention would be held. It was a mix of oil and water for the representative of each group held a firm conviction that would not, under any circumstances, be changed.

One thousand delegates filed into the San Francisco meeting hall. Tables and chairs were positioned for

Earth - Mars

private discussions. Each group appointed a speaker and lots were drawn to establish the roster of presentations of particular points of view on the subject of abortion.

There were opinions concerning population explosion, the unmarried teenager, welfare rolls, physically and mentally defective infants, the right to kill and who would bear the responsibility for the killing. The problems were classed as economical, medical, psychological and moral.

How could the government bear the expense of providing services? Where and how would institutions set procedures for mass slaughter? Who would treat the trauma of the raped and the indigent poor? What legal standing would either party have in the cases where a woman chose to be a single parent or chose abortion without the man's consent? What human gods would overrule a woman's decision to do as she pleases with her own body? The discourses became debate among those drawn together by the issues of abortion but a sense of wellbeing pervaded the atmosphere. The scent of spring wafted across the hall on the cool waves blown from the air conditioning system. A sense of rebirth converted strident argument into stumbling uncertainty; a glad-to be-alive feeling silenced the conventioneers as they searched their consciences.

A curly-headed blond young man in a light blue suit strode to the podium. "What I have to say will take only a few moments," he announced. His voice spread from the loudspeakers, intruding and insidiously breaking the communicative silence.

"I represent all of you," he told them. "If you stop and think about it, all your views are right. Who are the authorities to tell you what you can or cannot do with your bodies? You do as you please. Who are the authorities to tell you that you cannot control your own destiny? They are your servants! Who is to say what taxes pay for abortion? Taxes must be spent for the welfare of the poor regardless of allocation.

Twenty million of you are in the abortion battle in one manner or another. That's a lot of taxes! Many anti-abortionists agree with capital punishment. What difference does it make whether killing takes place in the womb or in the electric chair? Many pro-abortionists believe in sustaining life at any cost. What difference does it make whether killing takes place in the womb or in the form of euthanasia?" He smiled a thin smile.

"Life cannot bring itself into the world; only a mother can do that. She has the right to determine whether or not she wishes to do so. Scientists and theologians cannot tell you when life begins, so why argue? If you want to have an abortion, do so. If you do not, then take your chances in this toxic, dangerous world of bearing a defective child."

He stepped down. There was a moment of stunned silence, then the crowd rose in a standing ovation. He strode through the hall amidst the applause, people reaching out to shake his hand and to pat him on the back as he went by and walked out the door. The questions flooded the air.

"Who was that? What group is he with? Didn't that make a great deal of sense?" Everyone agreed. Some ran outside to call him back but the blond young man was nowhere to be seen. In the ensuing chatter of a thousand voices, the hall suddenly went dark. No one spoke as a soft light appeared that turned into a rainbow over the rostrum showing an ovoid with a head plainly discernable. A flash of light enveloped the form and the fetus took shape.

As a scalpel thrust through the sack and then

Earth - Mars

systematically cut the fetus into small pieces, it squirmed and writhed but to no avail. A light flashed and the form was still, offering no resistance. There was blood. The audience was sickened; attempting to close their eyes, turning away their heads from the hologram. They gasped with relief when the it was done and a new form came into view.

An egg was developing. They watched in awe, when suddenly a long needle three times pierced the ovoid. Blood spilled and the egg collapsed. Caught by surprise, viewers gagged and wept.

Weakness pervaded their limbs; some wanted to rise and run from the hall but could not raise the strength to do so. Their eyes were riveted on the spot where the holograms had appeared. With great horror, they saw a new scene emerge that raised disgust to hysteria.

Hands, legs, heads, chunks of unidentifyable flesh rose in a huge mound. Blood flowed from the hologram to the floor and spread through the hall. People raised their feet, pulled up trousers and skirts stricken with fear and nausea.

In the center of the mound appeared a face distorted with a terrible rage. It brought with it, the sweet, acrid small of death. The voice was fierce, a whisper and thunder.

"Just as you are, these are my children! What have you done?"

The face, the bodies and the blood disappeared and the audience was released from the weakening immobility, psychologically and emotionally empty. They felt drawn to one another by the shared experience, comforting the hysterical, consoling the weeping and helping those physically ill; yet, always turning their eyes to the source in disbelief and fear.

The Library

Just as order and reason began to return, the walls of the hall began to dissolve. Cringing in obedience, one thousand people accepted their places in a grey fog of nothingness. Gradually, the fog lifted and they realized the vastness of the Cosmos with beautiful, glittering stars about them.

They beheld the earth as they had never imagined it, lush forests and hordes of blossoms. There were cities thay had never dreamed, shining in a clear sweet atmosphere. There were no trains, automobiles, airplanes; no ships at sea. They observed one place where an interstellar vehicle rose slowly and disappeared into the darkness of space.

An angellic voice softly told them there was no crime and no reason for it. One after another, a thousand worlds were shown where mankind was learning and growing. Then there was a view of the Cosmos that mankind had not yet reached. The hologram was replaced by the vision of the Angel who had been speaking.

"That is where you should have been, but you destroyed the intelligence that would have made it possible." The Angel faded from view.

Pale-faced and shaken, the Abortion Conventioneers returned to their hotel rooms, boarded their planes and trains, drove their cars to their homes. The following day, every organization's office was flooded with resignations.

****

The crystal globe darkened and the six switched the terminals to the main frame quietly waiting until all was transferred. Sadly, they had witnessed similar events in their collective dreams. Their mission of recording human events now included the history of any living or non-

Earth - Mars

living sentient entities that they might encounter in the universe. It was no small task.

While recording pre-twenty-second century developments, they were simultaneously recording present activities. They doubled efforts to streamline the efficiency of the operation in both the input and the preservation of the library system. During the next planning session, the six sensed the Presence before the crystal glowed with its acknowledgment. They seated themselves at the terminals and the globe became a visual transmitter of the U.S. Supreme Court planning an agenda for the next session.

The Chief Justice led small talk about affairs of little import as the Justices settled comfortably in leather chairs. They were in office for life and their salaries could not be reduced which created a pomposity which fostered inertia. They seldom sought decisions, but waited until a question of constitutionality was raised. Secure in their situation, life was as good as it could be.

The long mahogany table was polished to a mirror-like finish, the crystal chandeliers hung in the proper places at the proper heights permitting the most myopic of them to read the briefs, petitions and legal documents before them. Here, they discussed their opinions of the constitutionality of law; the final opinions were written in chambers.

Every member arrived fully robed. A feeling of anticipation swept over them. They were waiting uncomfortably without an obvious reason. Quiet descended; the street noises faded; the desultry talk ceased; the rustling of robes was stilled.

Suddenly, above their heads, white-centered lights with colored rays streaming from them appeared. The moving orbs circled the room with increasing speed until they merged into one circular line that closed over the center of the table. The Justices sat frozen in their chairs.

An Angel appeared in the center of the circle and each Justice was sure that he was the one whom it faced.

"I am Raphael from the Most High. Do you not remember the rebuke He gave to the Scribes and the Pharisees in ancient times? You conspire with the Dark One to heap upon the people greater burdens than they heap upon themselves! You have done to the people that which He said He would not do! Do you consider yourselves higher than the Most High? In your desire to create equality under the law, you have stepped beyond it. Cultural change cannot be legislated nor enforced.

Where is the free will promised to mankind? Can your decisions enforce the law - Love ye one another? Are not the words *All men are created equal* enough for the schools and the churches?

The scribes of ancient times passed laws of restriction, laws of mandatory action, which were approved by the Sadducees. Have you done differently? Laws of desegregation caused shock and trauma for the children it was supposed to protect. Would it not have been wiser to mandate the brotherhood of mankind?

The ones you would make legally equal are the ones you forced to be more than equal, creating a greater inequality than existed before. Have you learned nothing?

Your attention to trivial questions has aided and abetted the Dark One in his insidious maneuverings. You approve the slaughtering of unborn innocents, yet waver on the issue of capital punishment. In the matter of fornication you have assumed the responsibilty for immorality by inhibiting inherent human conscience. You have ruled in favor of lewdness and pornography. He that sells the seed is responsible for the crop although he may not do the planting!

Earth - Mars

There is more to the law than words; there is the spirit of the law."

The Angel faded from sight. Confounded by the vision, the Chief Justice spoke softly. "Let us retire to chambers."

Outside the Supreme Court building, the sidewalks were filled with people hurrying to their destinations. One woman stood on a corner handing out small pamphlets to passersby, but she was mostly ignored. Those who accepted the pamphlet would discard it after five or six steps.

Sarah was tired. Most of the time she went to the bus terminal, the train station and the airport. That morning the group-coordinator had said,

"We have to stand up for our rights. We are not second-class citizens."

Sarah had never thought about it one way or another. No one had ever told her she was less than anyone else, but if the coordinator said it was necessary to hand out pamphlets, she wanted to help.

Walking beside a concrete wall with a high scrolled ironwork fense embedded in it, she stopped for a minute, then sat on the edge of the wall. Her feet were swollen; she had a run in her stocking. Altogether, she didn't give a hoot if the world considered her a second-class citizen because she was a woman. She longed for the luxury of stretching in a hot bath and not thinking about anything.

Sarah was a pretty girl with brown shoulder-length hair. She stood five feet three inches and weighed one hundred and twenty pounds. She had a mind of her own and believed that she had a right to choose what happened to her own body. She was going to have an abortion. It wasn't really her fault as the pills she had taken had not worked, although she had lived for three years with her young man and had no problems before now.

The Library

At a job interview, on discovering her pregnancy, she was told there were others to interview and she knew what that meant.

The doctor at the walk-in clinic had agreed she was about six weeks along and asked her if she wanted to have the baby. She had said,

"Oh,no! It can't be! What will he say?"

The doctor asked who "he" was; she knew the doctor was thinking about who would pay the bill. She didn't answer but walked dazedly out. A woman dressed in slacks stopped her outside.

"I am a member of the the National Organization for Women. You've just been given some news that doesn't sit well with you. I'm going for coffee. Would you like to join me and talk about it?"

Over coffee, they talked about how women were underpaid in the job market; how bosses considered them fair game; how men were always promoted over women; how women always carried the burden and paid the price for making love.

"There's no reason for you to carry the burden or pay the price. Having an abortion is a simple thing, nothing to worry about."

Sarah looked at this woman with short-cropped hair and a square chin.

"Isn't it expensive?" Sarah asked.

"Not at all," the woman replied."It's over in fifteen minutes or less. And if you are unemployed you qualify for government aid as this state has a law of abortion on demand." She also intimated that if Sarah joined their organization and worked to further the cause of women, they would be able to help her. Sarah agreed to think it over and give the woman a call.

When Sarah told him of her pregnancy, he was

Earth - Mars

furious. "How could you get yourself caught? Didn't you take your pills?" On and on, then he suggested she get an abortion as quickly as possible. "You can't afford a kid and besides, that's not what I bargained for."

In the following week, Sarah cried, but he was firm. Abortion was the only answer. Sarah contacted the woman who headed the local pro-abortion group, or was it the right-of-choice group? Sarah was confused and undecided; the pressure was too great. He was on one side with the group and on the other side was her maternal instincts. She felt it wasn't right, but she finally agreed to have the abortion and to help the cause.

At first, her tasks in the office were sweeping up and little go-fer jobs, then they had given her a bag full of pamphlets to distribute. Sarah didn't mind; it gave her a sense of purpose. She read one of the pamphlets and it said that she had the right to decide for herself whether or not she would have the baby. She considered all the trouble she was encountering from him and she made up her mind to have the abortion. She told the coordinator and asked if she would help with the arrangements.

"Go to the clinic where you were examined," she was told, "and the same doctor will do the abortion for you."

Sarah handed out her last pamphlet, checked in at the office, then went home determined to get things back to normal again.

That night she told him what she had decided and he became tender and solicitous all evening. He had won, but she didn't care for it was better than the constant bickering.

The next morning Sarah arrived at the clinic in a highly nervous state. The nurse gave her a shot to calm her as she laid on the cold white table. That was the last thing she remembered until she regained consciousness.

The Library

The nurse was standing beside the table and asked her if she felt alright.

"I have a stomach ache," Sarah told her.

"That will go away after awhile," the nurse replied. "The doctor said you should take these pills and come back in three days. Let's see you stand up now."

Sarah stood beside the table, feeling weak but able to take a few steps. She sat in the waiting room thinking she wasn't as strong as she had thought, but then she slowly walked out the door and hailed a cab, the first one she had taken in a long time. Feeling weak and tired, she went straight to bed when she arrived at home and immediately fell asleep and never awakened.

When he came home from work he found Sarah's body and telephoned the doctor, who told him to call the coroner. Sarah was quietly buried.

****

The crystal darkened and the Angel appeared to them. The Angel spoke but it's lips did not move. Each of the dreamers heard the voice inside themselves.

"Return after twelve hours. I shall not appear until the transition. Return to your dreaming; pay close attention to the occurances so that they will be recorded correctly."

The Angel disappeared. The six prepared their favorite food and placed it with a pitcher of water near the computer station. They went to their couches and slept soundly for exactly twelve hours. When they arose, they sat at the round table and went immediately into the dream state. The crystal glowed.

The scene was of the mid-west farmlands; miles of open flat land planted with crops. The Grange meeting was

Earth - Mars

usually held on the third Wednesday evening of the month, but this month it was the second Thursday. Henry Cooper, president of the local Grange for thirty years, made the first change that anyone could remember. The members who received notices went about their farming chores with a good deal of muttering that it was not right to change things without a vote. Old Hank must be up to something, they agreed. "It ain't natural to change tradition without a durn good reason." The men usually made a night of it. After the business meeting and the County Agent's talk (through which many of them dozed), they would sip a little from the refreshment bar and play cards. The talk would be about farming; crops, pigs, cows, horses, chickens, prices and the weather.

The history of the Grange, officially titled the Patrons of Husbandry, is one of the greatest farmers' organizations in the United States. After the Civil War, the GRange grew to represent national agricultural interests. It cooperated with the Federal Bureau of Agriculture and with state departments to disseminate farm education.

Henry hated to call the meeting when he did, but the State Committee had received notice from the National Committee to have the meeting on that particular day at that particular hour with the county and local clergy invited as honored guests by the Chaplin. The County Agent said he would attend but that he had no additional information to discuss.

Henry was not a poor man, but then he wasn't rich either. He owned two thousand acres of the best farmland in the county and raised wheat, corn, barley and alfalfa every third year. The other two years, federal subsidies paid him not to plant in order to maintain market price levels for those who did grow farm products to make a profit.

The Library

Henry did not like to not grow crops when he had the machinery and the land to do so. He would wander over his ywo thousand acres with his hands in his pockets, kicking clods of dirt, looking at the sky automatically to see if there were rain clouds, even though it made no difference to him.

Once in awhile, to show the irony of not planting, he would plant a huge flower bed somewhere within his two thousand acres. When they were in bloom, he would sit at the edge of the field on the fence and laugh.

During one of these times of rebellion, the air in front of Henry shimmered and the far side of the field wavered and rolled like waves on the beach. Henry rubbed his eyes, looked again, but the shimmering was still there. He stuck out his hand to see if it was a fluke heat wave, but it didn't feel any different than when he had his hand at his side. The shimmering disappeared and suddenly, someone was sitting beside him on the fence. Henry jumped off the fence and landed about four feet away.

He looked at the stranger. "Where in tarnation did you come from? " he asked. The stranger was dressed in coveralls, straw hat, heavy shoes and had the hands of a laborer. He didn't quite look like a farmer, nor did he look like an ordinary farm hand. His eyes were a piercing pale blue and seemed to look right through Henry.

"Come back here and sit," he said." Makes no difference where I come from; it's where we are going that counts."

"I ain't going anyplace," Henry said as he returned and sat beside the stranger on the fence.

"Worried 'bout the meeting you called for the Grange?"

"You bet I am,"Henry replied. "I got a funny feeling about it; ain't a good feeling, ain't a bad feeling.Just a feeling I ain't had before."

Earth - Mars

The stranger laughed. "You love this land, don't you?"

"Yep."

"Well, suppose you let me talk and you listen, then I will take you on a little trip. It won't last long; just a few minutes, and you won't even have to leave the place where you're sitting."

"You been drinking?" asked Henry

The stranger laughed again. "No," he said. "You sowed those flower seeds in your little garden. Your small rebellion against practical reality? Look at them now. "

The seeds shot into full grown flowers with perfect blooms and twice as tall as Henry had ever seen.

Henry became apprehensive."I just put them seeds in the ground this morning! Say, who are you? Better yet, what are you?" Once again Henry was four feet away from the fence. "You one of them magic fellas?" he asked with a scowl.

"No magic," the stranger replied. "I just speeded nature up a little. Who I am is not important; what I am might help you to understand." The stranger was suddenly clothed in shimmering white garments with beautiful wings whose tips touched over his head.

Henry was a church-going farmer but he didn't put too much stock in Bible thumping and bellering that went on Sundays, so he usuually managed to get a little snooze. But like most farmers, he understood nature and believed there must be someone or something that made things grow, but this was different.

"You an Angel?"

"Yes, I am. But this is not my real form. I look this way because man imagines me to be this way." The column of air around him shimmered."This is my real form" the Angel said. Instantly an Atom appeared with whirling electrons and protons and neutrons in combinations never

The Library

seen on earth. Henry wasn't a coward, but he started to run away. A voice called to him, "Henry! There is nothing to fear."

Henry looked over his shoulder. The stranger was sitting on the fence. Henry walked back saying, "You the same thing as those other things or am I getting too much sun?"

"I am the same. I just wanted you to know who I am. I have a message for you to pass on to the other farmers at the meeting."

"Okay," Henry said. "But you sure do scare the dickens out of a man."

Henry settled on the fence and the Angel began to speak. "I want you to close your eyes and think about the county; the entire county. Imagine that you are looking down on it from the clouds."

Henry closed his eyes and immediately he seemed to be sitting beside the stranger on a fence between two large clouds. The Angel gestured with a hand and a white line outlined the county. Within the outline, blue lines appeared.

"This shows how many crops were produced three years ago." About one third of the county turned blue.

"This shows last year." About one half turned blue.

"This shows this year." About one half turned blue. "All the black spaces are the lands that could have produced food but did not.

"I know," Henry said. "We can't plant all the land. We won't be paid enough to be able to plant next year. The government pays us not to plant; that's easy money."

"Is it easy money, Henry? If it is, why do you walk through your fallow fields? Why do you plant flowers in your two thousand acres? Is the money easy, Henry, when you see this?"

33

Earth - Mars

The Angel showed Henry masses of children and the elderly of foreign countries that were starving; hollow eyes dull with loss of hope, bloated stomachs, skin-covered bones, swollen joints, sickness and death, piles of bodies that no one had strength to bury.

"The wheat and barley that you do not grow would feed them and their livestock. It would help them to help themselves. The Most High gathered together in this great land the different children that he scattered at the Tower of Babel, but the purpose has been lost in the chaos of greed and selfishness. If the great purpose of this land is not regained, the world will be the loser, as will the solar system, the galaxy, the cosmos."

"I think I see what you mean," Henry said.

"Humanity is the seed the Most High planted on this planet. Can you imagine one planet to which man can travel without learning about his own? Or will all of you find only more emptiness than you already feel?"

"What can I do about it?" Henry asked helplessly. "I am only one farmer in one county in one state and there are forty-nine other states. I can talk to the men at the meeting tonight, but those farmers being paid by the government will think I am out of my mind and throw me out."

"Henry, you don't care about the selfish ones or the lazy ones. There are many who love the land as you do and all they need is a push. Besides, you are not alone. There are Angels talking to every Grange leader in the United States just as I am talking to you. I suggest, Henry, that you read the parable of the mustard seed. It may help you to do what you think is best."

Henry turned to reply and he found himself all alone sitting on his fence on the edge of his two thousand acres.

The Library

"Well, I'll be plowed and planted," he muttered. "If that don't beat all. I must have dozed off, but that sure was one heck of a dream!" Easing himself off the fence, he caught sight of the flower bed and walked to it to get a closer look. "By golly! That sure was no dream!"

The flowers were taller than he had ever seen and the blossoms were twice the normal size. As Henry strolled around the bed, the petal-laden plants seemed to lean toward him. Henry shoved his hands deeply into his pockets and walked slowly toward the house, deep in thought.

He was quiet during supper and when his wife spoke to him, she got a grunted answer. She thought something was bothering him, but held her tongue, knowing he would tell her about it when he had it worked out. When she cleared the table, Henry helped her carry the dishes to the kitchen. She knew then that it was no small problem.

"Grange meeting tonight?" she asked.

"Yump. Gonna be a big one; lots of arguing."

"Trouble?"

"No, not trouble; 'cepting with some. Gotta change things and most ain't gonna like it."

"Can I help?" she asked.

"Not afore; after, maybe." He put the last dish in the sink, grasped her shoulders in his big hands and looked into her eyes. "Yep. After, you can be a big help. I gotta go now. Be home as soon as I can."

The clergy was already there when Henry arrived at the Grange Hall, huddled together in a corner, talking earnestly, but Henry couldn't quite hear. Henry went about his duties; set up the podium, arranged the chairs, set out pencils and paper as he had done a thousand times. But tonight the chores seemed more important. A clergyman turned to him and called out.

Earth - Mars

"Henry, could we talk to you a little before the meeting?" Henry sauntered over.

"Sure," he said as they moved apart to let him have a seat. He had been busy with his own thoughts and was now surprised to see that these were not local clergy but included a bishop or two from a county away. "What can I do for you?"

"We would like to speak at the meeting tonight; not to give blessings or to call down help with the crops. We mean to speak plainly about farm subsidies which are of great importance to farmers."

Henry was taken aback and blurted out, "Did you see him too?"

"See who? What are you talking about, Henry?"

Henry caught himself. "Nothing; nothing. Just some stranger I was talking to this afternoon." He was saved from further explanation by the arrival of the County Agent and other farmers who filed in making thumps on the pine floor with their heavy shoes, clad in overalls, chattering about things farmers hold dear; slapping some on the back whom they had not seen for awhile. The County Agent immediately sought out Henry.

"Evenin', your Excellencies," he greeted the clergy. "Henry, can I speak to you for a minute?"

"Sure, Paul, be right there. Excuse me, gentlemen," he said to the Bishops. "What's up, Paul? You look like storm clouds."

"Henry, after you open the meeting, I have some official news. Can you call on me before anyone else? It's important."

"I'll just do that," agreed Hnery. He walked to the podium, banged the gavel a few times and the audience grew quiet.

"Men, the County Agent, Paul Cramer, who you all

The Library

know, has some news from the government. You all know the rules. There will be a discussion time and a question and answer time, so let's keep things in order. The good clergy will also have something to say. Now, here's Paul."

Paul Cramer stood at the podium and looked at the mass of windburned, craggy, weatherbeaten faces. Here, he thought, is the breadbasket of the Americas, in fact of the world. I wonder if they will be my friends after tonight. He took a deep breath.

"Gentlemen, my boss, the Secretary of Agriculture, on orders from the President, has informed all state and county agents that there will be a phase-out of the farm subsidy program."

There was a stir and immediately some hands were raised. "Not yet, gentlemen," Paul continued. "There is more to this than just farm subsidies. Let me explain. The National Debt is the largest we have ever had and the President must do something about it. Farm subsidies take a whopping bite out of the agricultural budget. The President will propose that you produce all that you can grow. " There were gasps and the hall grew quiet.

"Henry here has two thousand acres. Every third year, he plants wheat, barley, alfalfa and a few other small crops. If Henry planted his crops every year, prices would drop and Henry would not profit enough to pay his bills. He would fall into debt and be forced to sell his farm. The way things are now, you plant one year and the land lies fallow for two." Paul took a deep breath. He was holding their attention.

"Henry is a farmer; his parents and their parents were farmers, just like most of you. You all love the land and plant your seeds at the proper time. But once those seeds are planted, what can you do to make them grow? Nothing. Oh, yes, you can weed and spray to keep the

Earth - Mars

bugs off. The Most High does the rest." There was a stirring, an inaudible questioning.

"At this time there are many countries in which people are starving and here we sit with good land standing in weeds that could feed them. The governnment has studied ten years of population growth in relation to market prices for your produce that includes all the variables of machinery, maintenance, fertilizers, spraying and price controls. The income was averaged for every given area and led to the decision to permit farmers to grow all that they can or wish to grow.

The surplus, that above the amount needed to stabilize the market will be given to the countries where the need is greatest. Those countries selected shall pay only what it can afford to pay to our government. Rather than a subsidy, you collect what the market would have paid for your normal crop. Now, this is what it means." A rustling moved among the farmers; grow whatever you want?

"First, you can plant everything you normally would, the best way you can. Second, if it is a year that you would normally fall under the subsidy growing-year, you sell your crops the way you always have. Third, if it is a subsidy non-growing year, you plant your crops, harvest them and the Department of Agriculture will arrange the shipment to needy countries. You will be paid the same as if you did not plant your crop under the subsidy. Fourth, monies paid to the government from foreign countries will be credited to the Department of Agriculture account to be dispersed underwriting the subsidy.

This will continue until the subsidy program balances and the program will be discontinued, except for the cost of shpping and handling. If, and when, the countries begin to pay normal prices, or if the program shows a fund balance, that surplus will be used to help

38

The Library

farmers who need loans.

You will lose in the beginning, but in the long run it will mean security for you and for your farms. Loans can be set at a low rate and all interest paid goes back into the fund. Our government will collect whatever amounts involved countries are able to pay, but the most important point is that *people will be fed!*

You have a choice; join this program or compete on the open market. It's up to you. Our government takes a chance that it will collect from foreign sources the money to pay you or the subsidies program shuts down. In the end, the most important thing is that we can feed some damn hungry people."

Henry took his place st the podium. "Okay, okay. One at a time. You first, Pete."

"I only got five hundred acres and I'm in the farm subsidy program. The one year I work my farm, I work hard. Sometimes I get a good crop and sometimes I don't. What happens if I don't get a good crop the year I'm supposed to farm and market? Right now, the money I get paid for not planting two years carries me over the one bad year. As I understand it, if my crop fails, I get nothing. Is that so?"

"That's right," Henry replied. "There ain't no guarantees for anybody. You ain't got any now, have you?"

"No, I guess not, but why do we have to do all that work for those foreigners? They ain't done nothing for me."

There were more questions, then the Catholic Bishop asked to address the group. "Sure, Your Excellency," Henry said. "Anything to help this along." Whispers spread through the audience.

"Now we get a sermon."

"What's he know about farming?"

"Gentlemen," the Bishop began, "I'm not going to

Earth - Mars

preach, although the subject lends itself to an excellent sermon. I could give you a ten hour discourse on farming, but I will not. I am going to give you some facts. You might not like them; you may accept them with some reservations; but you cannot deny them and remain a human being." He drew himself up and surveyed the Grange membership.

"I am not concerned with a nation or government. I am concerned with the Kingdom of Heaven. I serve one Master, the Most High. I do not seek earthly power. All ministers here believe that we are our brothers' keepers. How can we say 'No' to a starving brother anywhere in the world? The pauper gives of his need; the rich man of his surplus. The question is *Will you give of your labor for your brother?*" The soul is equally belittled by the one who does nothing as it is by the one who does wrongly. Will you help to feed humanity or will you turn your backs on the rest of the world? Health has no politics."

The Bishop stepped back from the podium. The clergy rose and filed from their seats to leave as a group. When they reached the double doors they felt a sudden coldness. They hesitated and looked about, each aware of the chill, confused by its presence.

A blond young man in a light blue suit sitting alone at the back of the hall smiled at them. He rose and profered his hand, but they restrained themselves from offering a handshake.

"Good job! Good job, your Excellencies," he said looking at them with wide blue eyes. "You tell it like it is. I wish you good fortune." They shrugged off the chill, and went to their cars.

The meeting grew noisy. Concerns were voiced about hazards, real and imagined. "Working a farm is hard enough without giving the stuff away." "What happens

The Library

when the machinery breaks down and there's no money to fix it?" "Suppose these foreign governments just don't pay enough money at all?" "I still don't see why we have to be the ones to suffer for the deficit; let the rest of the country do without something."

It was late when Henry rose and spoke wearily. "I think we ought to adjourn this meeting. Take a few days to think it over. What say we meet here next Wednesday at the same time and then we can take a vote on it. All those in favor, raise your hands."

Everyone agreed and raised hands. The blond young man was nowhere to be seen. Henry stayed behind to straighten up. He set the chairs in place, turned out the lights, locked the door and went home. The blue-eyed blond young man appeared in the center of the hall. His grin was wider than before.

In every Grange Hall throughout the United States, the same message was presented by the Secretary of Agriculture and the clergy. There were the same arguments and the same conclusion. The decision was to be made the following Wednesday.

The evening was warm and the night sounds were soothing as Henry walked the mile to his house from the Grange, thinking about the different feeling in the hall tonight. He walked the dusty road, looking over his land. Weeds and rough grass had grown in the past two years. "Like a bum," he thought, "down on his luck. A downright shame."

"That you, Henry?" His wife called from her chair in the living room.

"Yep," he replied, joining her. "Got a lot to talk about and not sure where to begin."

"The beginning is usually a nice place to start," his wife told him with a smile.

41

Earth - Mars

"It started this afternoon when I was in the west field thinking about planting. Don't know where this stranger came from, but," Henry told her the sequence of events through the Grange meeting and the peculiar feeling he had when he was in the hall. Henry's wife had begun to sew, but had put down her needle and listened quietly.

"You've had quite a day! So that's what was on your mind at supper." She added thoughtfully, "What do you want to do? For my part, I don't mind the extra work to help those poor people."

"I don't know at this point. I do know that I don't like to see the land lay fallow. I can't lose nothing but some sweat."

"Let's sleep on it," his wife suggested. "Things might look different in the morning."

Henry awoke with a sense of urgency the next morning. Everything had fallen into place; the guilt concerning the land he had not tilled, the sights of starving masses on television, two years of rust on the equipment just to do one year's work, neighbors who had lost their farms because they couldn't pay the mortgages, the sense of total helplessness.

The program that Paul Cramer had outlined made sense and Henry decided to support it. Once his mind was made up, all thought went to getting the job done.

He lit the fire in the stove and the kitchen was warm when his wife came in dressed in robe and slippers.

"I'll take over," she said. "You get your chores done; by then I'll have breakfast ready."

"Right," Henry said and gave her a hug. "Lots to be done today."

Smiling, she knew he had made up his mind to help the poor. I hope, she thought, that the rest will too. Henry fed the stock and milked the three cows. He was

The Library

happier than he had been in a long time. He whistled a little returning to the house for a breakfast of pancakes with butter and maple syrup, ham and a couple of eggs.

Over a second cup of coffee, Henry asked,

"Remember last night when I said you could help after? I need you to call the women you know to pass the word around. Some of 'em will convince their husbands. We only got until next Wednesday. Meanwhile, I'm going to clean up the machinery and get everything ready to go."

"I'll be happy to help," she told him. Henry went to the shed, planning ahead, when suddenly he stopped, threw back his head and roared with laughter. He had just recalled the flower bed sitting absurdly within his two thousand acres. He would plant around it. It was there to stay.

That same day on large and small farms the bang of hammers and wrenches was heard as farmers prepared farm machinery to operate. There was an underlying happiness; the consensus of working farmers had already made a decision.

County Agent Cramer, making his rounds, found that many of the machines were broken and needed parts. It was a problem. His lists grew longer and he promised to speak to the local supplier and have him call as parts were ready. A half-dead and dying land was coming back to life. Cramer had much to smile about.

Neighbors were calling to see if they could help each other. Large farms with a stock of spare parts offered to help less fortunate farmers with repairs. Dairy farms offered piles of fertilizer at no cost and with mutual efforts erected drying platforms.

Farm women called local colleges to discover what clothing was needed in several foreign countries and sewing circles were formed to produce what to them, was

Earth - Mars

odd kinds of wearing apparel. The farming community of the United States began to get well again.

On Sunday, churches were filled to overflowing. There were new faces as well as regulars not seen in a long time. The clergy rushed to hang loudspeakers so that all could hear and handed out extra hymnals so all could take part. Henry's church was the same. A revival swept across the farm country. For the first time in a century wives did not outnumber the menfolk who rose to give the women their seats.

Psalms were sung, scripture readings presented and blessings were called down from the Most High on the people and their efforts. The Bishop came forward to speak, when suddenly, the rear of the church was in flames.

After the first shock of awareness, the panic hit. Women in the pews ran screaming to the front doors, pushing, shoving, trampling, while some men broke the windows and helped others to escape. By the time the Fire Department had arrived half of the church was in flames. The firemen pushed back the people who were milling about looking for loved ones and turned forceful streams of water on the fire whose flames only burned more fiercely. The church was now totally engulfed; even the concrete front steps were blazing. Two small storage buildings nearby burst into flames and in the next ten minutes, they and the church were reduced to a pile of ashes. Not a charred board remained; the concrete foundation could not be found.

Some worshippers had been injured; some could not be found. Henry had managed to get his wife out through the window and they both suffered cuts and bruises, but nothing serious. He led her away from the site, up a small rise of ground. Something was nagging at him; what was wrong? What was it? Then it struck him. He turned to

The Library

his wife, who was quietly weeping. He told her,
"Wait here. I must talk to the firemen for a minute."
"Don't go, Henry. I'm scared."
"It's alright," he told her and walked to the firemen who were rolling up hoses. The Chief looked up.
"Hi, Henry. We sure weren't much help on this one," he said.
"You did what you could." Henry consoled him. "Did you notice anything odd about this fire ? *There wasn't any heat!* I didn't feel any heat at all. Another thing, there's only ashes left. There ain't no charred nothing! The pipes, the concrete foundation, eveything completely burned. The only thing left is ashes. And the people who didn't get out? Did you see any bodies? This big building was burnt to ashes in ten minutes!"
The Chief laid down his hose and pulled Henry aside a few steps. "You are absolutely right. I already have those things in my notebook. Come with me. I was just getting ready to do this when you come up to me."
They went to the pile of ashes where the church had stood. It might have burned a week earlier; there was no change in temperature as they stood beside it.
"There are no hot ashes," the Chief noted. Henry added,
"There are no hot coals; nothing but ashes."
The Chief agreed. "Connect one of the hoses and bring it over here," he called to a nearby fireman. The Chief directed the man to spray the ashes with a direct stream.
"Might as well make it easier for the coroner," he remarked. But there wasn't a body, no bones, nothing but ashes. "Okay, turn it off. Put the hose on the truck."
Other men joined them, searching for a sign of those who had been trapped in the church. One of the men ran

Earth - Mars

to Henry who was standing by the Chief.

"Henry, I can't find any of them," he gasped, white and shaken. "Not one of the clergy! They nust not have gotten out. Lord, Henry, what does it mean? This ain't natural!"

"Keep looking," Henry told him. "We need to be sure first. Don't say anything to anybody."

Once again the Chief took Henry aside. "Now that's peculiar," he said with a puzzled look on his face." He looked Henry in the eye. "There ain't no smell, no burnt smell, no smell at all! And now that I think about it, there wasn't any smoke either. Did you see smoke come up from the fire? There ain't none now and there wasn't any then when it was burning."

Henry looked back at the church site and the terrible chill he had felt last Thursday returned. "I'm getting my wife and I'm going home." he told the Chief. "You will have to figure that out. I can't think anymore. Too much has happened to this poor farmer."

Henry found his wife still crying softly; she could not find her best friends. He took her home.

Sorrow descended over the county. It's silence spread to the crickets and the night hunters. At nine o'clock that evening while Henry and his wife were sitting in the living room, the lights went out.

They had been on the telephone the better part of the day. Twenty were missing, presumed to have perished in the blazing church. That number included all the clergy and a number of very helpful lay people. When the lights went out, Henry exclaimed,

"Oh no! What next!"

The wind began to blow. The weather station had given no indication that there would be a storm, and yet, the wind blew from the east growing stronger every minute

The Library

until it reached sixty knots. It blew for one hour from east to west in a straight line, then stopped as quickly as it had started.

The lights came on, and in the sudden quiet, the crickets made their usual sounds and the night hunters could be heard.

Henry went outdoors with a strong light to see if any damage had been done. He walked by the outbuildings, inspected the stock, looked at the fences. No harm had been done.

The blond young man in the light blue suit stood beside the flowerbed. The smile was still on his lips, and then he disappeared.

The flowers died.

****

On Monday morning when Henry had finished milking and was entering the back door, the telephone rang. His wife was just laying out breakfast so Henry picked up the receiver. "Henry speaking."

"Paul Cramer here. You had breakfast yet?"

"Nope. Just sitting down."

"Henry, I gotta show you something. Eat your breakfast and come over to the church site."

"I hope there ain't no more funny goings on," Henry turned to his wife. "I'm getting a little tired of this." He finished his hotcakes and ham in silence. His wife busied herself about the kitchen. She knew that Henry usually arrived at the proper answers, so she didn't worry too much.

After breakfast, Henry climbed into his pickup and drove to the devastated church property. Paul Cramer was sitting under a tree with his back against the trunk, his

Earth - Mars

hat tipped back on his head, his arms crossed over his bent knees. Henry stepped out of the truck and walked up to Paul.

"What do you make of all this?" Paul asked.

"I don't know. How long you been here?"

"Since sun-up. I came to see if I could clean up some of the mess and I found this, just as it is now. I haven't touched a thing."

Paul and Henry walked slowly around the area where the church had stood. There wasn't a bit of ash in sight. There wasn't a sign that a building had even stood there. The surrounding grass was green right up to the place where the church had stood, but in place of the church, there were flowers; thousands of flowers, packed together tightly forming a colorful mass.

"Reminds me of a patchwork quilt; sure is a beautiful sight." Henry added, "They are even growing where the two sheds stood. You have a big wind over your way last night?" he asked Paul.

"Sure did. Like to blew the house over. You too?"

"Yep," Henry replied thoughtfully. "Well, I gotta finish my chores."

Paul turned to walk to his truck also. "Strange goings on, Henry" he remarked.

"Yep," Henry answered, recalling another flowerbed in the middle of his two thousand acres. As Paul drove off, Henry walked up the slope at the rear of the church site. It was a short cut to the flowedbed he had planted. He topped the rise and looked down the slope to the center of his acreage. The flowers were dead.

He walked to the patch and picked a handful of the dead blossoms. They crumbled into ash and blew away in the gentle breeze. Henry brushed his hands together, climbed the fence and sat on the top rail. He felt sad

The Library

and empty. "What in tarnation is going on here?" he asked himself.

"A war, Henry."

Henry was moved four feet away. Sure enough, there was the stranger, rough clothes, shoes and all.

"I wish you wouldn't do that!" Henry exclaimed. "You make me jumpy as the dickens." He went back and sat on the fence.

"Sorry, Henry. You asked a question and I felt obliged to answer."

"I guess I'm jumpy from all the stuff that's been happening the last few days. All hell's busting loose. You know about the church? This used to be a peaceful place.." Henry saw the light. "Hey, what do you mean, a war?"

"Yes, Henry. The church is a part of the war. I can explain."

"I'm not too sure I like the last explanation I got," Henry grumbled. "Ain't had a peaceful minute since then."

"That's the point, Henry. You are not supposed to have a peaceful minute, depending on what you call a peaceful minute."

"That don't make sense," rejoined Henry. "Either things are peaceful or they ain't."

"Know much about the history of humans, Henry? Don't answer; your history is slanted by those who wrote it. Humans have been at war since Adam and Eve left the Garden of Eden and even that is allegorical."

"Alli what?"

"Allegorical; profound and complex truth explained in simple language and with examples so that the hearer can understand it. I'll go back a little further. When the Most High created the Cosmos and Earth, there was only love; no violence, hunger, anger or hate. All of his creations existed on the purest of food, Love. There was no need to

Earth - Mars

eat or to go anywhere. The lion lay down with the lamb, the fox with the hen. The music, or what you would call music, was the fabric of space. Each was in its place and there was a place for everything in creation. That, Henry, was peace."

The Angel continued. "Because you were very special to Him, the Most High put the earth and the Cosmos into a little piece of eternity which was His expression of love. Humans call this place a different dimension. The Most High created a special light to shine on His treasure which outshone all the others which you call a rainbow.

The rainbow is His sign both to Heaven and this dimension that He made everything as close to His own perfection as was possible. This was to exist for Eternity, but something happened."

"A beautiful entity named Lucifer (which means Morning Star or Angel of Light) was sent to guard the rainbow. He began to consider himself as powerful as the Most High. Some angels were saddened by this, but others agreed with Lucifer. The Most High called the Archangel Michael to Him, handed him the shining sword of His power and commanded,

"Drive from My face and out of Heaven, Lucifer and his followers into the domain of the Cosmos and the Earth."

"This Michael and his legions did in a great war. Lucifer upon leaving Heaven was immediately darkened and his beautiful shape twisted and filled with pain at the loss of his glory, as were his followers. But the Most High relented and caught Lucifer's descent halfway between earth and the Cosmos, for He still loved all His creations, which is why He gave them all knowledge and free will with the transdimensional ability. The Most High gave Lucifer and his followers the opportunity to repent and to ascend to Heaven but they chose not to.

The Library

Banished, Lucifer and his hordes fell to earth and the Cosmos. Lucifer became Satan and his angels were called demons."

"You see, Henry, everything and everyone that ever was or will be belongs to the Most High. All must face judgement eventually. The Most High thought the earth and the Cosmos surrounding it so beautiful that he created entities from the earth, but with each containing a little bit of Himself when He breathed the breath of life into him and gave him free will."

"He created them in His own image, but don't misunderstand, Henry. The Most High does not look like a human being; the word image means he put a little bit of himself into each one of all human beings."

"He sent Satan to earth also, but by using the earth to create mankind, He balanced His creations with the gift of free will in the choice of which master to follow. The Scripture says that you cannot serve two masters; for you will love the one and hate the other."

"Adam and Eve were doing alright for they were friends with the most high and the earth was a paradise. The first children of the Most High had all the knowledge of eternity and could have lived in Paradise throughout all eternity.

"The Most High did not reveal two things to them; the negative knowledge concerning Satan and the immortality in this dimension. He reserved that knowledge for Himself and buried it in the essence of two trees."

The Most High walked with His children and told them of all things in creation and He let them name various creatures He created."

Satan was jealous of these children destined to inherit the Kingdom of Heaven, so he conspired with the

Earth - Mars

demons to get them to disobey the Most High. Satan made the fruit of the tree of his negative knowledge, that of himself, the most beautiful and enticing. Adam and Eve ate of the fruit and when the Most High came to walk with them, He was angry with them for they had become as Satan wanted them to become, disobedient. He drove them away from the place of peace and told them they would know hunger and be like the beasts, except that they, like Satan, would have a chance to earn their way back into His good graces."

Henry turned and looked at the stranger. "Why did all those people in the church, the house of the Most High, die?"

"Death is a human word," the stranger replied. "It is a word for your sorrow and your love that is incomplete. They are with the Most High, casualties in this great war."

"Henry, look at it this way. You have seen the lowly catapillar emerge from a cocoon as a lovely butterfly. Why do you think the Most High created this small transition? Nothing is created without a reason! It is a living example for human beings if they would only observe and think! There is no death, only transition. The body is a shell; in itself, nothing, for it is of the earth. Do you understand?"

"Not all of it," Henry said. "If this is true, why do we have to worry about starving kids and old folks? They ain't gonna die; they are just on the way to a better life."

"All human beings are in transition; it is the manner of transition that should concern human beings; whether it is easy or painful. The brotherhood of man is an opportunity to ease the transition; to care enough; whether gold was the controlling factor or whether love was the driving force."

There was a short silence. The stranger looked at

The Library

the desecrated flower bed sadly. Suddenly a grin appeared on his face.

"He missed it!" he said. "Watch, Henry."

In the midst of the wilted blossoms, a green shoot grew and grew until it was the largest oak that Henry had ever seen.

"Whoever killed the flowers missed the little acorn buried beneath the bed."

In a time-lapse sequence, the oak tree had grown four feet across, it's branches spreading shade over an eighth of an acre of land.

"You did it again," Henry marvelled. He jumped down from the fence and walked slowly around the tree. Then he backed up about fifty feet, looked at the top of it and frowned.

"What's wrong, Henry?"

"I was just thinking. You put that durned tree there and I'm going to have to cut it down," Henry turned with a twinkle in his eye, "cause I can't waste space if I'm going to feed all them kids."

The stranger laughed. "I think you will have enough acreage to plant. Your rebellion is as strong as an oak tree."

"Yeah", Henry said noncommittedly.

"Henry, you were picked by me because you were least likely to go off the deep end and confuse that which is natural with superstition. There is a reason why farmers have these things happening to them. The reason is the earth; it all begins in the dirt. Everything originates in the soil; the bed you sleep in, the food you eat, the truck you drive, your pitchfork, your clothes, jet planes; everything started in the earth."

The stranger shifted on the fence. "Even illnesses that you must endure results from something someone

Earth - Mars

should not have done, or failed to do. It all begins with farmers working the earth."

"Henry, I won't be seeing you again until after your transition. You have a fight on your hands. There are those who would twist what you are doing and who will try to stop you for their own ends. But, keep the faith and do your best."

The stranger stepped down from the fence, walked a dozen feet from Henry and as he turned to face him, he became a golden, winged, white-clothed Angel.

Henry's mouth fell open in astonishment. The Angel's right hand held a sword of blue flame, his left, a highly polished silver shield.

"I am Michael," he said, then vanished.

****

Farmers in all the states were ravaged by some kind of catastrophe. With slight variations, they were all in the sense of natural order, negative and unexplainable. In terms of science, they were completely unpredictable. It was as though nature had gone berserk. Wide crevices opened in the middle of the fertile farmland; sections of corn and wheat crops withered; churches burned to ashes; violent east to west winds blew farmhouses into piles of broken lumber and glass stopping as suddenly as they had started. Schools suffered the same destructive fates, sometimes with students in them. There was no predictable geographical pattern, no way to prepare except to pray, for these calamities occured on the third Tuesday, the day before the Wednesday evening Grange meetings.

Farmers meeting in Grange Halls were dazed and shaken. Doubt and resentment grew about the program outlined by the president. Leaders of the Grange Halls,

The Library

who themselves had the same experience as Henry, rose to speak in one voice. The Grange Hall in Henry's county was filled with farmers, but there was little of the usual smiling and glad-handing. The unexplainable nature of recent events had a sobering effect on them.

Henry banged the gavel more from habit than necessity as the hall was quiet.

"You all know why we are here tonight," he began gravely. "We have a big decision to make. You all know I'm not much given to making up stories or letting my imagination run away with me. So here goes. You've all seen my little fower bed of rebellion against farm subsidies and this is what happened."

Henry told them about the stranger appearing beside him on the fence, of the flower bed, and what had been said about an on-going war. He ended solemnly,

"If we think about the havoc, it appears that *someone or something* just doesn't want us to help those people. I for one can make up my own mind what I want to do. I'm getting mad as hell! Discussion?"

As Henry talked, the eyes of the farmers had narrowed, taken on a hard look. They were not quick to anger, but once provoked, their anger was not a pleasant sight. A sense of determination was setting in.

One of the farmers stood up in the rear of the hall.

"Henry, it does seem that the things goin' on ain't natural. You tellin' us you talked to an angel? That there's demons at work here in the county?"

"That's my answer, Zeb, unless you got a better one. We felt caught in the middle, but now, we can go one way or the other. Let the people starve and help one side, or do our best to feed them and help the other side. Sort of like doing right or wrong."

"But, Henry," Zeb asked, "how do we fight demons?

Earth - Mars

It's hard enough just farming!"

"I don't know," Henry answered honestly. "Maybe the answer to that might be in what we decide tonight. The wrong side is trying to keep us from deciding; so you all have to decide for yourselves. Me, I'm just going to start farming and trust in the stranger."

"Okay, Henry, putting all the strange stuff aside, there's a lot more to think about and that is the government. It's going to give us the same as we get now. The only difference is they want us to grow crops anyhow and what we harvest is to be shipped to the countries that have starving people. The money the government gets from them countries could eventually get back to us. What happens if we get another president?"

"We take our chances, just like we are doing now. Nobody gives guarantees, you know that, Zeb."

"Somehow, I thought you'd be saying that," an old farmer said ironically, "but, I'll go along with it' if everyone else is willing."

"Anyone else?" Henry asked. He waited a moment."I propose that we give this thing a try for a three-year period and see how it goes. If we are doing any good as far as the national debt is concerned, we continue. If not, then we can consider just going on the open market. All in favor raise your hands."

There was unanimous approval. They had helped each other recover from the havoc and now that they understood a possible cause, Henry's speech clinched their cooperation. Henry closed the meeting. Card tables were set up and refreshments passed around.

Walking home, Henry listened to the night sounds. The stars were bright. Henry's uneasiness had passed and he felt at peace.

****

The Library

In the state of California, a place called Badwater, Death Valley, 282 feet below sea level, is the most desolate part of the United States. The blond, curley haired young man appeared. There was no smile on his face. He hated this place. It reminded him of home.

It was 125 degrees and the thermal waves distorted the landscape. Heat waves danced to some hidden tune in the vast silence. The dark purple circle before him was joined by varigated deep red circles. Each contained a ball that rotated around the other circles. It had the semblance of an atomic structure. Centered in the revolving circles was the face of an old man that shimmered into the vision of an ancient dragon, changing from one to the other, wrinkled and shriveled, with thin lips and the coldest of green eyes.

"You failed!" the harsh voice accused.

The blond-haired young man winced and crouched against a rock wall. "No, I..." he started to say when the rock behind him exploded and he was smashed against the opposite cliff, falling one hundred feet to the canyon floor. He was immediately hurled against the cliff. This was repeated forty times. His blue suit was in shreds and his blond hair was burning with a bright blue flame that caused him unimaginable pain, although it gave off no apparent heat. He screamed and snarled. The sounds of fierce hate echoed along the one hundred and thirty mile canyon.

"Don't fail again." The old dragon-man snarled a warning and was gone.

****

Word had leaked out from the Department of

Earth - Mars

Agriculture in Washington, D.C. that farm subsidies were to be discontinued. The president was accused of using the farmers as scape-goats to help reduce the national debt. Newspapers reported that the president was using the little people to pull his irons out of the fire when he could tax large corporations and big businesses instead.

The facts were slanted to say what they wanted to hear; facts that fit a particular political or sociological belief. Not one newspaper reporter, or television newscaster or commentator applauded the action, nor did they look seriously at the information received "...from a highly-placed official source. "

The president, hearing the questions from staff journalists, was tempted to remove all reporters from the White House and to charge profit-making news corporations for the use of space, telephones and all other equipment including electricity. The White House was a public building utilized by a profit-making business. It was illegal for profits to be made from public tax-maintained structures. He felt that press releases could be delivered to corporate headquarters and journalists could submit questions in writing to the administration with the guarantee of an answer.

The president sighed and dismissed the novel idea. Telephones rang in every section of the Agricultural Department as Senators demanded to know what in blazes the Department was trying to do? It continued through Monday morning, afternoon and late into the night.

The governors of all fifty states called Department heads demanding explanations of the Executive Order. Somewhat mollified, but still uneasy because of the bad press, the Governors took a wait-and-see attitude, declining to make public statements.

Little was said by the members of the House of

Representatives. Asked for comments, they would reply, "No comment." or "I'm not informed of the complexities of the issue, but as soon as I am, I shall have something to say." Later events made comments unnecessary.

The United States exported that year two billion bushels of corn and one billion bushels of wheat to three West African nations and three Central American countries.

The ships were unmarked, as were the bags of corn and wheat. The ships also carried several hundred tons of corn meal and wheat flour ready for immediate conversion to food products within the areas. One of the African countries was landlocked, so permission was obtained from the port country to tranship overland. When the usual under-the-table graft was demanded, the captain immediately ordered his cargo to be reloaded. The port country objected, so the Captain who had carte blanche authority called his crew aboard and waited.

Later, the American Ambassador and the country's chief executive asked permission to come aboard. The Captain led them to the Board Room.

"Make yourselves comfortable, gentlemen. There is coffee on the sideboard. Help yourselves."

The Captain was not impressed by their credentials. "Now what can I do for you?" he asked impassively.

"Why have you stopped unloading your cargo?" the Executive asked.

"Your people asked for graft to tranship free food to your neighbor. You are getting free food, or only as much as your government can afford to pay. We are trusting you and you try to *make* us pay. I'll load my cargo and take it somewhere else."

"You can't do that, Captain." The Ambassador's face was white. "You are under contract to the United States government. You are in this country's waters which

Earth - Mars

places you under their control and I am the representative of the United States government. You are under our control legally."

"Mr. Ambassador, I have orders from the Department of Agriculture, counter signed by the President, that if any interference is met, if a profit is demanded from this cargo, if I am prevented delivery of it to the country consigned, I am to go elsewhere. If I cannot deliver it directly, *I am to dump it!* I have a list of priority countries. As a last resort, the Secretary of Agriculture will tell me where to dispose of it."

The Captain rose and stood by the hatch-way. He broke the silence. "Gentlemen, I am going up on deck to reload my cargo."

The boom man had swung the loading boom over the dock when the two men joined the Captain on the bridge. The Executive Officer said stiffly,

"Captain, you will have a free hand in delivering your cargo to it's destination. I will sign an Executive Order and there will be no interference within my country. Your Ambassador has said this may quiet the unrest in this region. Perhaps full stomachs are less susceptible to contentious influences. Three countries border us. We will try to regionalize our efforts, but that is for later. Distribute what you have. My country needs some of your cargo."

"No." The Captain's voice was firm. "This cargo is destined for the three border countries."

The Ambassador asked sharply, "Why unload your cargo here, if it is not for this country?"

"Mr. Ambassador, I suggest you contact your boss in Washington, D.C. I have my orders." He turned to the Executive. "Do I still unload?"

The Executive Officer gritted his teeth. "Unload your

The Library

cargo, Captain and see that it is delivered to those three countries. I will send you a written order."

The two men walked off the bridge and the Captain signaled the first mate to proceed with the unloading. Within the hour, the written comfirmation was received. Army trucks loaded the cargo and departed in three different directions with two of the Captain's crew in each of the lead trucks.

At the borders, they were met by American ambassadors and passed through without delay. They drove to the nearest army bases and off-loaded the cargo into each country's army trucks. The Americans travelled with the food for they had been briefed by a representative of the Agriculture Department, who in turn had been briefed by the C.I.A. The food was delivered directly to locations where starving people were gathered. Only then did the crewmen return to their ship.

****

The Foreign Affairs Committee met the following week, and the Chairman gave a brief report.

"Gentlemen, the Food to the Starving Program is successful. The following points have been executed and the developments for which we hoped have evidenced themselves. Six maritime companies were contacted and given tax considerations for the use of their ships. The Captains, along with their crews, were briefed directly and individually concerning encounters at each port of call and how they would respond to possible obstacles."

He paused briefly and continued with a slight smile. "Countries not receiving food deliveries, but needed for access to those countries that were, provided an opportunity for officials to be cooperative to a

Earth - Mars

humanitarian cause. These countries are now forming regional cooperatives out of necessity and interdependency. At the suggestion of the American ambassadors, these governments have formed a cooperative monetary fund to pay the United States at least fifty per cent of the market price of delivered food."

A rumble of satisfaction came from the group. He continued,

"There have been, to this date, (one month from the inception of the Program) ten farmers in the mid-west who negotiated farm mortgages and were saved from bankruptcy. The President has this report in hand. Are there any comments? No? Then, the meeting is adjourned."

The Angels smiled.

****

The six returned to awareness and looked at each other. "That was a darn good solution!" Peter exclaimed. "I hope it continues."

"Our concern," said Glorene, "is to make sure it is part of the record."

They transferred all the data into the main computer, ate, drank some water, then settled back in their large chairs. The globe turned dark, began to glow and they resumed their dream state, joining minds and watching closely.

****

The United States House of Representatives was in a great debate concerning a bill presented on the floor by Rep. Hikiluna (D.) from the state of Hawaii. His bill would guarantee every living person in the United States

The Library

three meals a day and shelter for the night, between sunset and sunrise. The arguments were rhetorical.

"Who will pay for this? How will it be paid?"

"We owe it to the people."

The debate went on and on. So intense in preparing their arguments, no one realized that as each speaker arose, the decibel level of the chamber fell slightly. In the middle of a speech by Rep. Palmer (D.) from the state of Ohio, no words could be heard. With a look of confusion, he left the podium and sat down.

An Angel appeared. "I am Gabriel." The voice thundered. "I hear the echo of empty words! Would you be the Dark One, leading your people down the path of idleness and dependency? You gather like the Pharasees and scribes of ancient times burdening the people with unbearable burdens. Helping those in need is the law of the Most High; but to make them dependent upon you is the trick of the Dark One."

The voice softened slightly. "You have a sacred trust in a pledge of allegiance to *One Nation, Under God*, but you deny the people the right to include the Most High in state affairs. You commit abominations while the great light of your nation grows dim and fails to recognize the brotherhood of man."

"Why do you turn your land into a wasteland? You pay the sower not to sow while people hunger. You foul your waters with waste, then cry out when plagues descend upon you. Your have slaughtered your children in the womb. You are concerned with profit. You have not protected the weak and the helpless. Remember the lesson of the rich man and the pauper; one gave of his surplus, the other of his need."

The voice once again thundered. "You hypocrites!"

A hologram expanded and obliterated the vision of the

Earth - Mars

Angel. The Representatives sat transfixed with fear and awe. Each one viewed his own state and the people he represented, experiencing the hopelessness, the anger, the kindness. Each wallowed in the foulness in their homelands, then they saw the beautiful cities that could have been. The holograph faded. In the pall of a heavy silence, the Representatives filed slowly out of the hall.

****

The six observed humanity taught by Angels to work harder, forming a base for the adventure into space and the solar system. The six condensed the data and then recorded it. New discoveries were registered and correlated for cross reference. They had indeed, become Librarians of the Cosmos.

In time, transition claimed them. Glorene and Peter remained in the library on the Dark Planet which was completely sealed. The only visible sign was the antennae that stretched between the two obsidian mountains. Two problems remained to be solved: the library had to remain hidden from unwanted visitors and the entrance had to be difficult to unseal.

Peter was writing the names of the planets while they discussed possible solutions. Suddenly, his wrinkled face and tired eyes lit up like a quasar.

"I have it! I have the answer."

He passed the paper to Glorene. "It's nothing but letters," she said queriously.

"Think! Look at the letters and think!"

"If you don't mind your manners, I'll give you some knots on your old coconut head," Glorene replied. Peter chuckled.

"The first letters of the names of the planets spell

The Library

JEMMPAVSUN. That could be the code that we need. The planet Mars is the only planet occupied and is the center of government. We can seal the letters in a circle of obsidian and send it to them. The obsidian is the clue to this planet. What do you think?"

"I think that's using your head. It will give them another mystery to think about."

In the laboratory, they formed a circle four inches across and one half inch thick of pure gold; then, they stamped the letters JEMMPAVSUN upon it. They sealed the golden circle in a ball of obsidian.

"Even if this planet is found, it will give them a few centuries of frustration."

"Now that robots are working in the fields," Peter said, "we can take this obsidian ball to one of them."

"Good idea! Tell him it is a key and that he is to deliver it to the Head of the Government on Mars." Then Glorene added, "You take it, Peter. I don't feel up to going outside."

"Alright. But you take it easy. We still have to find a way to replace that obvious antennae that we have now."

Peter took the obsidian ball and went to the Flitter. He knew where to find one of the robots. One had taken over the care of the large dome generator, freeing the men for other duties.

Peter landed the Flitter beside the dome and approached the entrance. The port slid open and out stepped a robot.

"May I help you, sir?" it asked politely.

"Yes," answered Peter. "Please give this key to the person called Jim. I believe that you will find him at Mars Central."

"I cannot leave my present duties," said the robot.

Earth - Mars

"You have a computer connection with Mars Central. Call them and have Jim pick up the key. Do not give it to anyone else.

The robot scanned the obsidian ball, found that it was not dangerous and answered, "I will do so immediately, sir."

"Good," Peter said, "and thank you." He climbed into his Flitter and returned to the Dark Planet. He found Glorene slumped over the large table. He touched her shoulder; she raised her head slowly. "I am very tired," she said. "I am going to my bed."

"I'll help you," Peter said, realizing that he alone would have to solve the antennae problem. He helped her to the elevator and when they arrived at her room, he opened the door and escorted her to the bed. When he was sure she was comfortable, he left her and returned to the workroom.

He activated the six foot screen and brought up a facsimile of the solar system. The orbit of the Dark Planet around the sun was at a right angle to the orbits of the other planets.

"Hmm. That makes things a little easier." In the automated laboratory he manufactured six ball antennaes and placed them each in the center of an obsidian block. Peter grunted with satisfaction. "That ought to do it."

Using the anti-grav projector, he loaded them into the Flitter. At the base of each leg of the towers, he placed one of the balls. He backed off in the Flitter and surveyed his handiwork. No difference could be observed between the antennaes and the surrounding obsidian. He sealed each ball in place with his laser, connected the wires and melted obsidian over them.

Peter returned to the Control Room, adjusted the input controls, then disconnected the tower antennaes.

The Library

The reception indicator jumped a little, but settled down to where it had been before.

"One more thing to do and then it will be finished." He entered the Flitter and stopped midway between the towers. Using his laser to cut the wires between them, he placed an anti-grav unit on one leg of each tower and turned on full power. Then, he loosened the foundation blocks and stood back.

The towers shook loose and silently rose into space. Peter smoothed over the holes and when he had finished, there was no evidence that anything had been there.

Peter returned to his Flitter, approached the entrance and activated both doors. He flew the Flitter into the large entrance hall of the library. When he dismounted, he went to Glorene's room and found her barely conscious. He clasped her hand and they silently looked at each other.

They were not aware of the stranger until he spoke. "Well done, Peter and Glorene," he said softly.

"Why do you do that?" Peter asked. "You always startle us and my heart is not so strong these days."

"Peter, you have had the strongest heart and mind in the entire universe. And you, Glorene, have had the most compassionate and understanding heart and mind. It was not easy for the six of you to isolate yourselves all these years. You did not falter in the work. This library is not for this generation, nor the next. Many generations will come and go before it becomes useful."

"And the records?" Peter asked.

"The records kept by the Computer Central on the Moon will have long disappeared. It took several thousand earth years to have the words of the Most High given to Moses twisted into an unrecognizable message. The original ten laws were just that: LAWS. They were not

Earth - Mars

to be interpreted by humans to fit circumstances, but rather, humans were to make the circumstances fit the law. There is no condemnation; only disappointment."

The stranger continued, "These records you have established of mankind's accomplishments will be sorely needed by generations of the future. But, you are tired and wish to rest. Peter, take Glorene's hand and help her rise from her bed."

Glorene felt a heavy burden lifted from her shoulders. She clasped Peter's hand. The stranger became a golden-winged Angel in a snow-white robe. The room disappeared and Glorene and Peter realized they were in space. They had started the transition.

"Look at yourselves," the Angel instructed. They looked at each other. They too had wings and snow-white robes.

****

Robot Floyd 4 was puzzled. This stranger has landed beside his dome, handed him a little globe and instructed him to call Jim. What was the purpose of the globe? His programming did not tell him. He transmitted the rquest for Jim to come to his work place, then gave his identification number.

On his arrival, Jim examined the globe minutely. "So, a human gave it to you? I'm to take this to Mars Central? What am I supposed to do with it?" Jim put the globe in his pack. "I'll take it and see what happens."

Jim called a meeting of the scientists, the independents and the corporation people. He placed the globe on a stand next to the podium, called their attention to how he had acquired it, and pointed out the fact that there was a gold circle of letters at its center. "I think

The Library

it is made of obsidian, but I am not sure."

One of the scientists rose. "I don't recall anyone finding obsidian on a known planet or moon. Could this be some contact by an alien?"

"Don't start that old line," Jim replied impatiently. "We lived on earth several thousand years and never completely explored it. We have only scratched the surface on this planet. So forget alien artifact or message. The encased letters are *English* letters. Someone within this solar system has left us a message. I invite each of you to study the globe; take pictures if you wish. Let's try to solve this mystery."

As scientists continued their work, they each carried the memory of the obsidian ball with golden letters forming a circle at its center. Jim believed that it was a clue to something important. He announced that anyone visiting Mars Central would have the opportunity to study the letters and the ball.

A silicon pyramid was constructed and exactly five feet above ground level, the ball was placed with the letters facing outward toward the entrance door of the main dome. "One day," Jim muttered, "someone would solve this mystery."

THE KEY

The Library was like a tomb without the chatter of the six librarians. The computers continued to record. Giant record disks were automatically removed, replaced and stored. Every five years, the doors would open and the computerized laser would carve another room to accomodate records of occurrances inpacting human history.

****

Kenneth Rackner was a bastard. His mother was a prostitute and she did not want this baby fathered by a psychopathic killer who was imprisoned for life in a mental hospital.

Kenneth knew nothing about his mother and father. It wouldn't have concerned him if he had known. Ken, as his few friends called him, was not even certain that his name was Kenneth Rackner. He was found in a brown paper bag in the grabage can behind Krasner's Restaurant when he was two weeks old by a drunk named Bill Rackner.

Rackner, a street bum for twenty years, hefted the bag and thought he had found a bottle. He stashed it under his coat and went stumbling down the alley in search of a place to examine his loot. When he looked into the bag, he was almost shocked into soberness.

The hospital was one block away and he staggered

Earth - Mars

to the entrance. When one of the nurses saw him, ragged and dirty with an infant in his arms, she grabbed the child and called an orderly. Rackner was ushered into the security office.

The child, suffering from exposure and hunger, was taken to the emergency room for treatment while Bill Rackner was questioned.

"What were you doing with this baby? Is it yours?"

"I found it in the garbage can," Bill told them. "I didn't know what to do with it so I brought it here."

"Does it have a name? Was anything in the bag to show who it belonged to? "

The endless questioning confused, then angered, him. He shouted belligerently,"

"My name's William Rackner! And the baby's name is Kenneth!" The name just popped into his whiskey-soaked mind. "I brought him here cause I didn't know where else to take him."

Security let him go and that was the last anyone ever saw of him. The baby was taken to the Social Worker and the name, Kenneth Rackner, was registered and filed with the City Clerk. Placed in a foster home, Kenneth grew into a dark-complexioned tyke with black hair and dark eyes that saw things no one else could see.

The Professor and his wife had taken Kenneth at the age of two. The Professor, a scholar who dabbled in applied physics in his basement, had objected mildly, but was overridden by his wife, a quiet woman who usually remained in the background. When she did insist on something, the Professor always gave in to her. So, Kenneth Rackner went to live with them. It was love at first sight for the professor's wife, and although he would not admit it, the professor was taken with the little tyke.

He joined the well-ordered household, bringing the

The Key

usual sicknesses and colds until he was six years old, one year before he was to begin his schooling. The Professor had an extensive library that contained most of the current science books and journals located in his den, which was off-limits to everyone. His wife, in the process of housecleaning, would not enter unless invited.

The Professor arrived home early one afternoon from a lecture and found the door to his den open. He looked in and saw six-year-old Kenneth studiously bent over a text on nuclear physics. The Professor assumed he was looking at the pictures, but then muttered,

"By thunder! He is reading the text!" He quietly closed the door and went to the kitchen for a cup of coffee.

"You're home early," his wife said.

"Yes," replied the Professor absentmindedly. He was excited with his thoughts, but was not one to let his feeling show.

That evening he made a series of telephone calls to friends, professors of various disciplines from sociology to physics. He made appointments then sat back and smiled. "We'll soon see," he mused.

The next morning he told his wife he would spend some time with Kenneth to prepare him for school attendance next year; to lessen the shock of new surroundings.

"Do you think it is necessary?" she asked.

The Professor replied, "Absolutely."

During the next few weeks, the Professor's wife dressed Kenneth the first thing in the morning, prepared his breakfast, and saw him off with the Professor, ostensibly to spend the day at the local park or at elementary schools.

In reality, the Professor took Kenneth to his friends'

Earth - Mars

offices who tested him to ascertain his I.Q. level. They were all astounded. Kenneth's I.Q. was above the 200 level. After the initial tests had proven Ken's intelligence capabilities, they gave him short texts to read, testing him on the contents. They found he had a photographic memory, that he had an unusual aptitude for mathematics, atomic structures and magnetics and that he grasped immediately the understanding of their applied uses. At the end of five weeks, the Professor told his wife.

"It doesn't surprise me," she answered, continuing her housework. "I knew he was a bright boy."

"Good Lord, woman!," he exploded. "Don't you realize we have a genius here?"

"That's nice," she replied. "Maybe he will fix the things that are broken around here when he gets a little older."

The Professor told little Kenneth that he could use his den and library whenever he wished and if there was something else he wanted, the Professor would see that he got it.

Kenneth spent the next ten years attending school, reading everything in the Professor's den. With an insatiable thirst for knowledge, he absorbed the Science Section of the Public Library. At age sixteen, he wrote a mathematical formula with equations that made it possible to build a self-sustaining force field that could protect anything from a bag of marbles(his application) to the largest city in the world. He was certain that it could encircle the world.

It converted radiation from the ultra-violet spectrum of the sun, regardless whether the day was cloudy or sunny. If there was any degree of radiation at all, it worked at full strength.

The Key

Government agents, happy to learn of his invention, were made unhappy because Kenneth made it's use conditional; it was to be used as a protective, not an offensive, weapon. Two months after he had presented his plans to the government, he published and advertised his equations in every major scientific journal in the world.

The media's response was overwhelming to the Professor's household. The President dispatched the Secret Service to protect Kenneth from abduction by foreign agents. Local police had their hands full with anti-nuclear groups who appeared to show their enthusiasm. Missile manufacturers, corporations that made enormous profits from defense projects expressed displeasure and would like to have throttled him.

The news media at first hailed him as a hero, then labelled him a traitor for giving the equations to the world-at-large. They predicted doom and gloom, but nothing they projected came to pass.

Kenneth, The Professor and his wife rejected all monetary offers, then refused to speak to anyone in the media. Kenneth couldn't understand what the fuss was all about. He liked to put mathematical things together.

The Professor's friends, dedicated to various disciplines, established an applied physics laboratory to test Kenneth's equations for other applications. Scientists asked Kenneth if the field could be applied to automobiles.

Kenneth had his learner's permit and when driving, studied the engine, the braking system and the steering mechanism. Then, he went into the den to think and to work on the necessary equations.. He sent the results of his exercises to the research lab.

Using his expanded equations, the scientists designed a black box to protect the vehicle that could fit into the trunk of an automobile. When the ignition key was turned

Earth - Mars

on, a forcefield immediately surrounded the car which only a gaseous substance could penetrate. Anything with a greater mass was immediately repelled, with the effect being operative at twelve inches from any part of the vehicle.

In the first test, the car ended up in a neighbor's living room. The forcefield not only surrounded the car, but also held it twelve inches off the ground and the driver had no control. That possibility had not occurred to Kenneth and he went back to work at it some more.

Although this field could possibly protect the vehicle and its occupants, the scientists were not happy. They wanted the force to propel the car. Kenneth considered all the possibilities with the applied science professors.

One morning, Kenneth was watching the news about the N.A.S.A. space shuttle that was having difficulties. The newscaster said that they had only two hours to hit the window. Kenneth's eyes widened with inspiration. "That's it," he muttered.

He changed his equation so that a window was formed around the tires of the automobile. Calculating the basic equasion, Kenneth stopped for a moment and grinned. He worked for two days, proving and disproving his equation; he believed that he was right. Then, he sent them to the research lab.

They were puzzled by the formula for when applied to the problem of the automobile, nothing worked. Finally, one of them went to question Kenneth. Kenneth apologized and explained that the new equation had nothing to do with automobiles.

"In fact," he continued, "the automobile may soon be obsolete. I was watching the blast-off of the NASA shuttle last week and was struck by the use of the term "space" window. I know what they mean. There is a

The Key

certain time that a given area of space is available for a space vehicle to obtain orbit. I tried to apply the window to the contact of an automobile tire to a given surface."

The scientist was intrigued. "And ?"

"I remembered the enormous noise and burning of fuel when the shuttle left the launch pad. This seemed to be a greater waste of fuel than the use of an automobile. The equations I gave you, from the perspective of a space driver, narrow the forcefield to a small area with it's force concentrated to practically throw a shuttle off the earth. It also can be reversed. It's power can be used to control easy lift off and an easy return."

Amazed at this new development, the lab professors moved into Kenneth's house and spent twenty-four hours a day working on the forcefield application.

Six months later, they built a small remote-controlled model and tested it in a large field. They found, after considerable practice, that it could take off slowly and soundlessly while continually gaining speed enough for orbit. Yet, it could be brought down in the same place as gently as a feather.

That night, they called NASA.

On Kenneth's nineteenth birthday, NASA launched a space shuttle with no fanfare, with no noise, with no blast of flame and smoke. The shuttle quietly lifted off the launch pad, circled the moon twice and quietly returned.

With amazement, they discovered that this space drive, for any given period of time, doubled the speed of the vehicle.

Mankind was headed for the stars. The Rackner Drive, whose inventor had been salvaged from a garbage can, led man into space.

Earth - Mars

****

  Scientists all over the world worked with the new mathematics of Kenneth Rackner. It opened new fields of thought as had the Einsteinian theories of the past. Another deeper level of reasoning, and a new direction away from conventional mathematics was presented for them to consider. The door was opened and many walked through it.
  A normal Space Drive was developed that could lift anything from the pull of earth's gravity. Only a small amount of power was needed to activate it. The American Society of Scientists developed a sub-space drive that turned millions of light years of distance into a short journey in actual time.
  Domes were designed and redesigned until they were so strong that they could be made impenetrable with a flick of a switch or the push of a button.
  Swedish scientists produced a laser that could be converted to the size of a pistol and was more deadly than any known weapon. Sweden, known for its neutrality and political independence, decided that if man were to explore the universe he needed protection from any undeterminable kind of wildlife he might encounter. It tried to protect the invention, but as it was whispered throughout the world, Sweden put it on the market to profit from its manufacture.
  Landings on the moon began and it was soon developed as a base of operations. Wastelands, once considered to be nothing more than a platform, were mined, and in some areas, agricultural experimentation under domes was undertaken.
  World governments involved with the Moon operations soon realized that they would require a central clearing house for all information processed and transmitted.

The Key

Neither the United States, nor any other one country, had the trust of the group to gather and relay data. The United Nations Organization formed a committee consisting of one scientist from every member nation to discuss the problem and arrive at a solution.

After weeks of deliberation, the decision was made to establish a Space Station midway between Earth and the Moon. It's orbit would follow the rotation of the moon around the earth and it would be of sufficient size to hold main frame computers to which each country would have an access code.

Engineers and architects spent months together designing the Space Station that would be maintained by no more than five people, as decided by the Committee. The final problem was one of authority: who would be the Executive In Charge of the Space Station? Arguments for and against were hot and heavy for it was an important post.

Indeed, to everyone's great surprise, it was the Russian representative on the Committee who suggested that the original mathematician be asked to supervise the Space Station; Mr. Kenneth Rackner.

Approval was immediate.

Kenneth Rackner agreed to meet with the Engineers to discuss the new Space Station's structure emphasizing composition, materials and shape. He was not asked to decide on supervizing its operation until he had presented his ideas and needs to the engineers.

The more he thought about the project, the more Kenneth liked it. He would have a place to develop new discoveries through the Station; he would have a well-equipped laboratory and a lounge. He would insist upon crystal windows to reduce distortion as he planned to study the stars as much as possible.

Earth - Mars

Kenneth went to the United Nations Space Development Center to talk with the engineers. The Chief Engineer met him as he stepped from the limo hired to deliver him.

"Good morning, Mr. Rackner. It's a pleasure to have you on our team," he said.

"It's a pleasure to meet you," Kenneth replied, shaking hands. "I hope we can come to an agreement on some of the ideas that I have."

As they walked through the front door of the Complex, the engineer chuckled and said,

"Mr. Rackner, I have talked with some of the professors that were in the original laboratory established by you and your father. I'm sure that we can get along fine."

They entered the architectural section and Kenneth generally outlined what he would incorporate in the Station. Everything received a nod of approval until he mentioned the crystaline windows. Eyebrows raised, faces frowned.

"Mr. Rackner," the Chief Engineer protested, "crystalline windows are very expensive and to be strong enough to withstand the pressures of space, they will have to be very thick."

"Two and one-quarter inches," replied Kennath. "That thickness will stand three earth pressures, or 11.1 punds per square inch."

"I will take your suggestions to the Committee. That is an extra expense, but I don't think it will be a problem. Still, I must get approval."

"There is one other small problem that you might present to the Committee. I want the authority to pick my own crew. The four people will be qualified. I do not want them assigned immediately, but will choose them as I need them. For the present, I want only one scientist

The Key

to accompany me, an engineer."

The Chief Engineer made notes and told Ken he would get back to him in the morning. When informed that his proposals were accepted by the Committee, Ken agreed to accept the position, saying he would provide the name of his engineer at a later date.

The architects sectionalized the Space Station on paper; the engineers manufactured the sections. Lifted into it's two thousand mile orbit, sections were welded together and in six months, the Space Station was finished.

The installation of the main frame computer and the communications equipment required yet another month. Meanwhile, NASA was receiving telemetry and radio data from domes on the moon.

Ken's first operation was the accumulation of all the records that NASA had acquired throughout the years. It was a full-time job, necessary, but boring. He asked for a computer programmer and technician and the Committee sent Dora Compton, a near-genius who had worked for IBM, until she found the job dull.

Dora contacted field terminals on the moon and on Mars, informing them of this new center for all data. They were to transmit all information to the Space Station Coordination Center. Information required by them would be available upon demand. The efforts of all scientists were being coordinated efficiently.

Dora grid-mapped the surfaces of the Moon and Mars marking the locations of all domes. She asked Ken to issue an order instructing all field-working personnel to code in their locations on the grid every four hours. Accountability of personnel was most important in coordinating efforts in any given direction or discipline.

Ken called Chief Engineer Robert Cramer and invited him to be his assistant. "I need someone who knows

Earth - Mars

every weld and bolt and machine. Will you accept?"

"I was hoping you would call," Bob laughed. "I like that piece of junk we've put up there. You people may be scientists, but you know nothing about keeping the Station running." He arrived the next day at noon.

The Space Coordination Center ran smoothly. Kenneth turned his attention to problems encountered by scientists with field equipment; to converting his mathematical equations fitting more practical applied scientific endeavors such as Moon to Earth Flitters for single passengers, Sand Crawlers for personnel on Moon and Mars and innovative dome structures for habitats.

Mankind was on its way to the Solar System, not haphazzardly, but methodically with an efficiency that kept accidents to a minimum.

****

The year was 2025. Fifty earth years had passed and the human race was climbing out of its cradle, beginning to understand what it saw. It was comprehending abstract implications of actions, building compassion, losing fear of the unknown.

With the use of the Rackner Force Field and the Rackner Hyper-Space Drive, the United States became the first nation to explore the Solar System of which Earth was one of the nine known planets. There were colonies on Mars, and on the moons of Jupiter, Saturn, Uranus and Neptune. Giant-sized Space Stations were established for scientific and industrial experimental purposes.

The Rackner Process Formula had proved to be a veritable key to the treasure of the Universe. Gravity on various planets was adjusted for human use within giant domes which contained the proper atmosphere. Personal

The Key

force fields made mobility possible. Exploration and discovery ran rampant all over the planets.

Earth became the benefactor of the discoveries. Scientific space stations and platforms became testing and development centers and the earth flourished. The combinations of minerals and chemicals of other planets with those of earth reconstituted diminishing resources permitting earth to bask in a rebirth. Most chemical forms of the planets complimented those of earth and produced new processes and new products. The people themselves developed different perspectives.

There no longer was hunger on earth. The addition of a chemical found on Mars made the deserts disappear. Seeds and grains, which the poor had devoured so quickly, showed a surplus used to develop their own crops which were now harvested four times a year instead of the usual two. New fertilizers and the use of agricultural domes fed the surplus which was transported via Hyper-Spatial Beaming to outer planets for sustenance until they became self-supporting.

There was no reason for war. There was a psychological change in attitudes due to the fact that anyone who wished could travel via space ship to any of the planets. In the beginning, few had the courage or the desire to make such trips, but after they spoke to those who had returned, many developed an urge to see for themselves. Perhaps it was the far-away look in the eyes or the sense of a subtle, but never-the-less, change in the travelers themselves. A great, unstoppable feeling spread across the world. Doctors and psychologists could not explain it for they, themselves, were affected by it.

There was an increase in the sense of purpose; people were less interested in the trivial. Greater understanding of the Cosmos grew and the role of human

Earth - Mars

destiny within it as more people traveled the universe. Contention, individually and collectively, became less and less evident.

This whole turnaround in attitudes toward space was the result of a law, made mandatory, that on each space vehicle an explanation of the Solar System was presented. It included the billions of stars that made up our Galaxy, and the billions of Galaxies of which we are just one. The totality of the Universe was shown.

The effects were amazing on earth. People of all ages returned to schools. Schools changed curricula to furnish a higher degree of learning. This in turn affected the understanding of the ultimate destiny of mankind.

The House of Representatives was streamlined into an efficient operative arm of the government. There were no longer protracted, politically motivated speeches. They represented the people and what the people desired or wanted to be done.

The great chamber, where they had met before, was used now occasionally; set aside for meetings with off-world representatives to discuss problems of relationships between them and Earth.

There was an annual meeting of all off-world government officials to discuss developing technology that might present problems to any given planet. The space stations were the major source of helpful information.

Each Senator and Representative had a suite of offices equipped with a direct-connect computer terminal to every member of Congress. Comment on any bill was initiated by pushing a button; a number was given in turn to use the terminal. All comments would appear on the screens of the Congressional membership. All business was recorded, filmed and stored in the Congressional Record. Any Congressional member wishing to recall a

The Key

particular day's business had only to call it up on his computer and it would flash on a ten-foot screen in his central office.

Special interest groups were no longer permitted to lobby in Washington, D.C. Nothing was to distract the members from their duty to their constituents. Such lobbying activity was confined to the home state of Congressional members.

When the law against abortion came before the Congress, the Supreme Court was asked to write indiviual opinions and to present them to each member of Congress. The individual opinions were all against abortion. Since there was life in the father and mother at conception, there had to be life as a result of their union. Therefore, the fetus was to be considered as having life.

The Congress passed an anti-abortion law in short order with a wide majority in both houses. With much ceremony, the President signed the bill into Law. It contained a requirement that all doctors report to police officials all abortions performed; the only acceptable reason was to save the life of the mother.

The report was recorded with the State Medical Board. An abortion performed, other than to save the life of the mother, was prosecuted as murder. Government funds were cut off and insurance companies cancelled policies.

The debate over prayer in schools finally ended when the Congress was in the process of drawing up a bill to permit it.

An earlier furor concerned the separation of Church and State. It was settled when the President had appeared on television stating that he was considering the recall of all American currency in order to reissue it without the words "*In God We Trust.*" He stated that it was the purest and the most profound hypocrisy for Congress to open it's

Earth - Mars

session with a prayer when school children were denied prayer in school and when public buildings were not permitted to display the word God.

"Therefore," the President said, "It would be removed immediately." In all public cemeteries, military and otherwise, maintained with taxpayers' monies there could be no mention of God. Crosses, angels and other religious symbolism would be a violation of the separation of Church and State. No state seal or official document could contain a word referring to a deity. In Courts of Law the term "perjury" would have to be redefined as there could be no *So help me God* as part of the sworn testimony.

The reaction was immediate and the uproar was great. The Mafia families had no manner in which to account for the money being laundered; quiet foreign investors were in a panic; the underground economy, noted for avoiding taxes, took a nose dive.

The public, when it found out that the cost to change the currency would be somewhere in the billions, began to think, and after many marches objecting to the action aided of course by the Mafia, soon quieted down. Senators and Congressmen soon got letters supporting the bill. It passed and was signed by the President, but the bill did not call for prayer in school as such; only for minute of silence at the beginning of each school day and the teachers would be permitted to encourage the students to pray to their God.

The first ten years after the inception of prayer in the schools did not seem to matter one way or another. Bishops noted a marked increase in church attendance, but it was a matter of debate whether this was due solely to prayer in school or not.

The exodus of mankind into space and the need for a

The Key

belief in something, a leaning post to make the unknown supportable and bearable, could have something to do with it. Man still found himself alone in the Universe for no other civilization had been discovered. He was exploring his own house, his Solar System, and he had not yet ventured beyond, to a different Solar System.

There were differences in the Bishops, Priests and Ministers of Christianity and in the Rabbis of Judaism and the Leaders of Islam. They no longer preached, nor taught, from opinionated human writings and interpretations. They preached and taught their basic scriptures. All taught the brotherhood of man and the Fatherhood of the Most High. They did not condone actions against governments or anything or anyone. Except, of course, evil. They did not preach against the profane world.

They taught that there was a time and a place, in this dimension, for everything. That it all pointed toward one direction. Toward Eternity. They taught much more, each in accordance with his basic fundamental belief.

All these things went with man to the planets.

The Rackner Dome, as the force field became known, created an enclosed area where weather could be controlled. Every farmer in the world used it to grow his crops. Chemical mixtures from the planets and earth were used in sprays to saturate the atmosphere to make it rain, for it was proven that the washing effect of rain was better for the plants than irrigation.

The earth, once again, was considered the Green Earth.

****

In Badwater, California, a Convention was being held. The City Fathers were happy about the whole thing, but

Earth - Mars

they were a little confused. There had never been a Convention in their town; in fact, most people avoided the place. Vacationers passed through or just stopped to take pictures of Death Valley. The heat was unbearable and there were few facilities for large groups.

But here they were, a large group of sober-faced young men and women led by a leader, a blond, curley-headed young man in a blue suit.

One morning, the townspeople awakened and found a chill in the air rather than the usual heat. It wasn't cold; just a coolness they had never before felt. They also found that the young, convention people were gone.

The large group of young people were standing silently in a desolate part of Death Valley. They were slowly looking older. Perhaps it was the result of the terror that showed in their eyes. The heat was twice the usual 125 degrees but they did not perspire. Suddenly there appeared before them and the blond young man, the purple and red circles. In the midst of their brilliant spinning was the face of the man-dragon, with the thin cruel lips and the cold green eyes rimmed by a flashing red.

"I warned you not to fail again!" The voice sounded like a rumble echoing in a hollow cave. "Your failure has given the enemy more power." The face was terrible to see. The young people shrank back, stumbling, falling, trampling one another. Jumping up, they fought each other, shouting blame on everyone but themselves.

The old man disappeared and in his place appeared a giant chasm. One by one, each person was changed into a red and black atom, then sent screaming into the chasm. Those observing screamed, "No! No!" but to no avail. They all fell into the depths and the chasm closed with a shattering noise like thunder. An earthquake shook

The Key

all of southern California. One square mile of the southern end of Death Valley detached itself from the earth and hurtled into space.

The Asteroid Belt acquired an additional asteroid.

****

Kenneth Rackner was bored. The Space Platform he had occupied for the past ten years was beginning to close in on him and his unlimited imagination was beginning to pall. He needed a change.

He had solved the problem of the Force Field Dome, the conversion of its mathematics, then the sub-space drive. These had given man the opportunity to crawl out of the cradle into the direction of the stars. His new mathematics became the basis for many other bright mathematicians to develop molecular formulae that helped to solve earth's human-induced problems.

The rivers and streams were clear and pure; the forests no longer suffered from the ancient acid rain; smoke stack industries were gone. The environmental ills of the past no longer existed. Sociological ills continued as man was still human, but they had been reduced without destroying freedom and choice. Innovation and imagination flourished.

The Great Scroll was accepted as the basis for all governments with the addition of one amendment that had been the subject of a speech by an early American citizen: *The best of governments was the least of governments, and that even the best was but a necessary evil.*

This encouraged the countries of all the planets to maintain as little government as possible, interfering in the lives of the people only when it was unavoidable.

Rackner looked back with amused reflection at all

Earth - Mars

that had happened in so short a span of time. He was sixteen when he had written his original equations and now he was forty years old.

Dora had departed for a better position on the Moon where she was in charge of all computer and material transmission equipment. He heard from her on occasion, but it was not her absence that was troubling him.

Why, then, was he so bored? He had everything he could want; his station was the best equipped in the entire Solar System. But the technology was useless without the inspiration to effectively use it. He wasn't sure that he was inspired; that it would be an impediment to innovation. Man had the habit of relying on what he knew and using it as a basis for development, instead of searching through his ignorance for inspiration.

Kenneth stood before the quartz window that stretched from floor to ceiling and was as wide. He could see the stars shining in all their glory. It seemed as though he was transcended outside himself, surrounded by clouds of stardust with millions of bright centers. Each of the centers was held in place by invisible hands of the planets that surrounded him. Under his feet was an invisible firmament.

He felt as though he could drift forever among the stars. There was no fear; no joy; no agitation; his feelings were in neutral. He watched objectively the changing scene and he knew within himself, that *everything* was alive, waiting for mankind to acknowledge the fact.

He was leaning with his hand on the quartz window. He sighed and crossed the room to a small couch, where with his head on one arm of the couch and his feet dangling over the other end, he fell into a half-sleep, his mind trying to rid itself of the boredom.

The Key

After a half hour, he suddenly sat bolt upright. "Why not?" He asked himself. "I have never been to any of the planets. So busy, I've never had the time nor the inclination. It's time to see new things and get new ideas."

Kenneth contacted his assistant, Bob Gantry.

"Hey, Bob. Call earth and tell them to send up a small interpanetary hopper. We're going to do a little traveling."

"Coming right up. By the way," Bob asked. "Where are we going?"

"Mars, first. It's the closest."

The year, earth time, was 2050 and Mars was approaching it's perhelion, the time when it was closest to the sun and the earth was between it and the sun. The approximate distance would be 35,000,000 miles from Earth to Mars. Ken's Space Station was two thousand miles above Earth, so the distance was not much diminished. But with the Rackner Drive it would take a relatively short time to reach Mars.

Kenneth studied his Space Almanac and found that Mars is the third smallest planet in the Solar System with a diameter of 4220 miles, a little more than one-half the size of Earth. With a sudden urge to make comparisons, he jotted in his notebook. Compared to Earth, Mars was:

Surface...	2/7th of Earth
Volume....	1/7th of Earth
Mass......	1/9th of Earth
Revolutions...	24 hrs/37 min/23sec
Orbit.....	687 Earth days
Axis tilt.....	25 degrees/12 minutes
Moons.....	Phobos, Deimos

Deimos revolves around Mars... 30 hrs. 18 min.

91

Earth - Mars

Phobos revolves around Mars... 7 hrs. 39.min.

Kenneth read and reread the figures. Something in the back of his mind bothered him, but he could not bring it to the surface. He continued to read and to make notes.

In the past, astronomers and scientists had studied Mars through telescopes and had taken pictures. They had reported clouds and light measurements indicating that the average atmospheric temperature was 218 degrees K.

During the 1970's, a probe had been sent and it had shown that Mars had no magnetic field and no radiation belts around it and that the surface atmospheric pressure was only about 3% of Earth's atmospheric pressure. There were no clouds in evidence at that time, and Mars appeared to be a round globe, pock-marked and cratered over it's entire surface. The only previous data shown to be correct was that the Polar Caps were thought to be ice.

Kenneth laughed. He knew what had been bothering him. If such mistakes had been made in the past by Earth's leading scientists before the Seventies and if most data had been proven wrong by the Mars Probe, could he be sure that the little he knew now was correct?

Facts that man thought true about Earth were still being disproved. Man was still finding startling truths about his own Earth. What bothered him most of all was that being a mathematician, something in his notes did not fit.

He closed his notebook, forgoing the problem until later. He packed his small computer it its case and placed it with the instruments he was taking with him. Then, he had the Communications Room notify the scientists on Mars that he would visit them within twenty-four hours.

The Key

Unlike space ships that most people imagine, the space ship from Earth was not a long, silvery needle-nosed vehicle. It was, instead, a series of boxlike structures with egg-shaped bumps here and there. It sat on a pancake-like structure that housed the drive section.

The loading was done, goodbyes said. The little ship did not enter Huper-Space, but accelerated to just under the speed of light. To those aboard, it seemed to stand still.

Kenneth was nervous with anticipation as it was the first time he had set foot on another planet. He walked out of the Space Craft and down the ramp, forgetting the lesser gravity that lengthened his stride and caused him to rise a little.

"Steady, Boss," Bob laughed. "This takes getting used to."

They walked across the landing to the reception area, a building shaped like a dome with the sides cut into arches so that the four corners were anchored in the red Martian soil. Behind it rose the tallest tower Kenneth had ever seen. It reached, with very little support, to the underside of the covering dome.

"What's that?" Kenneth asked.

"That's the molecular beam receptor and transmitter from here to Earth," Bob explained. "It's the transport system between us. You should know. You helped to develop it."

"Only the mathematics and the theory," Kenneth muttered. "I've never seen one before."

They entered the building and were met by the Station Commander. Every station, off-Earth, was controlled by the military with the scientists as advisors. This Commander was impressed by the world's most well known scientist, but tried to hide it.

Earth - Mars

"Good morning, gentlemen. If you will come with me, I'll see that you are issued quarters numbers and ration tickets. I'm sure you realize that everything here is rationed and we must keep a strict account of all goods."

He handed them each a small circular piece of metal about the size of a quarter. "Be sure," he instructed, "to keep this with you at all times, even when you sleep or bathe. It tells Central where you are and reports your physical condition. We have not lost anyone yet, and I would not like to break our record."

Ken put the instrument in his tunic pocket, then followed Bob and the Commander out of the building and into a ground car. The Ground Cars of Mars were well known and other planets were trying to duplicate them. They ran on magnetic rails, using negative current for the rails and vehicles, but were powered by converting solar radiation into electrical energy. The system was coded and computerized so there was little danger of accidents. The cars were constructed of silicon and cadmium mixed with an aluminum alloy. Above the seats, the curved roof was silicon crystal and almost invisible.

The top and the doors closed with a gentle whoosh and the air-pressure began to build to Earth normal. "Why the pressure build-up?" asked Kenneth.

"So that there will be no adverse effects when you leave the dome," the Commander answered. "It is not absolutely necessary, but we do it to be sure there are no air leaks. There is a light on board that will flash if the pressure drops. We have never had a leak, but if that should happen, an automatic alarm will be set off in Central Control and all other vehicles will clear the track. Then the Board will show the shortest distance to the nearest dome."

Kenneth had presumed that to be the case, but had

The Key

asked because this was a learning trip and with his recorder on, he wanted as much information as he could acquire. He changed the subject as they began to glide with ever-increasing speed over the rails.

"Have you, or any of the scientists, found any evidence of the canal system like the ones thought in the past to have existed?" They sped along the iron oxide surface.

"There have been none reported by the scientists, but of course, everyone has a pet theory or idea. I've been here since the beginning, five years ago, and so far there has been nothing proven. There are some lower areas that could be called valleys, I suppose, but nothing definite."

Ken watched the landscape, fascinated by the redness of it.

"Iron oxide," he mused. "In other words, rust. If I think of the material in terms of earth science, I would immediately think of oxygen and hydrogen. Oh well, I'll investigate later."

Ken had often wondered about the far-away look in the eyes of those who had travelled in space. He could never understand that look, that all-knowing look of peace when anyone mentioned the Cosmos or travel through the Universe. It was as if they had seen things of an indescribable beauty or of the terror of things not understood. He had felt as though he were less an insider and more of an outsider of the human race.

As he stared at the blackness of space, the myriad of stars, the redness of Mars that did not reflect in the vacuum around him, he began to comprehend why they had that look in their eyes.

The ground vehicle arrived at the Scientists' Dome and was admitted. They stopped at the top of a flight of

Earth - Mars

stairs and were immdediately overwhelmed by the sound of applause. The scientists had gathered to greet one of their own, and possible the best. They shook hands and treated Ken and Bob like long lost brothers, insisting that they dine with them that evening. Ken and Bob readily agreed and then took their equipment and luggage to their quarters. Once inside, Bob remarked,

"I hope this doesn't happen every time we move."

"I imagine we'll get used to it," Ken replied and went to take a shower. He stripped off his Mars suit and stepped into the cubicle. There were no water valves, but a set of buttons that read "On" and "Off" and a sign: "Be certain to close the door firmly before activating the shower."

Ken made sure the door was shut properly and pushed the "On" button. He expected to be drenched by water but instead he felt a tingling over all his body. There was a slight draft of air across his feet from a one inch opening that appeared on both sides of the cubicle. The tingling left him and an ultraviolet light filled the space. When the light went out, the door clicked. He pushed the "Off" button, stepped out and donned his Mars suit.

"Hey, Bob," he called, "You like these showers?"

"Call it a shower if you like," came the answer, "but I prefer the kind with water."

Ken laughed. "I guess there are many things we shall have to get used to on this trip."

They went to the dining area to meet the scientists. The food was plain and simple. Liquids were consumed through tubes because of the gravity. It was not null gravity, but being one-third of earth's gravity, liquids had the tendency to slop around while in the glasses. The solid food slid and moved very quickly if a knife or fork were used too forcibly. During their last tube of coffee, one of the scientists asked Ken,

"When was the last time you were earth-side, Mr. Rackner?"

"About two months ago," Ken replied.

"How is the environmental situation? Are there problems we can help with?"

"The last I heard, things were pretty much under control, but they are running into sociological problems. The one concern with the physical world is about domes and the jet stream. There are no domes allowed north and south of the 75 degree lines from the Equator in both directions, due to the possibility of melting the ice caps. Well, it seems that a few countries are experimenting with the establishment of domes deep into the ice pack. This in turn, could cause difficulty with sea levels in the future, and then in turn, with the tides. It is actually more of a sociological problem to make the population understand the limits of technological developments."

Other conversations had ceased and the scientists turned to listen. "What people are doing this?" asked one.

"The people mostly involved are anthropologists attempting to trace human history and animal genetics. There has been a law passed in some countries that anyone establishing a dome in the Arctic or Antarctic will be exiled to one of the colonies in the Solar System."

"How does this relate to the jet stream?" asked another.

"The jet stream is nothing more than the movement of air caused by the earth's rotation and it's direction, both north and south, is controlled by the earth's tilt and various differences in temperature and atmospheric pressure. It now seems that domes we have already established are causing a greenhouse effect outside, as

Earth - Mars

well as inside, by interfering with atmospheric circulation. And of course, people are using domes for uses not originally intended, so we shall have to enact more laws to control their use. It seems that when we solve one problem, two more spring up." Ken turned and asked,

"Are there any adaptibility problems here on Mars?"

"None" replied the scientist, "as long as we remain inside the domes or wear cumbersome space suits. It seems a shame that we cannot convert Mars into a livable world. There is so much that we need to learn."

"Have you tried to break down the soil?" Ken asked.

"We have sent soil samples to the Lab on Earth because we don't have the facilities here to do a complete analysis. The atmosphere is mostly carbon dioxide and water, what there is of it. The land itself as far as we can determine, is mostly rust. We can't be sure what kind of oxidation has taken place, or why, or even if it covers the entire surface of the planet."

Another spoke up. "It is possible that melting ice caps somewhere below the surface are causing the red-brown coloring. The ice cap in the northern pole does not completely melt in the summer and does reconstitute itself in the winter; while the ice cap in the south melts completely in the summer and reappears in the winter. These actions take place at exactly opposite times of the Martian year. One melts and the other rebuilds, then they reverse the process. A check of the thin atmosphere flow, the winds, essentially follow the same timetable. The thin layer of clouds you observed when approaching Mars is the result of CO_2 ice (dry ice) and minute particles of dust flowing north or south."

All of the scientists joined in with their speculations and with their discoveries concerning Mars. All decried the necessity of wearing space suits although

The Key

they admitted that they were not uncomfortable in pursuit of their investigations.

Ken and Bob agreed that they were a group of frustrated scientists who would need help in settling the planet. Ken took notes and said he would consult them when he returned to his Space Station.

During the next week Ken and Bob travelled between the domes of Mars. They acquired samples of Martian soil, from planet dust to coarse aggregate, and stored them in their small ship. They travelled to the north and south Polar Caps and discovered that the melting caps did not leave any liquid. When the temperature rose, the "ice", which was a combination of CO_2 and H_2O, turned into a gaseous state and was blown away by the movement of the thin air.

But, Ken wondered, blown away where? Nothing is destroyed in Nature, it only changes form.

They took many pictures of the light and dark areas with both natural light and with infra-red film. Each time, they returned to their dome, very tired, and longing to see something other than the red or red-brown color.

Alone in his cubicle, Ken wrote a list of the planets in the Solar System as they progressed from the sun to the furthest known planet:

Mercury, Venus, Earth, Mars, Jupiter, Saturn, Uranus, Neptune, Pluto. In that order, from the sun outward, he also listed the Asteroid Belt that was between Mars and Jupiter. He sat and stared at the lists.

"What am I looking for?" he mused. "I don't know. There is something here that makes me uneasy. There's something I should be seeing; some combination, some mixture. There is something unbalanced in the equation of parts."

He reflected on the time he had solved the

Earth - Mars

mathematics of the domes. He recalled what had happened with the toxic waste dilemma and how it was solved. Everyone wanted to bury it in someone else's city, town or state. Then reserach teams had tried to combine it to produce a product or at least to neutralize it, but that hadn't worked either.

Then, one intelligent scientist had taken small vials of every known toxic waste, and along with other wastes, had fed their atomic structures into his computer. He determined which of the atomic elements would lend themselves to electrovalence, which would be compatible to covalence, which would form ions with the same valence to produce Ionic agglomerates. In covalence, the atoms interpenetrate to form molecules.

The process was difficult because inert materials became active in certain combinations. He filtered out the inert materials, then recombined the elements of the various compounds into useable material.

His work resulted in the discovery of many new compounds that, with imagination, could be substituted for raw materials that were being mined on Earth. The manufacturing of these substitutes proved to be less toxic and the overall process turned away from one that wasted much to one that wasted little.

"Nothing in Nature can be destroyed; it only changes form." If that were true, Ken thought, then it would be logical that the Solar System would follow the same law. Maybe. Ken would need all the data he could get about the planets.

He called Bob. If they could determine, using Earth as the norm, what was missing from each of the planets, there was a possibility of supplying some of the missing parts. Then, let Nature take its course.

Jupiter and Saturn were believed to be two enormous

The Key

gaseous planets, but it was not known if they contained nuclei which could be the surfaces from which to measure altitude. Because their atmospheres were similar, Ken linked the two. They contained, chiefly, Hydrogen Gas, about 90% and 94%. Helium was next most common, followed by methane, amonia, water. hydrogen cyanide, carbon monoxide, phosphine and germane. Saturn's atmosphere was also thought to contain methyl acetylene and propane.

The data accumulated meant very little to Kenneth or to Bob, but they believed that the computer would be capable of making the necessary comparisons. They also included moons of the planets.

Packing all their notes and the samples of the rock strata, they returned to Mars-Port, checked out with the Port Commander, and in the little flitter, returned to the Space Coordination Center, Ken's Space Station.

They began their studies of the collected data and cataloged the information they had gathered.

****

During the summer, Professor Bontor worked for the Government in one of the Space Domes on Mars, and if something extraordinary needed analyzing, he would take a sabbatical to get the job finished. It was on one of these sabbaticals that his work made it necessary to visit Kenneth Rackner at his Space Station Laboratory.

Mars was a difficult planet to investigate or to prospect, for analyzing it's mass was like analyzing Earth rust. Scientists could not arrive at an answer as to what had caused the minerals to change to a rusty red - whether it was natural or the result of oxidation.

The Professor was told to find the chemical

Earth - Mars

composition of a series of disks that had been found in a small tunnel in one of the dark areas that formed areas of the canals. The circular objects were thought to be stone at the time of their discovery. They were registered and put aside for further consideration when time permitted. While storing other objects, a scientist glanced at the disks when the light had been at the right angle and he noticed markings on their surfaces, so small and so fine he had to look closely. He turned them over and found similar markings on both sides.

The Director of Research called Earth and asked for the Professor's help. He wanted an in-depth analysis of the disks' physical structure before a study of the markings should begin. The Professor, finding that the Mars Field Domes did not have sufficient equipment for his work, asked Kenneth if he could bring them to the Space Station Laboratory. The answer was affirmative. Little did either realize that one of the major questions of centuries was about to be answered.

※※※※※※※※※※※※※

George Cramer was ten years old, developing physically as any ten-year-old, but mentally, George was in a world of his own. He did not like a world where he could see everything's atomic structure. He did not like a world where everything was normal to everyone else and a double world to him. The former frightened him; the latter disgusted him. He reacted to the way he felt because he didn't understand his gift, nor it's implications for his own life and for humanity.

George was sitting on his porch with two rocks, one in each hand. He was looking at the molecular structure of each and was trying to put them together. The instant

The Key

the electrons touched, he met resistance.

He twisted and turned them, trying to get them to mesh or combine, but no luck. He didn't understand. They were the same, but they were different and George knew little about nuclear physics or molecular physics. If anyone had mentioned these scientific disciplines to him, he would not have known what they were talking about. He was a little boy and even though his brain contained a complete college education, there was a gulf as wide as the Grand Canyon between having the knowledge and understanding the application of it.

George had left behind quite a record for the short time he had sat in college classes. He had also made quite an impression on the Chemistry Professor. In a fit of anger and disgust, both of which came easily to George, he had demonstrated his ability to detect the atomic, molecular and chemical components of a small piece of material brought in by this Professor Bontor from N.A.S.A. The Chemistry Professor was naming the components of the chemicals it contained and George, being bored, had risen from his seat and named them all, including a couple that the Professor did not know. Professor Bontor called the Space Agency after class was dismissed to verify and found that George had been right. It was a lesson the Professor would never forget.

****

Professor Bontor arrived from Mars with the disks and was welcomed by Bob. "I hope we can be of some assistance to you," he said. "You must realize that the best equipment is on Earth. We do have a competent technologically sophisticated lab, but the very best is at the University of California."

Earth - Mars

"Yes, I know. But I think your equipment will be sufficient."

"I'll show you your quarters. Ken will meet you in the Lounge and then will show you the Lab." Bob led the Professor along the outer corridor to a room that had a large quartz window providing a breath-taking view of the stars. There were lounge chairs and small tables and a desk with a computer.

"This computer is tied into the Computer Central at Space Command on Earth as well as to all the computers in off-world locations. A log in the top right-hand drawer will give you the call codes, including the main one here on the lower levels. The banks have twenty billion storage units and they contain everything we have learned from day one of the Space Program. You are free to use any of the information on record," Bob said as he walked toward the door. "Good luck! We'll see you in the Lounge when you are ready."

The Professor unpacked his bags, removed the disks from the sealed bag and placed them in the top left-hand draw of the desk. He changed his mind and slipped one of the disks into the pocket of his single unit jump suit. With a sigh of relief, he laid down on the couch for a nap. The first leg of his soon-to-be-momentous journey was finished.

Two hours later, the Professor joined Kenneth and Bob in the Lounge. Ken had spread a pile of papers before him on the center table and was calculating the atmosphere of various planets. Intent on his work, Ken had a tendency to be short when it came to conversation.

"Ken," Bob said, "this is Professor Bontor from Space Agency. Professor, this is Kenneth Rackner, Director of the Space Program, Off-Earth."

"Very pleased to meet you," said Professor Bontor.

The Key

"Likewise," muttered Ken. "Take a seat. I'll be right with you." He continued his calculations. The Professor looked at Bob with raised eyebrows. Bob smiled, shrugged and motioned to a chair. Ten minutes later, Ken sighed and put away his calculator, pushed back his papers and smiled at the Professor.

"Sorry. I was in the midst of some critical calculations and I didn't want to lose my train of thought. What can I do to help you with your work?"

The Professor reached into his pocket and removed the disk. He placed it on the table in front of Ken.

"This was found," he said, "in one of the dark areas on Mars. I must analyze the structure of these disks, so I would like to use your laboratory equipment."

"Help yourself. If you need anything, just call on Bob or myself. All of our facilities are at your disposal."

"Thank you. By the way, I used to be pretty good at math. Is there anything I can do to help you?"

Bob laughed aloud. "I think you are going to have your hands full with those disks. Say! What are these markings on this one? It looks like a series of straight lines in groups and the groups are in rows."

"Yes," Professor Bontor replied. "We have noted the markings but are taking one step at a time. If the material is of natural origin, that poses one set of questions; but if the disks have been manufactured, then we have a different set of questions. I must determine the origin of the material."

"I see," said Ken. "I'll be interested in what you find. Please keep me informed. Perhaps we can work together to find the meaning of the marks."

"I will indeed. Bob, can you show me where the lab is located?"

"Sure." They left the lounge and Ken returned to his

Earth - Mars

work. In the lab, Professor Bontor was cleaning one of the disks. He placed it in a large glass dish and brushed it gently to remove extraneous material. From an eye-dropper, he carefully dropped one drop of water on the edge of the disk. The result startled him! The edge of the disk disappeared the instant the water touched it. It did not melt nor run down into the dish. It just vanished!

He raised the disk to see if the piece had dropped off, but it had not. He removed the disk from the dish and brushed the extraneous material into a small pile. He then carefully dropped a single drop of water on the pile. The water was absorbed and part of the material disappeared.

The Professor carefully and thoughtfully put all the disks into an air-tight plastic bag and sealed it. He sat and stared at the lab wall while he considered what to do next. He could not afford to make a mistake and have all the disks disappear altogether!

A thought crossed his mind...his most embarrasing moment with a young student. What was his name? Calner? Carmer ? George? Yes, George Carmer. No. George Cramer. "I wonder if his parents would let him help me. I had better speak to Mr. Rackner."

Ken was still hunched over his papers in the Lounge. "Mr. Rackner, if I may disturb you for a moment, I'd like to ask a favor of you."

"Shoot."

"I had a student in one of my classes. He was ten years old, but he was brilliant. He had this ability to discern the atomic and molecular structure of any material. He would save me a lot of time and work. I guess he is eleven or twelve now, but he was a character. He seemed to think the world (Earth) is a lousy place and

The Key

this was reflected in his attitude toward everything.

"Sounds interesting," Ken replied, recalling his own youth. "I'll see if I can make arrangements, but you must be responsible for him and his actions, once he is here. My work demands quiet and a lot of concentration."

"I'll see that he won't bother you." To himself he thought, "The trouble will be to get him to say or to do anything with his attitude."

Professor Bontor went to Communications and requested the University for the full name and address of George Cramer. He also requested that Cramer's parents be contacted for permission to have George visit the Space Station, for whatever reason they thought applicable.

George had never thought about space in his eleven years and when his parents broached the subject, his reaction was a hard, staring silence. He walked out of the room, went to his own room, sat on the edge of the bed and thought about it. It was not much good here on Earth and most things disgusted him with their simplicity.

He often looked at the sky, in daytime and at night. He'd adjust his sight to the atomic and molecular vision he possessed, but all he could see was the molecular structure of the atmosphere; and that was all.

He wondered for the first time in his short life what he would see if the air didn't get in the way. Maybe this was a chance to find out. A small stirring of interest began to replace the disgust and anger that constantly filled him.

He jumped off his bed and went back to the room where his parents were still talking to the representative of the University. His face was bland and passive.

"I'll go," he said. "When do we leave?"

"Tomorrow too soon?" The Dean of Students asked. He spent some time convincing George's parents that it

Earth - Mars

was safe, that he would be in good hands. Then he offered a substantial payment for George's services as consultant.

"I'll be ready," George told them.

The university limo picked George up in the morning and delivered him for the trip to the Space Station. It was uneventful, except to George. He was astounded at the darkness of space and the difference in the molecular structure from that which he was accustomed. The beauty of space left him breathless, in both the natural and the gifted order of his sight. He was quiet, subdued, when they landed. Professor Bontor considered it George's usual behavior, but if he looked into George's eyes, he would have seen that George had changed.

****

The Secretary of the Department of Health, Education and Welfare was a worried man. With the influx of students of all ages into the educational system, the budget of the Bureau of Education had risen beyond all reason. Adding to the problem was the fact that any subject currently taught changed constantly with the discovery of new theories and possibilities by the scientists scattered throughtout the Solar System. He had to devise a way to incorporate this new data into the curriculum and to also make it available to those who had graduated.

The curriculi were set by the state and there were few federal regulations to be observed. It wasn't the state laws or federal regulations that posed a problem. It was something else.

The Secretary hung his hat and coat on the office coat rack, seated himself in the high-backed chair at his

The Key

desk and swiveled around to stare out of the window. He could see the Potomac River and the Fourteenth Street bridge; the Treasury building loomed on his left. To his right, an off-world transport was landing at the National Airport.

A thought in the back of his mind continued to escape him. He sighed and turned back to his desk. The Secretary jerked upright in surprise. A stranger dressed in old clothes and rough shoes sat smiling across from him, with his caloused hands folded.

"Good morning," he smiled. "I'm sorry to have startled you."

"Who are you?" demanded the Secretary. "Who let you in? How did you get past my secretary. Miss Johnson!" he shouted and pushed a button on his desk.

"Please don't get excited," cautioned the stranger. "I'm not here to hurt you and Miss Johnson has gone for a cup of coffee. Your button will not work as long as I am here. You have a problem. Perhaps I can help."

"I still want to know how you got in here," the Secretary said indignantly. "I do not receive visitors until the afternoon."

The stranger sighed and became an Angel with golden wings and a white robe. The Secretary had heard tales of earlier Angel visits but had never believed the stories. He was startled, let out a long "Oh-h-h-h" and rubbed his eyes because of the brightness. When he looked again, the roughly clad stranger was seated in the chair.

"Mr. Secretary, please sit back and listen to me for a few minutes. No one will interrupt us and you may turn on your recorder if you wish. Just remember that no one can hear it but you. Ever."

The Secretary sat back in his chair and agreed.

Earth - Mars

"When the exodus from this earthly cradle began, most of the travellers returned to schools to better their understanding of the new technology and to be able to survive on the planets. It was a challenge. Everyone managed to get through high school, but when it came to college, older generations found it an expensive proposition. The younger generation also found it expensive but they had the advantage of youth and employment to help pay expenses.

Then, someone remembered that back in 1958 the Congress had passed the National Defense Education Act intended to raise levels of knowledge in science, mathematics and foreign languages, as well as to improve testing, guidance and counciling. Students could apply for education loans which they repaid after graduation at very low rates of interest, and in some cases, no interest at all."

The Secretary recalled some of it and the stranger continued.

"Mr. Secretary, I suggest you look at the records and see how many of the older generation applied for these loans compared to the younger generation. Then look again to see how many of the younger generation have repaid, or attempted to repay, the loans. A very high percentage have not. To their thinking, why should they? They believe that the government has a lot of money. Now, they have migrated from earth and their first responsibility is to the planet they now occupy. The younger generations with higher education have left earth and the older generation remains behind.

I am not passing judgements; I am relating historical facts. Honest, dedicated students wishing to acquire higher education will develop personal integrity. They deserve to be helped and should be encouraged to obtain

The Key

higher degrees. This does not mean the learning of facts, or the use of the imagination to expound on new theories alone, but also the acquisition of an ethical approach which should be the integral part of professionals in all disciplines. Human beings are not only physical entities, but are balanced as spiritual entities as well.

The subjective parts of education are not being taught; nor are there good examples being set by those who teach. One cannot do away with, nor even reduce the educational system, but a move must be made to address that which the system lacks."

"Therein lies my problem," commented the Secretary.

"I suggest that you establish a one-time-fund for student loans deposited where it will earn interest. The student, after graduation, cannot be given permission to emigrate from earth until full payment of the loan is made. Colleges accepting students under this program must accept the loan as a trust to be administered by them providing tuition, dorm, food and lab fees. Whatever else is desired will require that the student work and earn the money to pay for the extras. A student loan fund is public money, paid by taxpayers and should not be spent foolishly. These things have happened in the past."

"And the older people?"

"I don't think there is much difference today as far as the older folks are concerned. A greater effort should be made to help the older generation for progress can be made when you combine experience with knowledge. There is a need to stabilize the exodus from and to other planets and the older folks might furnish that which is missing.

One last thing; set a basic amount of investment and do not add or subtract from it. Make students responsible for maintaining it and if the fund should be depleted, inform the public by publishing the names of the students

Earth - Mars

who have not repaid their loans."

"Those would be considered very strict rules. Congress would give me a lot of trouble."

"Did you take the position of Secretary to coast, to walk the middle of the road? If you do nothing, your troubles will be greater. Don't you think it is your responsibility to teach integrity along with your other duties?"

"You are probably right." The Secretary sighed. "I'll have to think it through."

"I have only made suggestions. You may do as you please," the stranger said, then turned into a vision of a golden-winged white-robed angel and disappeared.

The Secretary sat and stared at the place where the stranger had been sitting. He was deep in thought, remembering his youth and his hard struggle to get an education. For all it's difficulty he could look back and say, "I did it with a minimum of help."

He leaned back in his chair, pushed the button to call for his secretary, then told her he was going to the White House to see the President. On his return, he would want a few memos sent out to department lawyers.

He left his office wearing a grin. This was going to be a battle.

****

The orbit of the Asteroid Belt around the sun passed between Mars and Jupiter. The largest asteroid ever discovered was fifteen miles long and five miles wide. There probably were larger ones than the one named for Ceres, but no one bothered much with the Belt except for a cursory observation in passing.

The scientists on Mars awakened one morning and

The Key

met for breakfast. The observation dome was suddenly lighted by blinding flash of white light which then turned purple, then a brilliant red. There was some concern that the planet Mars might explode.

"What the hell are we going to do now?" a physicist shouted. "We can't get off soon enough, and if we did get off, it would catch us and burn us to a cinder before we were a thousand miles away!"

"Check the seismograph!" another scientist yelled.

They ran to the laboratory, but found no disturbance in the surface that was abnormal. They returned to the dining room and peered through the observation dome. Everthing was calm; there were no lights visible. They transmitted inquiries to all other stations on Mars and to Jupiter's moons and the response was immediate. One of the Asteroids, Ceres, had exploded and left in it's place a black hole in the Asteroid Belt.

The explosion was recorded and the scientists went back to their work.

****

On earth, night had fallen, a night when the moon reflected no light, but the stars were brilliant. About midnight, an unusual display of comets reached from coast to coast, millions of comets, very small that didn't fall to the earth. They resembled an exhibition of Fourth of July rockets.

The brilliant display lasted about two minutes, then the sky was once again filled with shining stars and peace returned to the heavens.

The blond young man in the light blue suit was standing on the sidewalk of a deserted street in Beruit, Lebanon. He shook himself as he recalled the half cold,

113

Earth - Mars

half heat, so intense it was beyond description. He glanced up at the sky, fear and dread mirrored in his eyes, which was replaced by a deep, fanatical hatred. He glanced away and surveyed his surroundings. He smiled. This was more like it.

****

    There is a profound pattern which humans deny with their words while their actions confirm it. They say they seek security and quiet, a condition called peace; but even as they speak, they create turmoil and violence. When they acquire a quiet security, they squirm in it. How boring it is. Most of their troubles have solutions in sight if they would expend the little effort to reach out for them. The Chinese have many words of wisdom, some constantly quoted, but the words most applicable to man's condition in the present society were uttered by Yi Fu Tuan. *All creative effort, including the making of an omelet, is preceded by destruction.*
    Thus it was with mankind after the peaceful interlude following the invention of the domes by Rackner. Humans could now control the natural environment, but controlling themselves was a completely different problem. During the few years of peace and contentment, the feeling grew that man could control his own destiny. He should have known better. Humanity forgot its own history, and as long as mankind retained its demonstrated mental attitudes, the vicious cycle of history would not change.
    The encroachment of domes into the Arctic and Sub-Arctic areas was resolved by all governments cooperating and increasing police forces. Older people continued education with the support of the Monetary School Loan Program. Happily, younger students discovered that the

The Key

development of a sense of integrity had its own rewards. Most of the student loans were paid with alacrity. An increasing number of the older generation now ventured to far-flung planets and all seemed well with the world.

****

George Cramer turned away from the crystal window and faced Professor Bontor. "You said I might help you with something."

"Yes." The Professor smiled. "Let's go to the Lab and I'll show you some disks that were found on Mars."

In the Laboratory, the Professor placed one of the disks in a glass dish. George looked at it with his atomic-molecular vision and recoiled in fear.

"What's wrong?" Professor Bontor asked.

"I don't know." George frowned. "I remember back on Earth I tried to push two pieces of this same rock together, but I never could do it. This disk is made up of a lot of little rocks and they are all passing through each other! This is not a single piece of matter. It is a mess of little pieces of matter and each is different from the other. Each looks like a little disk by itself, but with my normal vision, it looks like one piece."

Professor Bontor recorded all of George's statements. "Look closer, George," he instructed, "and tell me if there is any similarity at all between the individual pieces."

George sat on the stool and looked at the Professor, his eyes reflecting fear and wonder. For the first time, George was uncertain, unsure of himself.

"I don't know whether I should." His voice quavered.

"It is alright, George," Bontor assured the youngster. "You know there are many things in science that we do not understand and it is natural to fear those things you

Earth - Mars

cannot comprehend. Look at one disk and describe to me one of the little pieces of matter.

Reluctantly, George slid off the stool and approached the table.

"Will you hold the disk up, so that there is no interference from the glass dish?"

Bontor picked up the disk, straightened out his hands and held the disk with his palms touching the curved edges. George stared, backed away, returned, and concentrated on one spot. He started to smile, controlled it, and continued to study the disk. He picked up a pad and pencil from the table and drew a rough sketch, then backed away from the table.

"That's as good as I can do," he said.

"Well, I'll be..." the Professor exclaimed. The amateurish sketch was a miniature copy of the original disk. George had attempted to draw the atomic structure. "George, have you ever seen a drawing of an atom?"

"No, but I've seen just about all the atoms that exist on Earth; the real ones, not drawings.

"You have seen the electrons that spin around the nucleus, but you have not seen the paths they travel. You have seen only the electron itself. Let me show you what I mean."

The Professor went to the Library and returned with a book on elementary physics. He turned to the page that illustrated a hydrogen atom in color.

"See? This is what I mean. Can you draw the atomic structure of a disk and mark the path of each electron a different color, like they did in this drawing?"

"I guess I could," George replied. "But it might take a little while."

"Take all the time you need. We are not in any hurry. If it comes out the way I think it will, the time

The Key

you have spent on it will be priceless."

The Professor made a holder for the disk with a plastic clamp holding each outer edge. Then he brought a padded stool from the stockroom. "This ought to make you a little more comfortable."

George surprised himself. "Thanks," he said, for the first time in his life. The Professor smiled.

"That's alright, George. We all change a little when we get up here."

At the graphics computer, Bontor entered the software he had selected, then placed the scribe and plate in front of George. He spent an hour explaining to a fascinated George exactly how it worked.

"Now, what else will you need?"

"I don't know. If I do need something, where can I find you?"

"I'll be in the lounge with Mr. Rackner." The Professor pointed as he went out the door. "Just follow this corridor. You can't miss it."

George drew the profile of each atom then filed it in the computer.

On the planet Mars, Senior Scientist Dr. Hardwick was searching for a sign that would show there had been water in the Noctis Labyrinthus, the Labyrinth of Night. He was an older man, his eyes still sharp and his drive for new discoveries in geology insatiable, but he had been wandering about for hours and was a little tired. He was permanently and irrevocably excited about Mars. It was a treasure chest of geological formations containing minerals and compositions of minerals about which he, or anyone else, knew nothing.

He spied a low outcropping of rock where he could sit and rest for a few minutes. Then scanned the red-orange sky, the result of dust particles, and sighed. The

Earth - Mars

blue skies of Earth would have looked good right now just for a change. As he started to rise, he felt, rather than saw, another presence and quickly glanced about. A stranger was seated, not one of his party from the dome, but a stranger, wearing what looked like a jogging suit and tennis shoes. His long, curley blond hair reached to his hips.

Dr. Hardwick was startled. "Good Lord, man," he yelled, "where is your space suit?"

"I don't need a space suit, Dr. Hardwick," he laughed. "You need one, but I do not. You are from this dimension; I am not."

"What is going on here? My oxygen is running low so I'd better start back to the dome."

"That won't be necessary. Look at your gauge."

Dr. Leonard Hardwick looked at the gauge and it read full. "I must be hallucinating," he thought. "A candidate for a rubber room."

"Fear nothing, Doctor. I came to see you and to talk for awhile."

"How can you stand there with no atmosphere and remain alive?"

The stranger emitted a long sigh. "Well," he said, "if you must... " He changed into an Angel with golden wings and although still in a jogging suit, a halo about his head. The Doctor had heard of angel visitations.

"By golly!" he exclaimed, "I'm delighted. I can't imagine what you would want to talk to me about." As he reseated himself, the Angel became the stranger once again.

"There is an Angel assigned to every planet in the Solar System; in fact, in every planet and sun in this galaxy and all the rest of the galaxies. Actually, there is an Angel assigned to everything the Most High has created,

The Key

from a grain of dust to the universe. This planet, Mars, is my assignment.

A strict order from the Most High states we are not to interfere with the efforts of humans, but since you are the Senior Scientist in charge here, I thought you should know about me. I have been here since creation, waiting for mankind to leave the cradle and to come exploring. Welcome."

The Angel became smaller. "I will be going now. Ahead of you, about five hundred yards, you will find some very interesting things."

The Angel became still smaller, changed into the atomic structure that he really was, then disappeared.

Dr. Hardwick walked ahead as directed, noticing that the rock structures had changed slightly. The further he walked, wider and wider streaks of silicon became more pronounced. Suddenly, there before him stacked neatly against the dead end of the labyrinth was a pile of disks similar to the ones that had been discovered earlier. The silicon streaks had widened to a large deposit of clear crystal that made up the sides of the labyrinth and the ten-foot long floor. A shaft of sunlight struck the crystal on the right side and the entire area glowed with a pure white light.

In the center, there were four stacks of disks.

The Doctor gasped. "How beautiful!" He squatted on his heels and as the sunlight poured into the area, the white light glowed even brighter. The disks, he saw, had become transparent and although they were about fifteen feet in front of him, they appeared to be moving.

The doctor strained to see. The disks appeared to be covered with insects or other small creatures that he could not identify. "The sunlight must have passed the point where it could illuminate the labyrinth," he thought

Earth - Mars

for the white light was slowly fading and as it faded, the disks returned to the reddish-brown material that he had first seen.

He didn't know what to do. The labyrinth walls blocked radio transmission so he had no contact with fellow scientists. He took the area map from his pocket and carefully marked the place where the disks were located. Walking back to the dome, he was deep in thought. He knew of no other crystalline deposit on Mars. Did the crystal have some significance with the disks? Did the sun's radiation and the crystal act as a catalyst activating the disks?

Hardwick arrived at the dome, activated his entrance key, and went directly to the communications room in the Laboratory. He told the operator,

"Inform all scientists that there will be a conference at two o'clock this afternoon. Call Mr. Rackner at Central Lab and ask if they have discovered anything about the disks they are studying."

Hardwick went to his quarters, removed his space suit, took an electronic shower and stretched out on his bunk. He was excited, awestruck and very tired. He dozed off.

The Communications Operator received Rackner's reply. "Nothing yet. Will let you know when we find anything." The Operator didn't think the message was too important, so he slipped the message under the Doctor's door.

****

Venus and Jupiter had taken their toll on explorers of the Solar System. Venus and its two satellites, or moons, being closer to the sun, had posed particular problems

The Key

because of excessive heat. Landings had finally been made by enterprising explorer-scientists using a series of reflecting mirrors as shields that deflected the sun's rays to form a pocket of reduced heat until they could establish their first dome.

It was necessary to change the dome controls to make the domes more dense, but with human ingenuity this was accomplished. These landing sites were on Eros and Geographos, two satellites that orbit between Venus and Earth. The heat shields were absolutely necessary when they were sun-side in their orbits, but the sites made perfect platforms for studying Venus and to plan for a Venus landing. Other satellites between Earth and Venus were used as storage units for supplies and equipment.

Explorers had set up domes on all twelve of the moons of Jupiter and were accumulating data to permit a landing. Different problems had been encountered on Jupiter than on Venus. Jupiter's surface was 130 times greater than that of Earth's surface. While it's volume was 1,300 times greater, it's density was only one-fourth of Earth's density.

Simply stated, it would take 1,300 earths to fill the space occupied by Jupiter, but it would take only 317 earths to equal its weight. A man that weighed 150 pounds on Earth, would weigh 396 pounds on Jupiter. Unable to cope with the weight factor, Jupiter explorers sent the problem to Ken Rackner, asking if an adjustable belt could be devised to offset the gravity problem.

Ken laughed and called Bob, the mechanical engineer, who was told what was needed before the explorers could land on Jupiter.

"Those guys are always coming up with something," Bob said. "but I must say, this is a good one. There is a question here though; what if they lean too far to one side?

Earth - Mars

I don't think a belt is the answer. They need something in the helmet and something in the shoes to keep balanced. The adjustment can be hung on the belt."

"It's your problem," Ken said. "Go to it. By the way, how are Professor Bontor and George coming along with their project?"

"Bontor's alright, but I don't think George will have any voice left if he doesn't stop cussing. I don't think he likes to draw and those atoms are giving him fits."

"Help him all you can," Ken laughed. "He's young and will have to learn to have patience. Does the computer he is using have the ability to straighten lines and make a smooth curve where necessary?

"Sure it does," Bob replied, "but I'm not telling him that until he is finished. I want to watch his face when he sees a beautiful line curve where he thought he had wobbled."

"Get out of here," Ken laughed again. "Go to work."

Kenneth had things on his mind which would soon require a decision. There was just too much data received from the nine planets and all the moons. Fed by multiple computers, the storage units were filling up. Should Central Control be expanded? Or some other planet? Mars, perhaps? Or should a stable moon be utilized for a storage site?

This major decision would need input from every government on Earth and the other planets. Kenneth placed a call to the President of the United States and requested that a conference be called to establish a Computer Central at a given location. Ken explained the need and the reason for such a meeting and the President agreed.

"By the way, Ken," the President added, "I understand that you have an accomplished young man up there named

The Key

George Cramer. How is he doing? His talent for seeing the atomic and molecular structures of material has the doctors here lobbying to have the young man studied. I was told he was adamant vocally and physically in his refusal to take tests. Keep an eye on him. I don't want anyone interfering with the work he can do for you."

"I appreciate that, Mr. President. At this moment he is helping Professor Bontor determine the composition of some odd disks that were found on Mars. He hasn't lost the use of his temper, but he is good and he is doing a good job. We are happy with him."

The conversation closed and Ken went back to his pile of papers covered with mathematical symbols and calculations. He had arrived at one conclusion; it would take an awful lot of money to establish an atmosphere on even the smallest of moons. There had to be another answer.

He got to his feet and walked to the crystal window. As he stared at the stars a flickering thought crossed his mind. In that den where he had first begun to read scientific journals; in the Professor's study it was an old magazine he had read. He snapped his fingers.

He remembered an article that mentioned Carbon Dioxide conversion to Oxygen and Carbon Monoxide but the details escaped him. At that moment, Dr. Hardwick called to tell him of the discovery in the Labyrinth. Ken decided to take the small space vehicle and attend the meeting.

Hardwick awaited Ken's arrival and greeted him with a handshake.

"Good to see you again, Ken. I hope you are in good health?"

"Other than a headache from lack of sleep, I am fine. It's you I worry about. You're not as young as you used

Earth - Mars

to be and knocking about these hills can be pretty strenuous."

"When I get tired, I sit and enjoy the view," Hardwick said with a smile. "The meeting is about to start and what is heard here might be of help to your young man working with the disks."

They walked to the meeting room, which was actually the library and terminal computer room. It was a convenient place for discussions and announcements of findings. The scientists waved in greeting or rose and welcomed Ken with extended hands. Ken took a seat and Professor Hardwick began to describe his morning experience. When he mentioned the Angel, everyone laughed, even more so when he told about the jogging suit and tennis shoes, but they were impressed by what the Angel had said, but reluctant to admit it.

The first question was concerned with the assignment of an Angel to every planet, solar system, galaxy and universe. "You mean there is an Angel who will help us wherever we land? No matter where it is?"

"I did not say that," the Doctor replied. "I said they were assigned to each part of the Most High's creation. The Angel said nothing, and I said nothing, about helping us. I merely said they were assigned to these places. What they do, I guess, is up to them."

The Doctor continued. "I know, and you know, Angels have appeared at various times and have offered suggestions. Documents have recorded the times they have read us the riot act when we have behaved stupidly. But that is not why I have asked you here.

I want you to recall the areas of your investigation. Have any of you seen any disks besides the ones found by Johnson that are now being examined in Ken's Laboratory? Johnson, were there any clear crystaline formations

The Key

around or near the disks when you found them?"

"I really don't remember," Johnson replied. "It was pretty dark and they were the last things I examined. The light was just right to accentuate the markings. I just picked them up and brought them in. I can go back to examine the area, if you wish."

"That would be a good idea. Any of the rest of you ever see any disks and just passed them by?"

A babble of voices arose. Nearly everyone in the room had noticed disks in particular places, but geology was not their discipline, so they had not paid attention to them.

"Okay, okay," Dr. Hardwick quieted them. "In the future when disks are found, mark your maps to show locations and indicate if there is a crystaline structure around them, or near to them." He looked at Ken. "Mr. Rackner, would you like to see the disks and the surrounding material that I found? I hesitate to disturb the site without some study of it."

"I would be happy to go with you, but can we put it off until tomorrow? I am trying to resolve a problem at the Central Lab and I need to discuss some details with a couple of your engineers; specifically a chemical and a mechanical engineer."

"Tomorrow will be fine. We should see it in the morning sun."

Ken turned to the waiting engineers. He wanted to know if it would be possible to create a more dense atmosphere on Mars, then told them about the article he recalled reading when he was young. The engineers became excited at the new challenge and began talking in the language of their disciplines, leaving Ken in the dark. Having nothing further to offer them, he left and went to his quarters. He wanted to establish an atmosphere on

Earth - Mars

Mars that was conducive to human habitation. The disks were a different problem that belongd to other scientists.

He showered, had a snack in the kitchen and went to bed.

Dr. Hardwick and he donned their space suits the next morning, checked the oxygen supply and headed for Noctis Labyrinthus. Arriving at the dead end, they found the pile of disks as the Doctor had left them, surrounded by the crystaline structure.

"Shall I remove the disks? Shall we take a sample of the crystaline?"

Ken inspected the edges of the crystaline; first one side and then the other. He walked to the disks, did not disturb them, but examined the seam where the normal rock and the crystaline met.

"If I were you," he told the Doctor, "I would try to take the entire thing in one piece. You will have to get some earth-moving equipment up here and try not to break any of it." Kenneth remembered what George had seen in his second look at the disk in his laboratory. "I believe you have an important discovery here. When you get the map reports from your scientists on disk locations, compare them and look for a pattern of some sort. I would not take the chance of breaking it. Of course, this is just my opinion, Doctor."

"Let's wait one moment. I want you to see what happens when the sunlight hits the crystaline."

They sat quietly on a rock escarpment and waited for about ten minutes. As the spot of sunlight moved upon the crystaline, the entire structure glowed with the same white light that the Doctor had witnessed.

"Watch the disks!" he said as he grabbed Ken's arm.

The disks appeared to be self-contained masses of small, moving structures, whether alive or not, they could not tell. As the spot of sunlight faded, the disks returned to the normal state before a closer look could even be attempted.

"I am more sure than ever that they should not be touched!" Ken stated. "Now, I only hope that those we have at the Lab have not broken a pattern. If we have, we should try to restore it. Please, be certain that the one who found the original disks marks the exact place where he found them."

"I certainly will," Dr. Hardwick said. They returned to the central dome, both deep in thought. They did not notice the blond-haired young man with a grin on his face that sat on the cliff above them.

****

The President of the United States sighed and sat back in the easy chair in his Oval Office. Heads of governments had received notices of the Conference; off-world colonies had received invitations to attend. All of the off-world colonies had accepted, but some of the earth-governments had declined for various reasons. The President sat and thought about the circle of history.

"Don't tell me we are going to experience the isolationist period again; the non-cooperation times, the nationalistic selfish posturing like the 1980's." He poured himself a cup of coffee. "Maybe they just don't care. Maybe life is too easy. The domes put a halt to this sort of thing in the past. What will it take to head off this trend in history? Maybe they will come around after the Conference. I don't hold much hope for that, but we can try."

The President instructed his secretary to notify all the countries and colonies confirming the Conference and

Earth - Mars

to enclose a list of those who had agreed to attend.

When the Conference opened in the United States Congressional Hall, the President received a round of applause as he entered and seated himself on the dais behind the Speakers Platform. The President of the United Nations Organization introduced him and when it quieted down, he spoke.

"Your presnce is gratefully acknowledged," he said. "I shall address you as 'Friends' for we share a very large problem. If our efforts in space exploration are to be worthwhile, we must devise a process to record and to store all of the information in the discoveries of all the colonies. In addition, we must have a centralized system capable of analyzing the data.

Our first decision entails the necessity to expend funds to construct and to furnish equipment to adequately perform the required functions.

Our second decision is to determine the location of this facility. I remind you that it must be built and maintained with funds from participating countries and colonies. This location must be free of foreseeable dangers such as floods or earthquakes.

We must rise above our own special interests. Every colony that now exists, and those of the future, will have access to all the data stored in the data banks via satellite access stations."

The President went on to describe the needs and the functions of the universal library.

"Friends, I will now call a two-hour recess. Discuss amongst yourselves what you wish to do and select a spokesman for your group. Personal views may be submitted to me in writing. When the first two decisions have been made, that is, funding and location, we will then elect an eleven person commission to

The Key

administer the construction and the dispensation of funds. Thank you."

The President seated himself and the hum of voices rose as representatives sought each other and headed for the refreshment stand in the lobby. Groups met, avidly discussing the proposals.

At the end of two hours, the meeting was called to order. The representative from the small country of Iceland came forward and introduced himself to the President.

"Mr. President," he said, "I have been elected to speak and to present their views." The President waved him to the speaker's stand. "Ladies and gentlemen, I have been asked by the majority present to present our thoughts on this proposal.

The construction of a centralized computer bank to house information sounds like an efficient solution to the records problem. We are willing to share the costs of the facility if they can be prorated on the demographic statistics currently available at the United Nations.

As to the location, we recommend that this facility be constructed on Earth's moon. The exact site should be decided by three geologists from the off-earth colonies as they have had the most experience in extraterrestrial investigation.

We recommend that the President of the United States be the Chairman of the new Commission and we leave the selection of the other ten members to him. Objections to any appointment by him should be submitted to him in writing. Thank you."

The Representative of Iceland left the podium and the President took his place.

"Friends," he said, "if you agree with the total proposal presented by the Representative from Iceland, I

Earth - Mars

ask you to please stand."

Ninety per cent of those present arose.

"I thank you for this vote of confidence. All Commission appointees shall be notified by letter. The entire membership shall receive the report of the Committee of Geologists when they decide on the site for the construction. Are there any further questions? None? I hereby adjourn this Conference."

The President struck the gavel once, then proceded to his limosine that was waiting outside the Hall.

All of the news media had been excluded from the Conference and a mass of reporters tried to question the President and members of the Conference, but no statements were made. The President remarked that a statement would be released by his press secreaty very shortly.

The Press Room, along with all the facilities enjoyed in the past, had long since been removed from the White House, a decision that had incensed the press. The President also refused to permit press people to ride in any government vehicle. They now had to travel at the expense of their employers rather than at the taxpayers expense.

The media had raged against the decision, quoting the first amendment, that the public "...*had the right to know.*" The President agreed with that, but added that the right to know did not include paying media expenses. Many articles appeared castigating the President, but the American public had agreed with his action and the order to abolish the press from the White House had stood through three presidencies.

The law still provided a president with television time, but the media found that the viewing public did not want their president's words analyzed nor interpreted after the president had spoken. People openly considered it an

The Key

insult to have a commentator tell them what had been said or what had been meant. When the media finally accepted that, they had to become competitive with no privileges, like the rest of the American business society.

****

George Cramer was tired, mentally tired and it sapped the strength from his young body. His cramped fingers had been aching for the past twelve hours but at last it was finished. He had drawn all the different atoms in the small molecules and had entered them into the computer.

Professor Bontor was in the next compartment and had just finished carefully brushing off the debris from the last disk when Geoge buzzed him.

"Professor, I have finished. What shall I do now? I don't know how to run the computer."

"I'll be right there," the Professor said and began to clear his desk. When he entered the Lab, he found a tired little boy lying across the Lab table with his head resting on his arm, sound asleep. "By all that's ancient," Bontor said, "I didn't think he would stick to it, but he did!"

He disconnected the graphic plate and ran the computer through the program. The designs that looked like scribbling to George began to appear on the screen, smooth and perfect in their relationships. The Professor keyed them together and the monitor showed a perfect molecule. Bontor registered the atomic structure and the resultant molecule in the main frame memory, then he removed the software disk and inserted a different one in its place. This was a special program that Ken had written and it's function was purely analytical, comparative analytical.

Earth - Mars

Bontor activated the main computer and called for a comparative analysis of that molecule with any substance registered in the computer. It printed a list of materials including rocks, vegetation and flesh, both human and animal along with a few gases. The Professor studied the printout then turned and look at the sleeping youngster.

"I hate to do this to you, little genius, but I have no choice." He shook George gently. "George, wake up."

George raised his head. "Yeah." He rubbed his face with both hands. "Did you run the computer?"

"I sure did. We are making a little bit of headway, but not much. We'll tackle it again tomorrow."

He showed George the atoms he had drawn, the resultant molecule and the printout. "We have a long way to go unless we get a break of some kind. You go get some rest. We'll do more later.

George didn't argue. He was tired and confused as well. What did it all mean? He was no longer disgusted nor angry. For the first time in his life, he was interested and challenged. It was a different world here, especially out there. He stared at the stars through the cubicle window. With his different mind, he imagined butterflies and dragons and all sorts of beautiful sights. On earth, these were far from anything he could imagine. George was growing up, in spirit and in body.

****

The geologists reported to the Commission of Eleven recommending that the Central Computer facility be built in the Sea of Vapors. They had excavated ten feet and had found the meteorite that had caused the sea to melt upon impact. It formed a solid foundation upon which to build the facility.

The Key

The Sea of Vapors faced Earth directly so there would be less chance of distortion in the transmissions. They also recommended that the reception/transmission towers be erected at the north and south poles and that auxiliary towers be adjacent to the Ocean of Storms and the Sea of Fertility.

Construction people and equipment were transported to the Moon and the work began. Transportation was not too expensive so excavated material was shipped for study to the scientific community on Earth in the Mojave Desert. In a record construction time of three years, the Central Moon Computer began receiving input from all sources. It was ten miles long, with thirty levels of solid concrete holding main frames and living quarters for maintenance personnel and scientists. Kenneth Rackner was very happy about the whole thing. He now had access to all information being relayed as it was discovered.

The two engineers working on the chemical and mechanical process to change the atmosphere on planet Mars were sending the results from their first experiments. When Ken arose from his sleep time, the first thing he did was to check for their reports.

They fashioned the same type of machine he had described to them, but with essental differences. It could be described as an electrolyic pump with an electric gill situated between any atmosphere and an oxygen collection system. The pump sucks in the atmosphere, filters out dust and non-gaseous products then feeds the gases into a separation matrix of tubes.

The gases are heated to the amount of degrees C. until each gas breaks down to it's component parts. The oxygen is migrated to a ceramic lung, then the lung breathes the oxygen into a circulatory system which collects the oxygen, cools it and saves it. The article

Earth - Mars

recalled by Ken used a small nuclear reactor or a radio isotope generater to power the equipment, but the two engineers had developed a highly efficient solar collector that utilized the sun's radiation for fuel.

They reported that they were setting up several of these generating machines in the Crater Clavius, which was 144 miles wide and 16,000 feet deep, to see how effective they would be in generating an atmosphere of the same chemical components as the Earth's atmosphere.

"At least we have a start," Ken thought as he went to the kitchen area for his breakfast. He found George and Bontor just finishing their meals. "How are the disks coming?" he asked. Bontor described in detail their first results.

"How many molecules do you think there are in one disk?" Ken asked. The Professor laughed.

"You know as well as I do," he said. "There are millions."

"Are they all the same?" Ken asked with a grin.

"Some are alike," George replied, "but mostly they are different."

"Don't we have an electron microscope here?" Ken asked.

"George can see them without the microscope," the Professor said.

"The computer can't. Connect the optical unit on the computer to the electron microscope and have the computer analyze the disk."

The Professor was stunned. "I never thought of that," he admitted, and a new thought came to him. "Come on, George," he grabbed the boy's arm, "we've got work to do."

In the Lab, he pushed some buttons and the wapp panel slid back revealing a state-of-the-art electron microscope.

The Key

"Here it is, George. Now we can get some work done."

He placed the disk beneath the instrument's tube, connected the optical unit to the computer and to the microscope, turned all units on and made some small adjustments to the focus. Bontor inserted the analytical software into the computer and commanded it to make comparisons and to register the molecules that were the same and that were different, then to compare it with data in the computer bank. The computer went to work.

Professor Bontor retrieved the disks from his desk and placed them beside the electron microscope. He decided to run them all through the process. The first disk took three hours to analyze; the printer began to reproduce the data. The Professor took one look and sat down.

"I don't believe it!" he exclaimed. The last sentence read: *Composition of all molecular structure present in all material forms known to exist on planet Earth.*

"George, run each disk under the tube and see if we get the same reading."

"Okay," George complied. One by one, each disk went through the process and one by one, each showed the same results as the first one. The disks were composed of molecules that existed on and in the Earth.

There were a few unknown and the computer had set the differences in a column to one side. Ken viewed the information and deposited it in the main central space station computer which immediately transferred it to the central computer on Mars.

The communications bell was ringing in the Com Room and Ken received the message:

"Regarding the Conference at Mars Central, all deposits of disks are surrounded by the same crystaline structure as the one that I found. Locations drawn on

135

Earth - Mars

local map look like deposits are integral part of larger design. This design forms the sign of infinity. Will leave all untouched until you reply."

"Sign of infinity?" the Professor asked puzzledly.

George recalled that he had seen it once when a group of students had gone to get their fortunes read. "It's two circles joined together. If you draw a figure eight and lay it horizontally you have the sign of infinity; no beginning and no end."

"George, go to the Com Room. Tell them to contact Mars Central to send a graphics map of the area."

"Including Mars Central?" asked George.

"Yes. Also include the dome locations with reference points."

When George returned from the Communications Room, he found Professor Bontor looking through the electron microscope.

"George," he said, "we must resolve the meaning of the disk marks. Do you need the microscope to see them?"

"No, I can see them plainly."

We'll disconnect the microscope and hook up the graphics plate, then you can copy the marks into the computer. I thought about taking photographs of the disks, but I don't want to disturb them with bright artificial light. The computer will be fast and thorough in analyzing and decoding them; it might even interpret their meaning in relation to the English language."

George paused momentarily, fighting his old nature of rebellion at the thought of all that work, but he shook it off and smiled.

"Sure, Professor, I'll be glad to do it." He removed the connections from the electron microscope and slid the scope back into it's storage slot, retrieved the graphics plate from the locker, hooked it into the computer and

The Key

placed the disks before him. He began to copy the disk inscriptions onto the plate. The Professor smiled. He had caught the hint of rebellion and was happy that George had overcome the thought. "He's growing up at last," he thought as he left the Lab to help Ken in the lounge.

INDEPENDENCE

The people occupying Earth were reaping the benefits of man's exodus into space. Interplanetary transmission stations that transported known ores, like iron, and new metals named by current scientists, were stockpiling surplus materials.

At first, a trickle came through, but scientists found many different types of metal-bearing strata beneath the surface of the moon. New minerals had to be classified because they had never been discovered on Earth. A Scientific Consortium was formed to develop research funds. As the private sector became interested, many corporations began contributing to the research fund. The Consortium Headquarters was based in Dallas, Texas but research laboratories were established in every state, except Hawaii, and thr results were amazing.

New metals and compounds, combinations of off-world metals and earth metals, were stronger, and in some cases, more pliable. With the construction of the lunar inter-planetary computer central building with all its towers and cables, stockpiling became a problem. A Pandora's Box had been opened for the people of the Earth and in turn, the off-worlders.

Human nature was still comprised of the dual system of good and bad, the peaceful and the violent. There was an underground cadre of scientists at work on weapons and and others on devices for securing secrets of other labs to sell to competitors. They learned how to intercept

Earth - Mars

transmissions and could redirect them to their own storage piles.

When the interceptor device was perfected, the rogue scientists set it up for testing on a plateau in the highest reaches of the Rocky Mountains. It was designed to bend the electronic singular polarity transmission line to their chosen destination. They did not realize that the result was not merely inter-Solar hijacking, but that the electronic line could not be bent. The result was a catastrophe.

The interception device cut off transmission over Denver, Colorado, and several hundred thousand tons of mineral-bearing ore fell into the heart of the city. The effect was even more disastrous because of the doppler shift in the transmission beam. It was broadened, dumping the large chunks of material and rocks over most of Denver. Several hundred thousand people were killed and most of Denver was destroyed.

The backlash effect completely destroyed many transmission stations of off-worlders. Domes were sealed immediately because they were self-contained in the power grid. The casualies among the people manning the towers on off-world stations at the time of the interference were two hundred.

Doctor Hardwick was at the central location of the disks in the Noctis Labyrinthus scraping dirt away from one of the radiating arms of crystaline. Curious about the composition of the material and why it had been used at all locations, he only felt the ground shake slightly but heard nothing. When the ground shook, the piece of crystaline cracked. Hardwick backed away a step or two and waited, but nothing further happened. He fingered the crack, then gently removed the small piece to examine it closely. It looked like pure quartz, but he withheld

140

Independence

judgement, carefully wrapped and packed it away.

"This is for the Lab," he concluded. Back at the dome, he was told that the transmission/receiving towers were gone and he recalled the shaking ground. Up to that moment, he had believed that his disturbance of the crystaline had caused it. Inter-planetary vehicles were already carrying construction crews and maintenance people to clear away debris and to rebuild the towers.

The blond-haired young man smiled as he surveyed the scene in Denver, then he laughed.

"Well, it's a start." His laughter echoed through the Rocky Mountains.

****

News of the destruction of the towers reached Space Central Labs four hours after it happened. Kenneth sent Bob and Professor Bontor to the Mars Cental dome to assist however they could, while he remained at Space Central to serve as relay for communications. Nothing could be teleshipped via tower transmission lines, so everything had to be lifted by space vehicles of which Earth had developed many different types. The highest priority was oxygen needed on the moons of Uranus and Jupiter.

Engineers experimenting with the atmosphere generating system were able to create oxygen for the Mars colonies and thus avoided an emergency. After four years on Mars, there was a considerable difference in the atmosphere which showed an increase in carbon dioxide. Although scientists were encouraged by the results, they knew it would be many years before the atmosphere could support human or plant life.

Work in the Crater Clavius had produced a chemical

Earth - Mars

change up to the five thousand foot level, mostly carbon dioxide and oxygen, but scientists decided to do no testing until it reached the ten thousand foot level. They expanded the plan by placing machines in other craters, beginning with the deepest and working up to the shallowest.

Bob was met at the Central Dome by Dr. Hardwick and taken to his quarters where the Doctor showed him the piece of crystaline.

"I was working carefully at the Noctis Labyrinthus site when the ground shook and the crystaline ray cracked. I know now that the destruction of the towers made the ground shake."

"Yes," Bob replied. "You did nothing to disturb it. If you don't mind, I would like to take this piece with me. I'd like Bontor to examine it for this crystaline seems somehow to go together with the disks."

"Not at all. I'll be glad when this is cleared up."

When his services were no longer needed, Bob returned to the space lab and gave the piece of crystaline to Professor Bontor, explaining how Hardwick had come by it.

"There has to be a connection," Bontor agreed. "But I shall set it aside as George has nearly completed his project."

The Doctor returned to the Lab and George greeted him. "It's all done. What do I do now?"

Bontor inserted a software cartridge into the computer. It was a language-interpretation program using every known language including heiroglyphics. He pushed 'run' and the display screen stated 'working.'

"Let's go eat," Bontor told George. "After lunch it might have something for us."

"I am hungry," George replied, but grumbled, "I wish you had something besides those food tubes up here."

142

Independence

"They are working on it," the Professor laughed. During lunch, George read a book from Ken's library on the structure of space.

"That's heavy reading," Bontor remarked.

"The words are easy to remember, but I don't make sense out of their meaning. I only studied basic physics and not astronomy and this stuff is deep. I want to learn more about the stars and what keeps them in place."

"Keep at it," the Professor told him. "If I can help with anything, just ask. Let's go back and see what the computer has come up with."

The Professor, astounded, hurried to the computer and pushed the print button after reading the screen display. The first message line was an explanation of the code referring to the disk markings. The second line was the middle of a message that must have begun elsewhere. It read,

"...leaving this planet for it can no longer furnish us with enough minerals or water to sustain life. The ships are ready and the people are boarding as this is written. What we have left to those who come after us is very little. These tablets explain that we were here and where we are going. It is to the third planet from the sun. (A diagram showed the Solar System.) It is a beautiful planet and we have been there many times. It is primitive and the natives, if one can call them that, are small and stunted while the animal life is large and voracious. We have used as food the largest, and to the people there, the most deadly animals. I'm afraid we have slaughtered almost all of the large, dangerous animals. The small native population will not be in danger now..."

The message ended. After carefully storing the disks,

Earth - Mars

Bontor and George took the printout to Ken and Bob. The four sat in a circle while it was read, then they sat in silence for a few minutes staring at the paper.

"The infinity sign," the Professor remarked. "We must start where the lines cross. That's where their history begins. What form it will take is anyone's guess, but that is where the beginning lies."

"Their history?" mused Ken. "Maybe it is our history."

"I can't believe that humans came from Mars," Bob said.

"Let us not draw conclusions from so few facts. Bob, you and Professor Bontor take this message to Professor Hardwick at Mars Central. Then ask him if he will agree to removing all the disks from Noctis Labyrinthus so you can bring them here."

Dr. Hardwick became excited when he read the printout and agreed to the removal of the disks. They were carefully stowed in a lined container in the exact order as they were in the crystaline pocket. When the last stack was placed in the container, the crystaline pocket and the radiating lines began to grow dull. The removal had caused some kind of physical, chemical reaction. They moved about twenty yards away from the pocket, stood quietly and watched.

The pockets became dull; little pieces began to crumble. The entire crystaline structure crumbled into dust before their horrified eyes. The small piece that Ken had carefully put away on the space station did the same; it crumbled into dust. Doctor Hardwick reached down and picked up a pinch of the material.

"Pure silicon," he said. "Sand. Whoever hid these disks here belonged to an advanced cicilization. That was a very neat trick."

"I don't think it was a trick," Bob said. "The disks were part of a material and gaseous compound. We just

Independence

removed the disks which were a part of the whole and the rest returned to it's natural state. I would bet, Professor, that the little piece of crystaline you gave to me is nothing more than dust also."

"You are probably right," Hardwick agreed.

Professor Bontor and Bob returned to the central space lab with the container of disks which were given to George.

"You know how to run the computer now and the Ion microscope. Make the same tests on the disks and copy the markings from each one. When you are finished, call me."

"That's a lot of work!" George complained.

"If I am right, " the Professor told him, "we have a lot more coming. So get busy."

George smiled and went to work.

****

Asmodius, the blond young man, was furious. He had insidiously planted the seeds of rebellion in the minds of the underground scientists and had been successful in having them form their own society. He had conceived their idea of intercepting transhipments of valuable materials from off-world. The fools had botched the whole thing! Now they were isolated on one of the moons of Jupiter attempting to make it habitable. Asmodius shuddered at the thought of the wrath he would face if he failed. He must do something.

The planet Uranus was getting hotter and hotter. Volcanoes erupted on all sides of its surface which affected the gravitational fields between Uranus and Jupiter. This was like poking a finger into a sponge; when the finger is removed, the sponge springs back. The eruptions,

Earth - Mars

which lasted two earth days, caused the twelve Jupiter moons to change orbit. Four, that were moving east to west, were pushed out of their orbits and the domes which had been erected on the Uranus side were completely destroyed. These moons narrowly missed a collision with the opposite-revolving eight moons, and in doing so, caused them to change orbit.

Havoc reigned on all twelve moons. Many of the domes were destroyed. Four thousand scientists and their families were killed. After three earth years, all twelve moons began to move from west to east.

When this bad news reached Earth, the exodus slowed down, but in two years, off-world quotas were once again filled with young, and not so young, faces eager to explore the Solar System. The President of the United States, who had made a decision, called Ken Rackner at Space Central.

"Kenneth," he said, "I have been studying computer printouts on Jupiter and I realize that we have a long way to go before colonizing can start to any degree. What do you think about slowing down this development and trying to develop Venus? The consensus of opinion among the scientists here is that the temperature of 400 degrees is the greenhouse effect caused by carbon dioxide, with a little nitrogen and a few inert gases.

If we concentrate on Mars and Venus, we will have the Asteroid Belt available for the mining of minerals. And it is just possible that we may divert some ice asteroids to the planet of Venus. Is it worth a try? What do you think?"

"It is worth investigating, Mr. President. We haven't paid much attention to the Asteroid Belt."

"You men are doing a good job out there and I don't mean to interfere with your plans. Just thought I would call you on this."

Independence

"Glad you did, sir. We shall get right on it."

Ken called Bob, related the President's message and asked Bob to contact Hardwick.

"I didn't think the old boy had it in him!" Bob laughed. "But it's a hell of a good idea. I'll get to Mars Central right away."

Meanwhile, a Mars Central technician was tranferring loads of disks from the caves of the infinity symbol, stored in sequence as much as possible, and delivered to George for decoding. When Space Central data banks were full, space was found on the Moon's Central Computer.

Each disk received its own code and entered in the software program with the disk data. When finished with the disks, George stored them in an empty bubble on the outside edge of the space station. When they were halfway through the infinity symbol, George had transcribed three thousand disks. He began to recognize at the beginning of each disk, the same symbol. This symbol appeared in his sleep and at times, when he rested his eyes by staring at the stars, the symbol would superimpose itself on the starry background.

"When I get these things done, " he thought, "I will probably be able to tell what that symbol means." He told Professor Bontor about it and the Professor cautioned him to be patient. When the disks were translated, they would know.

George went to the crystal window in the lounge and as he looked at the stars, Earth came into view. He noticed a bright spot in the Middle East area. It grew brighter and brighter.

"Mr. Rackner," he called, "I hate to bother you, but I think you had better come and see this! There's an unusually bright spot on Earth!"

Kenneth came to his side. "We are two thousand

147

Earth - Mars

miles from Earth and if we can see it, it must be a disaster."

He hurriedly had the Communications Room operator contact Earth Central.

"What the dickens is going on in North East Africa?" he asked.

"It's the Underground Scientists," Earth operator replied. "They have established their headquarters in Iraq and have built a nuclear power reactor to power a different kind of dome. We don't yet know the purpose, but it won't make any difference now. They have set off a melt-down and it is spreading. If it reaches Earth's core, the whole planet will explode!"

"Why don't you explode it now?" Kenneth asked. "Drop an atom bomb in the center of it."

"I'll mention what you said to the President."

Bob and Bontor joined them at the crystal window.

"That's one heck of a mess," Bob exclaimed. "Why are those idiot's monkeying around with nuclear power? They must be out of their minds!"

"They want power, control," the Professor said. "Political power. I'm just curious as to how they got back to Earth from exile on the Jupiter moon."

They were startled when a huge mushroom cloud obliterated the bright spot momentarily. The President had ordered an atomic bomb be dropped on the meltdown. The little country of Iraq no longer existed. There was nothing but a large black hole where it had been.

It was fortunate that the wind was blowing from the east and the blast fall-out dropped into the Mediterranian Sea. Only the Island of Crete received a light dusting, but the meltdown reaction was neutralized and stopped.

The blond haired young man stood on the side of the crater and smiled. A stranger in rough clothes stood on the other side and stared across at the young man.

"This makes two times," the stranger said. "You have only one more to go and then I will be there, wherever you are."

The blond haired young man sneered. "The next time there will be nothing left for you to meet me on."

Late that night, when herdsmen were asleep and the night sky was dark and quiet, a long bright streak of light appeared in the sky, then slowly faded into the darkness. There was a thud as a meteorite landed and filled the hole made by the atom bomb.

One of the Asteroids from the Asteroid Belt disappeared from its orbit. It fit nicely into the hole left by the bomb. The desert winds moved the sand. Shepherds arose at the light of day and could not find the huge hole that had been Iraq. Praise Allah! Word spread quickly. Scientists from Egypt ran radiation tests, but there was none. The Angel had selected the Asteroid that could neutralize the entire area.

All the world and the off-world people became aware of the visit of the Angel or the act of the Most High. They marvelled, for two months talked of nothing else, then their interests changed and they forgot all about it.

The Computer did not forget; the occurance was a part of its chronicles.

****

The blond haired young man stood in the same place where he had stood before in Death Valley and he was just as frightened. The purple and red shades spun again before him and the cold steely eyes looked at him from the same lined face.

"You never seem to learn," rasped the ugly voice.

Earth - Mars

"This is my land, my planet. You are supposed to be the best - the best what? I am very angry!"

Checkers of ice and flame appeared on the young man. They became hotter and colder at the same time and his screams echoed in the valley. His skin began to split very slowly, and although the openings would close as soon as they opened, not a drop of blood was lost. The openings moved over his body like small snakes, then he was slammed into the side of the cliff. The old man vanished.

The blond haired young man sat on the highest peak on Mars. He was brooding.

****

The waters of Earth slowly became clear and life-bearing again. The sparkling waters of mountain streams, the swamps and rivers of the delta and the plains were once more free of contaminants. They flowed to the mighty seas with little flooding. Dams built to supply power and water to drought-stricken farmlands were no longer needed and had been destroyed.

Solar power was an enending source; the winds had been harnessed. Power generators had a capacity that far exceeded man's requirements and the choice of use was given to the individual.

Human beings were no longer throw-away entities. Manufacturers of products from steel smelting to food preparation had no need for landfills nor sea-dumping. Physical scientists developed systems of carbon extraction from everything that man could produce and very cheaply. The system was solar-powered. Household units were the size of an antique garbage disposal, industrial complexes required larger sizes. The final system was a molecular

Independence

disrupter that returned all waste to its original elements, then flushed them back into the environment.

Humans were finally learning the fundamental lesson given to them in the beginning by the Most High. *'Go forth and subdue the firmament.'* For thousands of years, mankind had abused the firmament.

Slowly, humanity was leaving the cradle, and the wisdom of the natural order was replacing the petulance of the child. Mankind was looking upward and outward at the rest of creation.

Off-world scientists were making progress with Mars and Venus. Dome structures on Mars had grown into a large metropolis. The mining of the Asteroid Belt was profitable and corporations were investing in permanent facilites. Some very peculiar factories were producing products that were impossible to produce in the heavier gravity of Earth. Medicine had leapt forward. Almost every kind of disease could be cured that was caused by man's disregard of the laws of natural order

Scientists discovered a basic form of life near the Polar Caps. Mechanical scientists were studying how to increase the fungus-like growths so that they could produce more oxygen from the carbon dioxide in the thin Martian air. And iron oxide was changing as more and more oxygen was generated.

Winds that were fierce and strong caused seasonal changes. Adjustments were necessary to the domes so that particles of iron and dust would not penetrate, but the domes were not strong enough to withstand the full force of the storms. Some of the force had to be dissipated by letting the winds pass through. After a five year period, it was found that the winds were getting less forceful. There was no scientific answer to this phenomenon, but most scientists agreed it was due to the growth of the

Earth - Mars

fungus and the added oxygen in the atmosphere.

The atmosphere was also getting more dense which encouraged the biologists. It also encouraged the three mechanical scientists in their conversion efforts. They called for more of the machines they were using.

****

George finished his task of transcribing the disks into the computer. He sighed with relief. It had been interesting once he got over his resentment at doing the work and he had tried to decipher the markings himself without success. He could recall each of the figures and when they occured again, make them more perfect. He stored the last disk in the carrying case, then took them to the storeroom. He disconnected the equipment, turned off the computer and sauntered in to the lounge where the Professor and Ken Rackner were in a deep conversation. He started to interrupt, but held back as he heard them talk.

"There are many geologists who believe that ferric iron was the basis of life's beginning on Earth," the Professor was saying. "At least the beginning of bacteria which used it for food. The bacteria itself was believed to come from meteorite fragments falling into the Earth when it was still liquid."

"That sounds reasonable," Ken agreed. "Especially if you consider the polar caps as being the beginning of the seas. Now as far as Mars is concerned, we have a similar condition. Two polar caps and the same rusty iron condition that must have prevailed on Earth millions of years ago."

"The thing that bothers me," said the Professor, "is that there is no sea on Mars. The surface is arid."

Independence

"Wait a minute," he mused, scratching a two-day growth of beard on his chin. "Do you suppose there could be an aquafir, or a large water table or even a sea beneath the surface of Mars?"

"That had not occured to me," Ken replied. "I have been thinking only about the surface. Let's get in touch with Dr. Hardwick."

"Agreed," the Professor replied. Kenneth went to the Communications Room, nodding to George as he passed.

"I've finished the disks," George told the Professor. "What do I do now?"

"We'll go to the Lab and run off a translation. I can't wait to see it!"

In the Lab, the software was inserted and the printer set for large print; then they sat back to watch the computer at work. It took three hours to print the translations of the disks' markings piling up six inches of paper. Together, George and the Professor scanned the printout late into the night. The next morning, Professor Bontor prepared abstracts of each of the eight parts which were called Chronicles in the translations. George ran off copies of the full texts of the Chronicles and of the Professor's abstracts which read:

CHRONICLE 1: To you who have found these Chronicles...

To read this, you must have deciphered our writings into your language which means you are an intelligent species. We have no manner in which to judge your development nor would the information be of any value to us. We wish you well.

This planet is dying and we are dying with it and it is our own fault. We did not understand in the beginning when it

Earth - Mars

was a beautiful planet and we came from a different star system. The temperature changes were a little extreme but it was a beautiful planet which suited us and was adequate for our needs. Now it is dying. For the last one hundred orbits around the Sun, the few of us that are left have been journeying to the third planet from the Sun to feed our people and to gather fuel for our ships. Now we are leaving for the Third Planet whose volcanic activity has somewhat subsided and where we should be able to survive.

All that is left of our civilization is ten males and fifty females. Winds and storms have destroyed most physical structures. We have two very old ships left. I hope they will carry us to our destination.

CHRONICLE 2: We are leaving these Chronicles behind us. I am the oldest and can do the least in preparing for the journey, so all have decided that I must write the record. It is very difficult for me as I am only five hundred years old, but we have been on this planet for approximately eight thousand years according to the preserved written history. Traditional oral history handed down for generations tells us we were driven from our original home and that it was impossible for us to return. All memory of that place and it's location was erased, but it was a place of peace and contentment.

It is said there was no need for material food, that we lived as part of the Cosmos; that violence and passion were conditions unheard of in all creatures. In the least, it is suspect. I, personally, believe that it is folklore since it is not part of the recorded history.

We have no memory of arriving on this planet, dressed in

Independence

the skins of an animal we did not know. We had nothing. We became aware only that we were standing in a large open area in the midst of knee-high grass with little seeds growing on the top of a long stem. We all suffered hunger and one of us picked a handfull of the little seeds and began to chew them, saying they tasted good. This wheat (as we later called it) didn't appear to hurt him, so some of us picked the seeds and the rest looked for a cave to shelter us. That was the beginning. We found other fruits and vegetables for food and soon we built shelters and planted crops close to them. We grew in numbers and learned to build shelters that were strong enough to protect us from the animals and the weather.

CHRONICLE 3: We discovered we could use stone implements to cut wood for our fires and to soften the grain and fibrous plants by grinding. It was during this period of the Stone Age when two men wanted the same woman for a wife. One man killed the other, took the woman and left the settlement with some of his followers. This was the first remembered act of violence and by it, we were separated into two settlements which became a conflict. In one settlement, the strongest ruled, but now it was us against them. When we met, we fought without a reason for doing so. I don't think anyone recalled what had caused the separation after a single revolution around the Sun.

I must proceed with the Chronicles. It is so easy to let my mind wander.

Separation introduced conflict and we soon learned to defend ourselves with spears and bows and arrows. We watched the substance spill out of the volcano and as it cooled it would sometimes bend and we hammered it into a

Earth - Mars

shape to use. Some of us found powder that would burn very hot and we could melt certain rocks into bowl shapes to hold water and fat melted from animals. Our spears lasted a long time with points that were very sharp and our bows also. We proceded from stone to metal.

CHRONICLE 4: The geography of this planet lent itself to division as there were two large continents and seas that reached from one pole to another. The land masses were almost equal in the capability to maintain agriculture. There were few mountains; land was mostly flat, overgrown with trees and brush. Tedious years were spent clearing the land to cultivate it and to produce food. By the time one third of the land was arable, animals had been tamed and sharpened sticks were used to plow the land.

By accident the plow was created. A man, whose animal was having difficulty drawing a sled, found that a piece of metal had slipped between the logs and had left a neat furrow in the field behind him. In time, improvements were made and an efficient method of plowing was developed. Before long, the wheel was produced and a new age of agriculture and industry began.

CHRONICLE 5: In the Agri-Industrial Era, trade grew from manufacture of goods and the growth of food products. Dishes and bowls were shaped from clay, fibers were woven into cloths, tools and weapons were shaped from bone, wood and metal. Many things were a great help to us on this planet, but when we used the material for wrong purposes, our downfall began.

The powder that burned was stored in a long-necked jar and in an accidental fire, when the jar heated to a high

Independence

temperature, it exploded. Quick-minded warriors created balls of clay filled with the powder that could be ignited by a fiber fuse. They used these to blow up houses in the neighboring villages in what was probably the first act of war. There was no division between the wars that followed in the next several thousand years. It seems that once we started, we could not stop. We would attack others, and they would attack us in a never-ending stream of bloodshed.

Thus we developed a civilization bent on industrial production with agriculture as a secondary base for the economy.

CHRONICLE 6: Schools were created to teach children the basic facts of early development and of history and there evolved a class called scientists. Some thinker devised the idea that everything encountered in the civilzation was a system or part of a system and to understand the total environment, one needed to teach that all systems or parts of systems had an effect on the total system. I could never understand that, but it soon caught on and everyone began to study the parts of the system that interested them. Scientists became specialists in their own system areas suited to their locations on the planet.

I supposed that it was good, as long as the development was for the good of all. Living became easier; wars settled down from major eruptions to local disputes over trivial matters. Laws set models to live by and there were those to make sure they were obeyed. Then the engine was invented. From large, heavy, cumbersome but simple machines, moving parts created "transportation" and some scientists decided they wanted to study that part of the system. From carts and wagons to automobiles and trains, the wheel sprouted

Earth - Mars

wings and flew. Before long, a conversion unit could change the sun's radiation into electrical energy that worked through a magnetic device. The scientist could now skim along in a small metal air buggy two feet above the ground. Scientific specialists idly wondered how high man could fly. The next step was space flight.

CHRONICLE 7: Everyone had air buggies; they were cheap, easy to run and they seemed to last indefinitely. Racing down one hill and up the side of the other was fun for a group of boys. One of them pushed his starting lever to the end of the slot to gain more speed. When he went up the next hill, the air buggy continued from the crest and rose to the heighth of a mile. Very frightened, he rode in circles until a nearby scientist duplicated his actions, came within shouting distance and told the boy to ease back very slowly on the throttle. They both slowly descended without harm, but the incident peaked the scientist's curiosity. He built a large, more powerful conversion unit and man was off into space.

But there was an unfortunate side to all this development. We had been on this Planet, fourth from the Sun, for about six thousand years and we had forgotten the environment that existed, the natural order that was here when we came. Unknowingly, we were slowly interfering with the natural order. There had been signs; bad water in some places, deserts developing in others, rainfall lessening and becoming impure. No one particularly noticed, so busy concentraing on society's selfish, artificial interests.

Hindsight is always wiser than foresight. We took from this beautiful Planet, but never gave anything in return. I suppose we were our own executioners.

Independence

CHRONICLE 8: The destruction of this beautiful planet is unforgivable. The things we did to ourselves, we deserve.

I have not mentioned wars very much; I am reticent about discussing them, but I have been told that I must. The first encounters were not large ground-shaking events and politically, they proved nothing. (I still believe that war proves nothing.) The first war began with the use of the explosive balls and there were twenty-five great wars after that. At the end of each, the planet was less beautiful and the people less human.

With the use of Solar Power for our machines and for our space vehicles, weapons became more vicious. There was vaster destruction over larger areas that took longer to heal; took more time to regain the natural order. The worst destruction was to the psyche of the people who became ingrained and selfish; lacking dignity and charity. The norm became "me, my and I" and the order of society became a laughable idea. Drugs developed by scientists to cure the ill became the playthings at social events. The darker side of humanity became evident as there was no respect for one's self nor for others.

Men had to be driven to fight the wars and the wars themselves turned humanity into wolf packs fighting for survival, even at the expense of their friends. The horrible end came suddenly. The enemy developed a bacteria that destroyed everything in its path. Then it too died. Everything is gone except we few who are going to the Third PLanet. Perhaps we can survive there. We have destroyed this planet...and ourselves.

Earth - Mars

CHRONICLE 9: There is one ironical thing left to write. It is my fondest hope that the melting waters from the Polar Cap never reach the infinity symbol. If they do, the Chronicles will disappear and there will be nothing left to show that our civilization existed. The last physical scientist alive manufactured these disks from the remains of things that had lived on this planet. There is no water left here, so he combined chemicals from the Ice Cap with chemicals derived from each plant, animal and human being. The result is a strong material easily destroyed by water. The disks will simply disappear. It is all we can do...

George turned to the Professor. "What does it mean? Are they all dead?"

"I think it means that our ancestors came from some other place in the Cosmos and settled on Mars. Then, they went to Earth. These people must be the first human beings. But, don't quote me on it! Let's get Ken and Bob and let them see what we have."

They went into the lounge and showed Kenneth and the others the work that George had produced. Ken read the abstracts, then told Bob to call Dr. Hardwick while he called the President. The President requested that the group come to the White House after all had read the complete Chronicles text.

****

They had assembled at the White House. Everyone had read the text, made notes and formed various opinions. Now they were eager to discuss the Chronicles not only as historical and scientific data, but as a warning to their own society. Their discussions were interrupted by a humming sound in the air and the rough-handed stranger

Independence

dressed in old clothes appeared before them.

"You have found the messages," he said softly. "Do you understand their meaning? Tell humanity about this history! All things are created in circles. You have completed one; the next circle awaits you." The stranger vanished.

In the ensuing silence, the President rose and stared out the window of the White House at the monument on the far hill. He laughed aloud and turned to the silent group.

"Gentlemen," he said, "we have not only completed the first circle, if this is the first, but I believe that we have gone a little farther into the next one. We can be proud of ourselves to a degree, but I hope we don't mess up the next one."

They all nodded in agreement. Mankind had crept out of the cradle and was exploring the house.

****

Humanity had found one chapter of its youth. "When I was a child, I thought as a child, I played with children's toys, and my world was a child's world. I am no longer a child, for I have found that my childhood was long ago. So long ago that I can no longer remember where or when it began."

Now humanity had something to compare with it's present and with it's near past. It was not pleasant and the feeling spread like a plague throughout all the countries of the world; the realization that mankind was traveling through another circle.

Many scientists and philosophers stated that it was not the same path; that there were many differences. Mankind, the scientists said, had more quickly developed into a civilized conglomerate of nations; that scientific

Earth - Mars

developments were far more sophisticated. Philosophers and theologians said that mankind had a more highly developed understanding of knowledge of the Most High. Extrapolations and points of proof offered by them merely justified their opinions, then after justifying, proved they were narrow-minded hypocrites at best, fools at the worst. They ignored the totality of the circle and selected parts of the arc to prove points.

The new circle of history was larger. The disks contained very few specifics. Those who studied the transcripts found only the fact that they had come from somewhere else, that Mars had not been their original home but merely a new beginning.

Theologians were intrigued by the idea as they pondered how many beginnings there had been. Their scriptural writings stated that a man and a woman were removed by the Most High from a paradise He had fashioned for them.

Scientists were not impressed with the manuscripts other than the fact that the molecular structure was the same as the total compilation of all the different molecules found on earth, and when placed in water, they disappeared.

Historians and sociologists were the most impressed. Their studies led to the inevitable interpretations of the philosophers; that man was doomed, again and again, to repeat his history.

But philosophy does not take into account that humans are predictable only to a point, that there is no telling what may happen, particularly when faced with a problem never before encountered, or with a new set of circumstances. Man has just a little bit of the Most High in him, and he could change his course by interjecting a new variable. In even the next same set of circumstances,

Independence

he may change the variable and set a new course.

The circle of human history, which most believed was just completed with the discovery of the infinity symbol, was not one that mankind took any great pride in remembering. Most pride could be felt only on an individual basis.

On even the smallest scale, very few nations could proclaim that they had made a positive contribution. The United States, a nation that proclaimed much and attempted much, failed in the long record of history.

Humanity had not yet learned how to break the old historical circle formed on territorial and land boundaries; the separation of good and bad with no basic definition of either, so that each man judged for himself.

The one great change had been in the written and oral news media. No media personnel were permitted on the space flights which caused an uproar. The First Amendment was often quoted and the "people's" right to know was repeated so often that the President finally told them they could ride with the astronauts if their companies or corporations would pay the cost of the flight. If it was of such importance, they should not object to paying for the news they might get. That, essentially, put a stop to the uproar.

Some Senators and Congressmen wanted to participate and were told the same thing, they could pay for the trip and ride whenever they wished. In the early days of confusion and outrage, the human condition seemed to breed the urge to explore space but at someone else's expense, namely the taxpayers. The President, and the ones that followed him, were adamant. No one boarded a space ship unless they were productive.

After the Mars landing and the construction of the domes, the ban was somewhat lifted, but all media reports

Earth - Mars

had to be cleared through the Public Relations Division of the Space Agency. Other countries set their own regulations, but most policies were similar to those of the United States. Democratic countries did not trust the media and totalitarian countries controlled their presses, so no international contention was raised over the edict.

The restrictions placed on the press made the media work on the positive side of human affairs. Discoveries were reported accurately and human activities on all planets were related as they actually happened with no slanted assumptions and no subjective meanings possible after an occurence.

Everything taken into consideration, humanity had indeed began to grow to adulthood.

****

In the year 2065 A.D., James Carpenter, one of the three mechanical engineers that Mars Central had sent to work on the mechanical atmosphere converters, was disgusted. The conversion machinery worked perfectly, but no matter what they tried, the new atmosphere leaked away into space and the part that remained was not breathable.

Carpenter stopped his sand crawler beside one of the electrolytic converters to check its operation. He climbed down from the driver's seat, stood on the red sand and scanned the locations of his other machines, then looked to the tops of the surrounding mountains on Clavius.

"There must be a better way," he thought, then opened his transmitter mike and called the other engineers. "Joe, Mike, can you hear me?"

"Yes, we can."

"Let's meet by Number Ten and talk a little. I'm

Independence

disgusted with the way things are going."

They met and dismounted at Ten. James removed a small machine from the rear compartment of the sand crawler. He set it on a pedistal surrounded by small rocks and turned it on. Within minutes, they were enclosed in a small dome. He activated the oxygen supply and they removed their helmets.

"What's this about being disgusted?" Joe laughed. "I thought you liked the pay."

"I do like the pay, but I also like to accomplish something and we don't seem to be getting anywhere with this project."

"What do you suggest?" Mike asked.

"I don't know. We need moisture in the atmosphere, even a tiny bit. You fellows go back to the Lab Dome and involve the others. See if you can come up with some ideas. I'll stay here. As the mechanical engineer, I can keep these things running. You, Joe, you're the chemist and you, Mike, you're the physicist; why don't you get into the library and see if there are things we haven't considered."

"Sounds good to me," Mike replied. Joe agreed, then looked at James. "We'll be gone at least two weeks. If we have no answers, we'll be back. You going to be alright while we are gone?"

"Don't worry; I'll be alright."

The two headed back to the Lab Dome and as the sand crawler moved out of sight, the loneliness of the Clavius Crater suddenly descended on James. He raised his head, looked at the black sky dusted with the bright spots of stars, then at the horizon where the red Martian landscape cut through the blackness of space.

He was an alien on an alien planet with nothing to remind him of home. The steep, red cliffs and hills were

Earth - Mars

obscene compared to the green hills of his home on Earth. Homesickness crept into his being, but he shook it off.

"If things go right," he thought, "This will be another earth and what an accomplishment that would be!"

He sighed, put on his helmet, turned off the generator, stowed the dome and it on his sand crawler. He made the rounds of the generators, checking working parts for wear, pressures on the dials, then moved through the maintenance routine. When it was completed, he returned to the campsite dome. The stranger in rough work clothes was sitting on one of the low cabinets.

"Hello, James," he said.

Startled, James jumped back, then recalled the stories told by Dr. Hardwick. "You really do exist!" he exclaimed.

"I certainly do," the stranger laughed. "Take my word for it. I understand you have a little problem here developing an atmosphere that will not leak away."

"That's right," James answered, amazed at his ready acceptance of the stranger. "We can only get a small amount of atmosphere up to the ten thousand foot level."

"Have you tested the ice on the cap?"

"We've been busy analyzing what we have here. No one has had the time to go to the ice caps to test anything."

"James," the stranger said, looking thoughtfully at him. "do you remember the college course you enrolled in called Modular Mechanics?" James nodded affirmatively. "Do you recall the basic fundamental of that course? *Everything belongs to a system.* Every problem, no matter how large, can be broken into subsystems or modules. Everything that exists belongs to a larger system. The key to solving a problem is to find the part of the system that failed and correct it. The rest of the larger system then

166

Independence

automatically rights itself."

"Yes, yes," James said softly. "Go on."

"You must keep in mind that there is only one complete whole in all creation and that is the Most High. Everything is part of His creation. Let me reduce this to a size you can comprehend.

This is the planet you call Mars; each planet and the sun are a part of the Solar System. Anything that affects one part of the Solar System also affects the other parts. This system is in a status of balance and only an outside force can change that balance.

This planet, Mars, is in a state of balance with itself and with the Solar System. Whatever you attempt to change must be done in a manner that its natural balance will not erect barriers against your efforts.

If, in the human sense, you exert a positive effort to improve the natural order, the planet will help you by following its own intrinsic nature. You are not dealing with a total, only a part; not just the surface, not just one little spot on the surface. Treat it as a whole system; do not take away from it, but add to it. The right solution to the problem is a change in one of the modular parts; this will indicate solutions to all the system.

I suggest that you and your people study the inscriptions on the disks and remember modular systems engineering."

The stranger's first mention of the college course set James thinking while he listened. The more that the stranger explained, the more he remembered. Then it struck him. They had not considered the problem from an academic point of view. When Jim looked up, the stranger was gone and in the place where he had been sitting, there was a glass of water.

He stared at the glass, his first impulse being to

Earth - Mars

drink it, that the Angel had left it for him to drink. But his scientific sense took over and he considered two things.

One, was it fresh water? Was its chemical contents the same as Earth water? He would send it to the lab at Mars Central for analysis.

Two, why had the Angel left it after the long speech? The atmosphere lacked humidity and humidity is moisture.

The only places on Mars where there was water were the North and South Poles. No, there was more to it than that. Think, man, think. Water table, that was it. If there was an ice cap, there must be a water table someplace.

James radioed Mars Central and asked for Dr. Hardwick. He told him,

"I think I have an answer, or at least part of an answer. Do you have any drilling rigs?"

"There are two from construction of the transmission towers, due to be sent back to Earth this week. What do you have in mind?"

James told him of the visit from the Angel and how it had helped him to think in different terms of the atmospheric problem. Dr. Hardwick agreed to send two crews to start drilling, but he reminded James, "We will have to send to Earth for pipe and drill heads."

"I'm down sixteen thousand feet from the mean surface level," James replied, "so get lots of pipe."

"I think we will start a little closer to the caps," the Doctor laughed, "and if we hit water, we will work down towards you. Signing off."

Dr. Hardwick summoned to his quarters the two operators of the excavation machines used to rebuild the destroyed towers and asked for a list of materials needed to convert their machines to drilling rigs. Both operators agreed the rigs would need a major overhaul to convert

Independence

them and that it probably would be cheaper to transport drilling rigs from Earth.

"I want those rigs stripped," the Doctor snapped, "and a list made of the parts you will need. Get busy!"

The operators shared a glance, then shrugged.

"Okay, but it will take time."

"Then stop wasting time by talking."

In the communications room, Dr. Hardwick called Earth Space Central to send crews who were experts on drilling. Then he called James to tell him that it would be awhile before crews and equipment would be on the two pole areas.

"In the meantime," he instructed James, "keep the atmosphere machines running. I'm going back to Noctus Labyrinthus to the spot where the infinity symbol lines crossed to see if we overlooked anything."

Hardwick donned his protective suit, hefted the oxygen bottle onto his back and connected the tube to the side of his airtight helmet. He felt a strong attraction to Noctus Labyrinthus, as if he had started a job and not finished it, as if there was more to be discovered there.

He would continue to return until he had covered the entire Labyrinth.

At Mars Central Library, Joe and Mike made copious notes concerning the impact that environment had on atmosphere, but they had not correlated them until the return to Clavius Crater where they could work with James. The flitter craft couldn't hold all the work, so while Mike flew in, Joe drove in his sand crawler. James was happy to see the flitter craft.

In order to find the best location for the drilling rigs, the area of both poles would have to be scouted and James hoped that something would indicate to him the best places to recommend to Dr. Hardwick for drilling.

Earth - Mars

The three men spent several days studying the research notes, hoping to find something to help their project move along. A Martian wind was blowing and even at sixteen thousand feet below the mean surface, they could do nothing outside the dome. The wind swirled down into the crater with a force that could cut through steel.

Water had to be the answer; water with a natural carbon dioxide conversion process. Green plants could do the job, but plants could not be cultivated until there was sufficient water.

****

Grousham Havenshaker was seventy-two years old. Except for his eyes which were bright and sharp as an eagle's, he looked about one hundred and ten. His hair stood out from his head like a peacock's tail, and from any direction, looked like a snow column returning to the clouds. His face, an uncooked prune framed by bushy eyebrows, sported ears that stuck out of his hair.

His frame was bent and hunched, but his hands were steady. He wore clothing that looked worse than an unmade bed; shoes sometimes matched, socks never.

He was a historian, the most renowned that ever lived. He was also the world's leading computer expert with a photographic memory. He had won every prize and accolade ever given on Earth, all packed away in a cardboard box in the attic of his small cottage on the outskirts of Oroville, California.

His home and office were now in the new computer complex on the Moon known throughout the Solar System as Computer Central,Moon,Earth. Everyone called him Old Grouse, but his temperment was mild unless he had difficulties with a hardware or software application. Then

Independence

Old Grouse became Attila the Hun; none dared to speak to him as he tramped the hallways mumbling to himself, or scribbling program language on the nearest surface. He was a brilliant, eccentric man.

Old Grouse had never studied systems engineering or modular systems engineering, but he was a systems man although he didn't know it. He viewed the total Cosmos as a system within a system, within a system, etc. Perhaps that was the reason for his renown.

He reviewed the incoming data from Mars that included geology reports, atmospheric reports, chemical analyses of the light and dark areas formerly called canals, mineral analyses, even medical reports and the psychological profiles of personnel working on Mars.

He had devised his own computer program using Earth as a control which made a comparative analysis every time he fed specifically reduced information into it. He used Mars as the system and all else as sub-systems but the analysis was not going well. There had been a major problem from the beginning and he could not think what it could be.

He stomped through the corridors to the screen of the main central computer data reception center, stared at the incoming data, snorted an invective, and then returned to pacing in the corridors. Staff avoided him at times like these, but as he turned a corner and spied a group idly talking at the water fountain, he was more irritated than usual.

"What are you doing here when you should all be working?" he roared. "A million problems must be solved and you stand there gabbing! Back to work!"

They walked away, mumbling. Old Grouse strode to the end of the hall, then turned to look back at the water fountain, the only one in Computer Central. He hurried to it,

Earth - Mars

pushed the button, put his hand under the flowing water and laughed aloud. Maybe this was it.

In his office, he fed terms into his computer. Ice Cap. Water. Humidity. Then he fed it into the subsystems and then into the singular system called Mars. He recalled each subsystem, then the total of all systems and sat there amazed. He had a ninety per cent success ratio in comparison to Earth. He had found the missing ingredient, but there was still a ten per cent unknown factor.

"Here we go again," he said. He sent a message to Hardwick at Mars Central. "Got to find a way to use water or you have no atmosphere."

Hardwick replied," You are a little late. We are working on it. Thanks, anyway. We shall keep you informed."

Old Grouse was taken back. "They are on the ball," he thought, then sent the following message,

"Computer shows a ten per cent non-success variable. I will work to find the discipline or the area where the percentage is located."

"I appreciate your work," Hardwick responded. "Please keep me informed."

Old Grouse went whistling back to his office. Seated at his desk, facing a relief map of Mars, taken from a circling satellite, that covered an entire wall from floor to ceiling, he had the feeling of not being alone.

"Hello, Grousham." Old Grouse whirled about and faced a stranger on sitting a stool, wearing old clothes and work shoes.

"Who in blazes are you?" Old Grouse demanded. "How did you get in here?"

"Don't be alarmed. I am a friend. Surely you have heard of me by now."

Independence

Then it struck Old Grouse. "By all that's Holy, this is the Angel that's been helping us out!"

"I'm supposed to be a historian," he said aloud, "but I'd forgotten how you helped us in the past. I sure can use your help now."

"No, Grousham, I cannot help you. I can only discuss things with you and make suggestions. You must decide what you must do and why."

"There is a ten per cent factor escaping me on the Mars water problem. I don't know where to look for the answer."

The Angel smiled. "I don't see how you could solve any problems running through the corridors with a scowl on your face. Since you consider everything as a system itself, or part of a system, or contained in a system, why not study the problem from a system view?"

The stranger pointed to a spot in front of Old Grouse and a hologram of the Solar System appeared with just the edge of the sun showing.

"Since you are not concerned with all the outer planets, let's change this hologram and include only Jupiter and Venus."

The image shifted leaving Venus, Mars and Jupiter with the Asteroid Belt between them. The details on the surface of Mars were clearly visible as it turned on its axis. The stranger said no more, sat back and waited.

"What am I supposed to see?" Old Grouse asked sharply. "There are only hills, valleys and plains; cracks and crevices, some of them deep."

"Think of the recent Earth history, the time when much of North and South Africa were desert wastelands. That was sand, mostly silicon; here you have oxidized materials. Why did Earth die in the last of the Twentieth Century? Water was important, but what else happened?"

173

Earth - Mars

Old Grouse frowned and the stranger continued.

"Do not consider who did what to ruin the land, think only how they solved their problem, how they had to change their thinking. Everyone manufacturing anything used Earth's resources to establish power, from new automobiles to nuclear power plants, and they created waste in achieving their ends. How did they solve this problem?"

Old Grouse listened thoughtfully, but for the life of him, could not provide the answer.

"Remember," the Angel said, "there are no unsolvable problems in the Cosmos. Sometimes, one must try harder to see an answer." He disappeared.

Old Grouse sank into his easy chair, thinking about the past human history of Earth that held the key to the problem. That and the transcripts that had been found on Mars which he had studied with single-minded diligence. He had made notes of the comparisons, the major one that both had changed from an agrarian society to an industrial society. The systems should have been compatible as one was fed by the other, but somehow the two became antagonistic and then, incompatible. What had caused this subtle antagonism?

Grouse poured himself a cup of coffee, stared at it a moment. Someone had to grow the beans, someone had to make the container, the cup. He considered both processes, agricultural and industrial. Land had been converted to a useable human product.

Coffee beans came from plants that did no harm to the environment. The companies that processed beans into coffee used wood, coal, gas, electricity to roast them and manufactured machinery to grind them. Stores occupied space.

Refined clay was converted to a cup using water to

Independence

shape it and the waste water contained natural elements that did not harm the environment. Baking in a kiln required heat. No harm there.

What was the key to the destruction of Earth's environment? What was the one activity that was to be avoided on Mars if humanity was to survive by breaking the cycle of history?

What had humanity finally accomplished that made it possible for them to remain on Earth while they explored the Solar System? The mathematical formulae that permitted man to leave Earth with ease had only allowed him to leave his mistakes behind.

They could not control the weather, but the erection of domes let them control well their immediate atmosphere and used judiciously, these domes were a boon to mankind and the environment. No harm there.

He recalled the period when the people of North America believed that Acid Rain was destroying their forests and woodlands. An idea grew. Grousham went to his vast computer library and called up all the information on Acid Rain. When he had read only half the information, he knew what had been ignored.

The environmentalists had blamed the industrial complex, the smoke-stack industries, but their charges were only partially true. Rain is water. The cycle to become rain originates from several ground sources. It begins as water in the oceans, lakes, rivers, streams and springs. It soaks through the ground to form acquifers, underground rivers and lakes. This water table is maintained in all areas from which the growth of plants forms evaporation. Cultivated crops, upon which pesticides were sprayed, add to the vapor content, which is the source from which the rain falls.

Waste had been ignored, toxic and non-toxic waste.

Earth - Mars

The waste material from the industries and the sewerage plants added to the normal, and natural, deterioration of the environment formed a deadly combination that had destroyed most of the plant life's ability to adapt or to reconstitute itself. Mankind, ninety per cent water in his physical state, was in grave danger.

The people in Canada and the United States blamed each other, argued for years but actually did nothing about the situation.

Corporations on both sides of the border reported to their governments that the installation of stack scrubbers to eliminate smoke from the air would be such a costly proposition that they would have to lay off many workers.

Environmentalists finally began to investigate where toxic wastes and solid effluents from sewerage systems were being dumped in, and out of, landfills. They trailed tanker trucks in every state from large and small manufacturings companies compiling evidence that they gave to both governments.

They proved that most water tables were contaminated, that most streams were killing the fish they were meant to support, that the oceans three miles from shore were being poisoned. They proved that it was a combination of all these things that caused the Acid Rain, and that the Acid Rain itself added to the problem by removing sulferic contaminents from the atmosphere and returning them to the water cycle. Toxcidity became more intense.

The United States and Canadian governments set up combined research teams of chemists and physicists to analyze all forms of waste products. Primarily, they wanted to neutralize the waste, then create a product that could be utilized in some way.

They had succeeded to the point where eighty per

Independence

cent was transformed to new products and the remaining twenty per cent was neutralized. In three years, nature adjusted to the revised conditions. Streams became clear and lakes, once again, a fisherman's paradise. It was no longer necessary to add chemicals to resevoirs and the transition provided new jobs as the old systems closed down.

The Waste Laboratory became economically self-sufficient by recouping original costs and showing a profit which was evenly divided between the two governments.

Old Grouse leaned back in his chair, pushed a button on his desk and said happily,

"Bring me the Mars transcripts. I think I have whipped the ten per cent!" He was thinking that if they did what he thought they did, then the trap could be avoided. In the Communications Room of Computer Central on Earth's Moon, he contacted Mars Computer Central and asked for Dr. Hardwick.

"Hello, Grouse." Dr. Hardwick was the only person who could address him that way. "What can I do for you?"

"Hello, Hardhead," Grouse responded. "You are planning to drill for water. Have you started yet? If so, where?"

"No, not yet. The drilling rigs arrived two days ago and are on their way to the sites. We shall drill one mile from the edge of the caps and in the middle of Clavius which is the lowest point, about sixteen thousand feet below the mean surface. Why?"

"I would like you to take core samples every one hundred feet and transmit the data to me here on Moon Central. I have a theory and the samples may answer several important questions."

"Will do, Grouse. I'll have to send a geologist with a computer to the sites, so I'll tell the crews to hold up

Earth - Mars

drilling until they arrive. Okay?"

"Thanks, Hardhead. We'll be glad we did this before we tackle the atmosphere project. Goodbye and good luck." Grouse signed off.

"Now, why does he want core samples?" puzzled Hardwick. "We won't be starting mining here for years. Well, the old boy must have a good reason."

Hardwick issued orders to the geologist and then transmitted instructions to the site drilling crews. He told the communications chief,

"I'm going to Noctis Labyrinthus and poke around a bit. If there are any messages, call me on the radio."

****

James Carpenter checked the atmosphere machines one last time, found them to be working well, then headed the Sand Crawler toward the Northern Cap where the crew was setting up the drilling rig. Joe and Mike were on the Southern Cap with a drilling crew, so James introduced himself to the project men and women who welcomed him warmly. There was a need for close bonds between extra-terrestrial humans who lived every moment in a dangerous environment.

The drilling rig was in place, so they started up the solar heaters in the dome nearby while waiting for the geologist. The site was flat, just below a range of mountains called Albis Patera. It was as good a place as any to start drilling on an educated guess.

Drilling began as soon as the geologist arrived. The first two feet went easily, but it got more difficult as they reached one hundred feet. They pulled the first core sample and laid the one hundred foot tube for the geologist's inspection. He took layer measurements, made

Independence

notes, and kept his opinions to himself while the crew drilled the second hundred feet. At a glance, there appeared to be no difference in the core samples.

At the Southern Cap, the site was also located on a flat plain below a mountain range called Charitum Montes. The first one hundred feet appeared to be the same as in the Northern Cap. Drilling was difficult at both sites as there was very little water to cool the bit drills, so they operated at one quarter of the usual drilling speed.

As the drilling progressed, geologists continued to examine core samples sending the information, via computer, to Mars Central. Mars Central, in turn, relayed the data to Earth's Moon Central.

****

Drawn to the area of Noctis Labyrinthus, yet not understanding the attraction, Dr. Hardwick knew it would take the rest of his life to explore it. He took photographs of the walls and the ground; with a geologist's pick, he collected samples of both and stowed them carefully in his pack. Each area of the infinity symbol was accurately marked on his map as he traced and retraced his steps of exploration. Nothing new had been discovered.

This time, he wanted to inspect the center area of one of the infinity loops. He casually flipped a coin and the north loop won, so he walked to the center where the lines crossed and headed due north.

He followed a crevice that appeared to be a little darker than the rest. "Blasted place is a little spooky," he thought. His portable solar battery floodlight could be focussed to a narrow beam, but he preferred it on flood so that he could see both walls. Almost at the center of the northern loop, the crevice widened and changed in

Earth - Mars

texture and smoothness. The layers were no longer jutting chunks of rock, but seemed to have been cut with a tool. He photographed as he walked and suddenly, as he rounded a bend, his light showed on the path ahead, a cave opening.

Hardwick paused, unsure of entering the cave. He took pictures and rock samples, then cautiously moved ahead. Ten feet inside the opening, the walls were smooth and unbroken; the path sloped downward with small cross ridges that gave firm footing. Hardwick moved down slowly with his camera working all the time.

The cavern branched to the left and to the right. Hardwick walked to the right and found the crystalline substance embedded in the walls. From a thin line, it became broad and soon formed the wall itself. An offset cut into the wall began as a platform two feet deep and two feet wide that ended at the ceiling. Standing in the center of the offset, was the statue of a human being, the form the same as his own. Both arms were bent at the elbows, palms of the hands upward as if in supplication. The eyes stared straight ahead in an impassive face.

Hardwick stepped before it to get a better photograph, but paused and looked to his left. There was another offset opposite this one holding a similar statue. There was something about the eyes that made him hesitate. Were they ornamental? Or, if he passed between them, could they be a trigger device of some kind?

He found a straight place in the wall and sat with his back to the cool surface, deciding to eat a snack lunch while he gave thought to the situation. Eating was a tedious process. He took a deep breath, opened his faceplate, took a bite, closed his faceplate; but he was used to it. He eyed the statues while he chewed, but he could see nothing electronic that resembled a trip device.

Independence

When he finished eating, he took his magnifying glass from his pack and made a close inspection of the tips of the outstretched fingers, but could find nothing different from the rest of the statue. Heaving a sigh of exasperation, he examined the two foot area below the statue, the areas behind and to the left and right of it and the rear wall. Nothing.

As he stepped back to pick up his pack, a faint glow came from each statue. He watched. It became brighter, and suddenly, a beam shot from both statues simultaneously, meeting in the exact center of the cave.

With a scientist's instinct, Hardwick looked at his watch. It was exactly twelve noon, Mars time and the sun was at the meridian. When the two beams met in the middle of the cave, a hologram appeared.

There was an illumined map of the cave and all it's branches with the same writing that was on the disks. Hardwick hurriedly shot as much film as he could before the light faded and only the statues remained. If his use of the camera was sufficiently expert, this discovery could be translated.

He was tempted to go further into the maze of side caves, but despite his high degree of curiosity, Hardwick was a cautious man in circumstances where he might destroy all, or part, of a valuable find. He stowed his camera, picked up his pack and retraced his steps out of the cave.

Back on Mars Central, he gave his film to the developing crew and instructed them to make eight by ten inch photographs. The series was transmitted to Computer Central on Earth's Moon. Copies in sets were sent to Ken Rachner's Space Coordination Central orbiting earth with a request for a translation of the writing.

Hardwick sat down to prepare a report of his trip,

Earth - Mars

then requested that a party of scientists study the report that would be sent from Space Central. While the cave hologram was still fresh in his mind, he drew single lines representing sides of the caves that he could remember.
There were some he was sure he had forgotten, but even as he drew, the design began to look familiar. He worked on it a long time, redrawing and trying to recall where he had seen it before. In disgust, he wadded up the last sketch and tossed it into a waste disposal unit.

On the oversized map of Mars covering his wall, Hardwick stuck minute samples of the rocks in the locations where he had found them. When the Photo Lab technician brought his pictures, he placed a photo beside the sample. The photographs of the hologram were astoundingly clear, clearer than all the others he had taken.

The light beams projecting from the eyes of the two statues did not meet, but formed a square about five feet on all sides. The design formed by the side caves *was* familiar. He booted up the computer.

"Well I'll be blasted!" he exclaimed aloud. "I was right! It is the Antares Solar System in the Scorpio Constellation! I wonder...is *that* where they came from? Or rather, is that where *we* came from?"

Hardwick mused, "We know very little about that star system, but if I remember correctly, if a line was drawn from the sun to each of the planets, it would look like an octopus. I hope we get the interpretation of those writings back soon."

Resigning himself to the wait, Dr. Hardwick transmitted the photographs to the Moon Central and to Space Central.

****

Independence

Kenneth Rackner had just completed a reading of Hardwick's findings in the caves of Noctis Labyrinthus, then he viewed the reproductions of the hologram photographs. He rose from his desk and stood at the crystal window staring at the stars. He felt uneasy and a chill ran down his back. His thoughts returned to his childhood when he had solved the equation that started this new era of history.

"Good Lord, what have I started?" he muttered. "Are we supposed to know all these things? Are we moving too fast? There are a million people scattered on Earth's Moon and on Mars. Can they survive? And for how long?"

He recalled a simple poem called "God's Reason" written by an unknown author that fit his heavy mood of doubt.

I don't know how to say it, but somehow it seems to me,
That maybe we are stationed where God wanted us to be.
That little place we're filling is the reason for our birth,
And just to do the work we do, He sent us down to earth.
If God had wanted otherwise, I reckon He'd have made
Each one a little different of a worse or better grade.
And since God knows and understands all things of land and sea,
I fancy that he placed us where He wanted us to be.
Sometimes we get to thinking as our labors we review,
That we should like a higher place with greater things to do,
But we come to the conclusion when the envying is stilled
That the post to which God sent us is the post He wanted filled.
And there isn't any service we rightfully can scorn
For it may be just the reason God allowed us to be born.

Earth - Mars

A voice spoke behind him. Startled, Ken whirled around.

"How do you know," the stranger asked, "that any place you are able to be, isn't the place He wants you to be?" He sat in a chair against the far wall.

"How did you..?" Ken began to speak, then recalled the tales he had heard about this stranger in rough clothes. "Are you truly an Angel?" he asked.

"Yep. Sure am. Why are you so doubtful about your accomplishments? You have done exactly what the Most High wanted you to do. You know, that poem you have remembered does not confine you to Earth. It was not meant to be confined to any particular place.

The smallest action taken can be as important as the largest Earth-shaking event. I remind you, as I have reminded others, that time is an invention of man. It means nothing; eternal destiny has no time. You use the word, immediately, and in our concept it could be when you utter the word or a million years.

The grand accomplishments of some human beings could have no effect on history, yet your past actions are of great importance to human destiny. You have given them the opportunity to leave the cradle and to enlarge their awareness of the vastness of creation.

The ancient ones thought the world in which they lived was the total creation, but they learned that the Most High created more than Earth. He does not create to create; there is a purpose to all He does.

The stars and the planets beckoned even to humans that lived in caves, although they were fearful to behold and considered gods of early spiritism. They were named to reflect early superstition, and names by which they are still called.

The Most High did not interfere for thousands of

Independence

Earth years, then He sent His Son to show mankind that they were fighting as children, turning their intelligence inward and ignoring the spirit that tried to show them their vast inheritance.

You have provided an opportunity and a challenge and they did begin to see beyond the bars of their cradle. Now they are starting to explore, to use an allegory, the rest of the house. Do not feel sorrow for those who make the transition to the eternal dimension. All the affairs of man must balance. That is the natural order of the Most High's creation and it cannot be changed."

"I often thought that Earth had terrible problems before, but looking back, they seem so simple," Ken said. "The problems we have now are so different and from so many directions, I sometimes doubt that we shall ever solve them."

"Have you read Dr. Hardwick's latest report?"

"Yes, I have," Ken replied, "but I've been so busy with the atmosphere project that I haven't had time to give the report serious thought."

"You will find it interesting. When the computer deciphers his findings, they may prove helpful to you. I want to leave you one last thought. In the known history of human beings, the Most High directly communicated with very few. He left mankind a promise not to interfere and gave him free will.

You have been blessed in a special way during your lifetime in this dimension for you have been chosen to do certain things. Some you have already done, but there are more. You will not know when He is helping you, for it will seem to come through your own efforts. Therefore, do not be downhearted. Encouraging mankind to seek greater understanding of the Cosmos is part of His plan toward expanding man's knowledge. Your inherent knowledge and

Earth - Mars

logical reasoning are abilities that have lost ground in Earth's society. Do not lose heart. We are with you."

The Angel turned into a blinding light through which Ken could faintly see the outline of an atom. In a few seconds, it faded and Ken was alone. For a long period, he sat and stared out of the window, experiencing an exhilaration that was hard to describe.

At last, with a sigh, he picked up Dr. Hardwick's report and began to read it. He immediately dismissed the likeness of the hologram to an octopus. It looked more like a starfish found on the beaches of Earth, a major difference being the starfish had five points and the hologram had nine.

Ken summoned George and Prof. Bontor to verify that their translations of the cave markings were accurate for they were simply the numbers one through nine. "Is there more information to be found in the photographs?" he asked.

"We shall go over them again," the Professor replied, "but I'm sure we got all that there was."

"Go over them again," Ken insisted. "If there is any doubt anywhere, call me and we shall try to figure it out together."

Bontor agreed and he and George went back to the Lab. Ken contacted Dr. Hardwick and relayed the results, then asked Hardwick from his map of the caves to give him the location of Cave One and the progression through Cave Nine.

"I would suggest," Ken said, "that you start with Cave One and see what you find. Keep in mind if there are disks, or similar artifacts, that the entire silicon structure collapsed into dust when we removed them. So take infre-red photographs when you go in. There may be a beam or radiation of some sort that might be interrupted if we move anything within the area."

"Good idea," Hardwick agreed. "I'll get right to it."

As Ken signed off, Bontor and George returned from the Lab. "Look at this," Bontor said. "Look what came up when we fed the photographs in for computer enhancement." He handed Ken a sheet. "I don't know how we missed it the first time."

"I'll be blasted!" Ken exclaimed. "If this means what I think it means, Old Grouse will have a lot of work to do."

One line of the sheet read *A.D.1000*.

"The A.D. and the zeros were very faint," Prof.Bontor explained. "If you don't mind, I'd like to go to my own compartment. I must be alone awhile to figure out how another culture with an off-world language knew about Anno Domini *BEFORE THEY WENT TO EARTH!*

****

The major mining corporations of the United States and a few other countries on Earth were sending team geologists to the Moon to explore for minerals. There was an unspoken agreement that if minerals suitable were located on Earth's Moon, large mining operations would cease on Earth to give nature the opportunity to reassert itself.

The surprising result of these explorations was the large number of unnamed and new composition minerals that had been found. All Earth governments demanded one particular field test: that radioactive materials must be processed on the Moon or on Mars and should never be transported to Earth until the material was stable and controllable.

A crystalline substance was found in the Apennine Mountains and scientists could not determine its origin nor its composition. It was not of a silicon base, not did it

Earth - Mars

have origins in oil or coal under pressure.

Speculating in an idle moment, an astronomer had a thought. Why was it found only in one place? Surely, if that were the case, it had to be the result of the mountain being struck by a comet or an asteroid. But, from where?

He contacted the corporations that had rights to mine the Apennine Mountains and asked if sonic soundings had been taken to record the size and direction of the deposit. He was told that that had been done and that a copy of the soundings would be sent to him.

He was excited; aware that somehow this was most important and that the puzzle of humanity was involved. When the soundings projections arrived, he laid a clear copy of the Galaxy over the top of it. The angle of the crystalline deposit in the side of the mountain range clearly showed through the overlay.

He drew two lines, one from the top of the deposit backward into the mountain and one along the bottom of the deposit back into the mountain. He measured the distance between the two lines at the bottom of the deposit, then the distance at the top of the deposit and drew a center line extending into space right. It ran right through the center of the Scorpio Constellation.

"Well, there it is again!" he muttered. "The Antares Solar System."

He sent his findings to Moon Computer Central and signed his name. The prime directive for use of the computers anywhere in the Solar System was that all information gathered and entered in the Computer Central must be signed and the sender identified.

****

Dr. Hardwick entered the cave complex. When he

Independence

approached the two statues, he consulted the make-shift map he had drawn to locate Cave One. He passed between the statues warily but nothing happened and he entered the first cave. About four steps into it, he realized that the walls were the same crystaline substance that formed the walls of the outer cave. He broke off a little piece that was jutting out and was surprised that it did not crumble. As he proceded, the cave became a square tunnel that reflected his flood-light so brightly, he dimmed it to one-quarter of its power. The walls and ceiling sparkled, but the floor was opaque and dull.

The surfaces in this tunnel were smoother than those at the center of the the infinity symbol. He constantly took pictures as he slowly made his way to the end of the tunnel where he found a large room cut from the same crystal. In the center of the room sitting upon a large block of the same material was a neatly stacked pile of disks.

On the rear wall of the room was inscribed, in a material that looked like gold, the Antares Solar System with circles showing the orbits of its moons. At least, that is what it appeared to be to Dr. Hardwick. He snapped photographs from every angle and as he stepped fully into the room, his eye caught a movement on his right.

Humanoid figures, of all shapes and sizes in every known color, appeared in the wall in one or another state of evolution. Slowly, they formed a complete circle just below the surface of the walls. Then above that, another circle began to appear from left to right. DR. Hardwick was startled as the entire room filled with the colorful figures.

Automatically, Hardwick continued to photograph the four walls, and when he ran out of film, he silently cursed himself for not bringing more. The circles of

Earth - Mars

figures began to fade and miniature scenes of developing civilizations appeared from tribes to villages that reminded him of the early history of mankind on earth.

"There's a magnificent history lesson here," he thought as he watched the unfolding panaorama that seemed to coincide with the humanoid figures. "I had better get this to Old Grouse. He will go out of his mind with delight."

The scenes changed on the lower level, then rose to the second level and as the wall filled from floor to ceiling, the vision faded and disappeared altogether. Behind the stack of disks, just beneath the Antares symbol, a single design emerged.

Hardwick hastily copied the design on the back of his pack as everything faded from view, leaving only the Antares symbol and the stack of disks. Dr. Hardwick, a geologist and not a historian, was overwhelmed by what he had seen. He recognized the progression of events and the evolution of a species, possibly Homo Sapien. With his flood light on, he sat with his back to a wall, looking at the pile of disks.

"There are eight more tunnels," he mused. "If they all contain so much information, it will take years to sort it out. Maybe Old Grouse and the computer can do it faster. I had better write my report."

He made his way to the central hub, passed the statues, then paused, turned and gave them a salute. "Thanks, whoever you are," he said.

Back at Mars Central he contacted Moon Computer Central.

"Hello, Hardhead," Grouse greeted him. "Do you have something for me?"

"Lots of information for the computer," Hardwick told him. I'm also sending you a batch of photographs. I've

Independence

found another set of disks, but I'll have them transported by carrier instead of the usual transport system. The last batch was delivered to Space Central. Orbiting Earth."

"Yes, I remember. Where did you find these"

"It will all be in my report," Hardwick laughed. "As a Historian, I think you will be pleased. There is a lot more in the same area where I found the disks. You'll have my report in about two hours."

"Yes, hah!" Grouse replied. "I'll send you a report concerning the crystals."

"Okay! Okay! Signing off."

Hardwick went to his office to write his report and just as he sat down, there was a tremendous explosion. Even in the thin air of Mars, it was extraordinary.

His com unit began to flash and he picked it up.

"Yes?" he shouted. The call came from the select astronomers who were conducting a spectrographic color analyses of the Asteroids to determine mineral content. "One of the asteroids has exploded! We saw the flash and it disappeared! You just heard the sound wave. Alert your people to take cover immediately. There is considerable debris and in about one hour, it will be raining rocks! Tell everyone to take cover!"

"Thanks," Hardwick said and instantly called the Communications official into his office. He directed him to open all channels and to continually inform everyone of the expected danger. He finished his report and ordered it to be transported. Hardwick had planned to make a trip to Noctis Labyrinthus, but he decided to wait until the rain of rocks was over.

Everyone on Mars was accustomed to the strong, hard winds that caused enormous dust storms, but the wind that blew on that day was beyond all comprehension. It caused greater concern that the fear of the rockfall.

191

Earth - Mars

Ten minutes after the sound of the explosion, fine sand began to whip across the dry seas, striking the sides of the mountains, zooming up in a circle then swirling down with twice the force. The coarse sand struck first like needlepoints, then cut like knives.

Before long, small rocks were hurled against the domes that protected the people. The dome generators whined with the strain of maintaining the force field to keep the domes inflated. Then the larger pieces of the exploded asteroid fell like hail from a New England Nor'easter, which in turn stirred up more dust and rocks. It felt like the planet had exploded and there were few places that were firm.

When the winds ceased and the rocks stopped falling, there was a dead silence.

Dr. Hardwick had survived although the dome interior was a wreck. No solid material could penetrate the dome material, but the wind did, and everyone was flattened against a wall, held by a large invisible hand. When the wind stopped, they fell forward.

Papers and equipment were scattered; three young technicians were killed by flying debris. Hardwick was fortunate that the radio tilted and was protected by a large desk. Feeling nauseous and dizzy, he righted the desk, retrieved the radio and after checking the Voltaic Battery connections, he contacted the network. It was a disaster of major proportions.

Technicians and scientists, who were caught in the open without protection, were slashed by the driving sand and cut to pieces, scattered all over the planet. Always called the Red Planet, Mars now lived up to its name. Hardly any of the Martian surface escaped the blood bath.

The few remaining posts in operation compiled the dire statistics. Of the five hundred thousand people on

Independence

Mars, a cursory count showed that two hundred thousand were alive, many of them suffering injuries.

Hardwick was spiritually and physically sick; the depression hit him like a sledgehammer. "All those people!" he groaned, many of them professionals in their fields and friends as well. "And I thought we were getting into the homestretch."

Hardwick sat with his head in his hands, hunched over, numb.

****

The blond-haired young man stood with fifty of his associates on the highest peak of the Noctis Labyrinthus facing the northern polar cap. Before them, the dark red and purple atom whirled and the face of the ancient one peered out at them.

"Don't expect me to approve!" the gravelly voice snarled. "You have done something you are not supposed to do. You are not to do it, but to lead them into *destroying themselves!* Get back to work." He disappeared.

They looked at one another, growling and knashing their teeth, then they too disappeared.

****

At the north ice cap, James and his crew had felt a change in the atmosphere and before the first gust of wind, James had herded his crew into the dome. Flattened hard against the sides of the dome by the terrible force of the wind, they were helpless and unable to move, but they all survived.

They did not know, until the wind stopped, how disastrous it had been. They went to the drilling site on

Earth - Mars

the edge of the ice cap and were sickened. The ice, filled with sand and rocks, was blood red as if sprayed with a paint sprayer. In the thin atmosphere, the stench turned their stomachs.

They rushed back to the dome and James radioed Hardwick."What the hell has happened here? We've got blood all over the ground and the ice cap!"

Hardwick explained that some three hundred thousand people had been cut to shreds by the wind and sand, but he cut James short as there were so many contacting others from Central.

James slowly shut down the radio. "Let's go," he said to his crew, "and see if the rig is still standing."

At the edge of the ice cap, the drilling rig was pitted and pockmarked from the storm of rocks. It still worked, but it was covered with blood. They stared at it, speechless for awhile. Jim shuddered and asked,

"How will we clean it?"

Then it came to him. He sent one of the crew to Mars Central for a large dome generator, one that could cover a square mile of surface. Two hours later, on his return, they set it up so that it just covered the drilling rig, but extended into the ice cap. The rigger had also brought a Solar Furnace, broken down into parts, which they quickly put together.

Every Mars dome contained a series of mirrors that could be adjusted to direct heat to all interior areas of the dome. The crew adjusted the mirrors to reflect on the ice cap and it began to melt. In the dome, the hydrogen/oxygen turned into water and the rest which was carbon dioxide, dissipated.

James had the crew fetch the waterpump-screened intake valve, and using the earth mover, they built a circular dam to hold the water. In a short time, they sprayed the drilling rig with melted ice. It worked fine. They cleaned the rig and a small area around it. When they turned it off, James radioed Mike and Joe, figuring they would have the same problem. The crew was exhausted. After lunch, they slept for five hours, which gave them time yet to start the drill before darkness fell.

The report went to Central Computer, as did all radio transmissions, and was recorded. Hardwick got a transcript of the entire operation.

Mike and Joe wanted to discuss the operation before they attempted to duplicate it. They and their crews set out, and when they were a mile away from James' camp, they called to announce their arrival. Parking their sand sleds, they approached the dome and Jim welcomed them into the shelter.

There was a babble of voices as the crews greeted each other and discussed the terrible destructive storm. A voice said,"Gentlemen!" Standing in the dome entrance was a stranger dressed in rough clothes who looked like a laborer. "Gentlemen, may I have your attention? "

They all looked startled and James blurted,

"O boy! I hope we haven't done something wrong! We've heard about you and we know that you're an Angel."

The stranger laughed. "No," he said, "you haven't done anything wrong. And if you did, there is nothing I could do about it. Everything in this dimension is yours to do or not to do. I can only make suggestions. At this time, I want to inform you so that you will understand what has effected you."

They gathered about and quietly waited.

"That terrible wind was an unnatural occurence that came as a result of a supernatural force. It was *not* the effect of anything natural. In your recent history, after the discovery of the mathematical formula by Kenneth Rachner,

Earth - Mars

humanity cared for its neighbors and, for all intents and purposes, abolished war. The negative forces of a different dimension interfered and caused damaging catastrophes to occur. We helped as much as possible and when the negative forces found they were not successful, their master forced them into a large piece of earth that was transported into the asteroid orbit where they have remained for many years.

The shower of rocks and the fierce wind was caused by the explosion of the asteroid. The negative forces have been released. Anti-humanity beings are once again on earth where they will try to prevent you from colonizing the universe. Be prepared.

The negative forces can do nothing by themselves for they are bound to the firmament and cannot invade a different dimension. Here, they will twist, distort and destroy for they are not in accordance with the natural order. They have an abhorance of becoming visible and are dedicated to your downfall.

The thousands of people who have lost their physical bodies gives them no satisfaction for they are after your souls which belong to the Most High. Your body returns to the natural order when it ceases to function, but your soul is of priceless value. Care for it and you will defeat the negative forces.

Return to your drilling rigs remembering that not all things which appear to be disasters are truly disastrous. Good can come from all things."

The Angel vanished.

James and the crews donned space suits, approached and entered the dome erected over the drilling rig. The entire floor of the dome was covered with a green lichen-like plant. They walked gingerly to the rig and gazed, awestricken, standing before the equipment. The rusty

Independence

sand surface was gone; even the air smelled fresh and clean.

"Good Lord!" James exclaimed.He wondered if the bloody surfaces that had been sprayed with water had combined with something in the ice cap to cause a chemical reaction on the oxidized machinery. "Get busy!" he told the men, then instructed Mike to deliver samples of the ground and the ice outside of the dome along with clippings of the lichen plants to the Mars Central chemical lab. "Tell Hardwick what has happened here," he added.

The crews started their sand crawlers and returned to their rigs. James and his crew set up the drilling machines to pull core samples. Not one gave a thought to the Solar furnace that they had set in operation.

The sand dam formed to hold the water melted from the ice cap was soon covered with the lichen growth. The water spilled over the dam and ran ten feet before it froze, then the water rose, spilled over and froze again, forming its own dam as the Solar furnace melted the ice. No one noticed that the pond was enlarging for it was between them and the dam area. The water found a crevice and drained to a lower area. Unknowingly, they had found a water table.

****

Astronomers on Earth constantly observed the Solar System. With all the conflicting data being published, they held a Symposium where it was decided to organize findings and observations before publication. Each participating country was scheduled to observe a particular planet, moon or asteroid belt and to report any occuring phenomena. The information was transmitted

Earth - Mars

monthly and all had the opportunity to comment on the impact of events in relation to the space effort.

The explosion of the asteroid was duly registered and the results of the wind storm noted. The astounding fact was also added that Mars was changing its color! A full spectrographic analysis was transmitted to the computer center.

An official of the computer center was conducting a tour for a local Bishop and a bored reporter who had been given the assignment because of his lack of experience when the startling information came through.

When the analysis flashed on the large viewing screen, all activity in the center halted. There were three parts to the report. The first showed Mars as it had always appeared; the second showed Mars as it appeared after the last observation; the third was a spectrograph of blood retrieved when the computer had searched for a comparison.

"What does that mean?" asked the Bishop, pointing to the spectrograph. The official ignored the question and strode over to the operator.

"Run all the associated data, reduce the size of the spectro and put the data beneath it," he instructed the operator.

"Yes sir," the operator replied, his fingers dancing over the keys. An image of the Asteroid Belt came up with a circle around an asteroid in the process of exploding. It showed the debris flying toward Mars, glowing as it hit the thin atmosphere, then striking the surface of Mars which was obscured by large clouds of dust. Statistics followed.

Population: 500,000 prior to windstorm.

Population: 200,000 after wind storm.

Surface contours had changed; some mountains were

Independence

smaller, some canyons were filled, crevices had disappeared.

The official forgot about his visitors, who backed away from the screen and turned to the exit. The Bishop was sickened, all those people! The reporter was elated; he had a story that would make him famous.

When the official turned, they had gone. "The fat's in the fire now," he thought and reached for a telephone to call the editor of the newspaper. The editor was aghast.

"Man, I've got the story of the century and you ask me not to print it? You have to be out of your mind."

"Do you realize the panic you will cause if you print this now?"

"They are going to find out soon enough, Doc. I'm going to print. Goodbye."

"The humanitarian press," he thought as he hung up the phone. He had the computer operator split the screen showing Mars before and after the windstorm with a spectrograph beside each one, then he sat and stared at the screen.

The evening edition carried banner headlines of the Martian disaster. The president declared a day of mourning as grief swept the nation. The churches filled and the Bishop was asked over and over why the Most High would permit such a thing to happen.

A week later, when his pressing duties had slackened, the Bishop sat in his study sipping a cup of coffee. He was deep in thought considering that question. Why *did* the Most High permit this to happen? A thought crossed his mind. He reached for his New Jerusalem Bible, the only one from which he would quote scripture, and turned to the second account of creation in the first chapter of Genesis. He closed the book, thought for awhile and then made notes for his next sermon.

Earth - Mars

He called his secretary and dictated a letter to be sent to all priests in his diocese inviting them and their parisioners to the Cathedral for his Sunday homily.

"I hope they will understand," he told his secretary. "In the climate of this present society, I feel like one of the Apostles going forth to preach the Word."

During the week, he refined his notes, but they changed little. He had to tell the truth, to explain and at the same time, to console. Although the Bishop usually celebrated Mass in private, on that Sunday, he called a public Mass.

After the Gospel reading, he surveyed the grieving congregation that filled the church. They sat silently, looking to their shepherd to ease their spiritual pain.

"If you expect an explanation of the actions of the Most High," the Bishop began, "you will go away greatly disappointed. Not even St. Peter could do that. I have been asked often why the Most High would allow such a terrible thing to happen. I can assure you, the Most High neither allowed it, nor disallowed it, to happen. Read all the chapters of Genesis in the Old Testament concerning the great flood.

When the Most High created man, he did something he did not do in the five previous days of creation. The first day He created in the darkness, Light. He created a dimension with barriers and set it aside.

On the second day, He created a void between Heaven and this dimension which we call space. Then He created Earth with land and the waters He called seas.

On the third day, He created all the self-producing vegetation on the land and in the seas. All these things He created from nothing.

On the fourth day, the Most High created the galaxies and the cosmos, the sun and the moon and the stars.

Independence

These He created out of nothing.

On the fifth day, the Most High created man *from the dust of the soil!* Into his nostrils, He *breathed the breath of life!* Thus, man became a living being. So that man would not be alone, He created animals and birds and fish, all things in a multitude. But man was still alone and the Most High thought that this was not good. He caused man to fall into a deep sleep and He took from him a rib and enclosed it with flesh and fashioned it into a woman and brought her to man. And man said,

> This at last is bone from my bones,
> and flesh from my flesh!
> This is to be called woman,
> for this was taken from man.

What has the first chapter of Genesis to do with such a terrible tragedy? It is this. The essence of man is not the body. The essence of man is the breath that God breathed into man to give him life in this dimension. This never dies. Those who died on Mars did not die. Those found acceptable to Him are with the Most High, just as you will be when you make the transition.

The physical part has returned to its natural order, although on a different planet. The Greeks who named Mars perhaps foretold this for the English translation of Mars is "the other Earth." It is difficult to think of the manner in which they perished. Three hundred thousand people were scattered over Mars and have not been found. The wind caused by the enemies of mankind have been used to make man's home there permanent.

From this great sacrifice have come reports of change. Areas in the south ice cap are reverting to green growth and the atmosphere is changing. Water may be

Earth - Mars

found in the deep sea areas. Perhaps you find no comfort in this, but at least remember that the catastrophe was not a total disaster; that good can come from all things, even from the bad.

The Most High loves His children and would not subject humanity to harm. We are at war with His enemy, Satan. We must be aware that this enemy is everywhere and that he will try to stop us from going forth into the rest of the Most High's creation. We must not let him."

A misty vision of an Angel's wings appeared behind the Bishop for a fleeting moment. He closed the Mass, returned to the chancellory. The worshippers filed slowly out of the cathedral, thoughtfully considering that good might come from this catastrophe. The image of the angel's wings had removed all doubts from their minds.

****

At the one thousand foot level, the drilling rigs hit water. It had taken three months of drilling through some amazing strata in the geological structure of Mars. At Mars Central, technicians had found traces of gold, diamonds, silver and other precious metals in the core samples. Rigging crews paid scant attention to the cores as they wanted to find a water source, or even some damp ground. They found water beyond their wildest dreams when they broke into an aquifir, an underground lake.

They radioed the news to Mars Central and asked that pumps be delivered to the three sites. Before long, water was pumped toward Clavis, the dried deep-sea, through pipes covered with thick insulation, lying in troughs lined with solar reflectors. Solar furnaces were situated just above the water level of Clavis and were

Independence

moved higher as the water level rose. This kept the small sea from freezing.

Wherever water landed or splashed on the surface, lichen appeared. There were other sproutings, but only an agronomist could determine to which family of plant life they belonged. It was as if the seeds had lain dormant for thousands of years in this thirsty land. Samples of all growth were sent to Mars Central and to Computer Central on Earth's Moon and it became evident to the scientists that within a century, life would return to normal on Mars.

What had caused the total desolation of this planet? If it had, at one time, flourished to the point where its people were developing inter-solar travel, what had then triggered the destruction of all life? Scientists searched for the answer.

George and Professor Bontor at Space Coordination Central were deciphering the last disks and were filing translations directly into the Central computer.

Hardwick on Mars was collecting and tagging disks from the crystal tunnels and sending them to be deciphered. He entered the ninth tunnel and noted that the pile of disks was smaller than in the other tunnels. He carefully stowed them in his pack and as he packed up the last disk the ground began to tremble.

"Here we go again!" he thought and ran back to the entrance. The entire area began to shake and rock as the crystal disappeared from the tunnels. Hardwick fled a safe distance from the tunnel entrance and when the shaking stopped, he returned but could not find the entrance. It was as though the tunnels had never existed. He turned sadly and started for Mars Central.

Beneath his feet, a short growth of lichen had taken root, slightly wet with dew. Hardwick looked up at the sky and shook his head in wonder. "I'll be blasted," he

Earth - Mars

thought. "It's working!"

He walked around the base of the Mars Central dome. Sure enough, the ground was damp with a fresh dewy accumulation. He smiled and went inside, keyed in his reports and poured himself a cup of coffee.

"Have you noticed that we now have dew?" he asked the other scientists nearby. They all looked up and smiled simultaneously.

"Yeeaah." Their sense of accomplishment was evident.

With the addition of moisture in the atmosphere, the higher cirrus and misty clouds of the troposhere lowered and became strato-cumulus clouds. Computer Central on Mars received a message from Earth's Lab that the planet was no longer visible in detail. The spectroscopic plates showed changes in the light spectrum. All of the information was logged in the computer banks.

Summer came to the Southern Ice Cap and it began to melt. Measurements taken in the aquifir showed the water was rising very slowly, not as fast as it should be with the ice melting. Scientists were stumped. The water was disappearing, but the computer calculated that it would return. Why and how would it return in winter?

New studies began and new explorations undertaken. A black area one half mile in diameter had appeared as the ice melted and one scientist took samples from different locations at its edges. Carefully briefed, he did not touch nor step into the blackened surface, but scraped up his samples and returned to the lab at Mars Central.

Lab tests showed the samples had a high degree of toxicity. The geologist taking samples was fortunate that he had not entered the area. It was deadly.

The remainder of the sample was sent to Space Coordination Center for analysis and as complete a breakdown as possible. Everyone was told to remain clear

Independence

of the black Martian area. A satellite used for pictorial mapping was moved directly over the site and a close watch was kept. Hourly photos were transmitted to Mars Central and to Computer Central on Earth's Moon for a historical record of its development.

George and Professor Bontor ran every conceivable test on the black material from Mars. They ran through every test known in the computer and carefully stored all the details. The computer results were shocking.

This black material was the accumulation of all the waste products of a modern city with a chemical reaction on the natural mineral material inherent in the planet!

George and the Professor exclaimed at the same moment,

"*Earth!*"

"Is this the result of what we are doing on Earth right now?" George asked.

"I don't know," the Professor replied, "but it sure looks like it. We'll file this information in the master computer on the Moon, but make no guesses or judgements. File data as it comes to us. Let others draw the final conclusions. We can ask at the end of our report, *Will Earth end as Mars did?*"

"Good idea," George agreed, then they hurried to discuss their report with Kenneth Rackner. Rackner looked thoughtfully toward the crystal window.

"Gentlemen," he said, "I believe you have forgotten one important condition in reference to your final question. On Earth at this moment, we have cleared 80% of the toxic waste material from the environment. We also monitor every private and public organizations that could, in any manner, begin the deterioration process once again. I believe we should extend the monitoring process to Mars and all other planets or moons that we settle."

Earth - Mars

"Yes, I see your point," Bontor agreed. "We had better concentrate on the toxic material found."

They returned to the lab and initiated a research program to neutralize the Martian toxic material.

****

The question of whether Earth was passing through another repititious cycle of history had entered the minds of everyone connected with off-world exploration. There were niggling doubts; there were subtle and some glaring differences. Earth seemed to be following the pattern of self-destruction as it had previously in the Chronicles of the disks. It seemed that man, wherever he went, caused the destruction of his natural surroundings.

Old Grousham, director of historical and computer sciences on Earth's Moon, finally received the completed transcript of all the disks that had been found on Mars. He sent for a pot of coffee, cleared everything off his messy massive desk and locked the door after informing his secretary that under no circumstances was he to be disturbed. If she disobeyed, he told her he would tie a rocket to her and send her earthward without benefit of a space suit. She smiled, punched two buttons that sealed the room and went to lunch.

As Grousham read, he made notes. There were many comparisons to be made. It took twelve hours to read all nine depositories and for the first time in his life, Grousham was subdued.

"I must think this over carefully. This could be dynamite if not handled properly." Grousham had been surprised on occasions in his lifetime, but never as surprised as this moment. If he was right, and he had no reason to doubt that he was, then mankind had a chance

Independence

to break the cycle of history. But he needed the key; an action, an event, a progression that had to be broken or altered.

Old Grouse paced in his office, aching to get to the keyboard of his computer, but he held off, knowing that any data entered would be recorded immediately in all computers throughout the system, becoming part of the data banks. He leaned against the top of his desk and when he moved his hand, it brushed some papers flipping one to the floor. He picked it up to place it on his desk but the words caught his eye and he read on. "Chemical Analysis of Deteriorated Mass Found Near Mars South Pole."

The analysis read that composite elements found in Exhibit One indicated a complex structure of all basic elements known to man, plus 20 elements that have never been found, nor identified, on Earth. Elements known to earth science are present in almost equal quantities. Toxicity is of such a high degree as to forbid handling in any manner, even to this lab. Two Doctors of Chemistry have been lost during the above cursory analysis.

Grouse turned to his computer. "There is no time to lose," he muttered. He cleared the computer of his personal data, then began to ask questions about the specific gravity of all known basic elements taken alone, then combined with water; what the resultant mixtures would form. Would they be heavier than water? Form their own layers? Would water tables and aquifirs carry the mixtures? If so, in what direction in relation to a spinning globe with a tabulation of one pound of atmospheric pressure per cubic inch?

One question followed another, combinations of answers posed new questions. Every bit of information formed a chain reaction that changed the previous answers.

Old Grousham worked four days, pausing only to

Earth - Mars

munch a few crackers and to sip his favorite coffee. He finally reduced the chemical components to three pages of closely handwritten mathematical symbols. "This is the beginning," he mumbled. "Now comes the hard part."

Someone was banging at his door.

"Wait a minute," he yelled. "Don't bust the blasted thing down!" He punched the buttons and it swung open. One of his junior programmers was framed in the doorway.

"Are you alright, Doctor?" he asked. "We haven't heard from you, but we know you are working at the computer. Do you want it registered and made part of the record or do you want it kept for your own files?"

"You people keep out of my personal files! If some of it shows up on your screens, ignore it." Grouse was irritated at the interruption. "I'll let you know when I want it put into the record. Have my meals sent in and send in my secretary."

Grouse slammed the door. The programmer went to tell the secretary that Old Grouse wanted her and left to attend to his duties. She found Grouse arranging a conference call with Hardwick, Rackner, Bontor and Hardwick's chief engineer, James. When they had all responded and were on the screens in Grouse's office, he began his explanation.

"Gentlemen, I have spent four days reading the disk transcripts. You know I am a Historian as well as a Mathematician, so I view things from a vastly different perspective than most scientists and I have arrived at some conclusions that scare the hell out of me. I need your opinions. Please read the transcripts very carefully and send me your reports concerning a comparison to the condition of Earth at this present time.

I realize this adds to your overloaded schedules, but this work is very important."

Independence

"I will as soon as I can," Hardwick replied and Ken added,

"I will also. This had better be important as I will have to postpone some work of my own."

"Rackner," Grouse said, "Nothing could be more important. One last thing, the specimen from the South Pole proved very toxic and killed two scientists. I believe that analysis should be made, taking stringent precautions, under the same atmospheric conditions in which the black specimen was found. The results will be a key concerning the future of the human race."

All agreed and Hardwick said he would instruct the Lab staff to procede. Old Grousham thanked them and closed the circuit. He remained at the terminal and called the Lab, informing them that the scientific community wanted them to procede with the Martian analysis but to improvise safer methods. The answer was profane and irritated, but they agreed to do it, somehow. They would have to relocate their equipment to the Mars site and that was not easy to do, but the need for control of the contamination was urgent.

Grousham turned to his huge library of world history and perused many volumes. He grunted in satisfaction and returned to the first volume. Then he entered the summary chapter of each volume into the computer as a basis for a comparison with the Martian disks and the history of Earth.

Somewhere there had to be a key to changing the course of human destiny. In the process he saw the last question posed by George and the Professor at the end of their report. He smiled.

"Rackner has some intelligent men working there. I wonder if they have the answer yet."

****

Earth - Mars

In the upper right hand quadrant of the United States a small patch of sandy soil appeared. On this half acre, the grass and all living things disappeared. The local residents noted the following year that the patch had enlarged to one acre. In ten years, it had grown to one hundred acres.

The blond-haired young man wearing a blue suit smiled. "Now let's see what they do with the rest of the continent," he sneered. Then he disappeared.

****

Students in Earth schools were taught the wonders of the Solar System. They not only learned the basics of reading, writing and arithmetic, they were also taught their relationships to the planets, moons, asteroids and the system that held them in place. Advanced students were taught about the fabric of space; the dust, magnetic flux, gravitational and centrifugal forces, and the balance that was necessary to maintain its stability.

Most importantly, children were taught to ask questions. It was not enough to memorize facts and observe pretty lights in the skies. They were taught to think about the facts and to attempt to contribute to the store of knowledge. They were taught to absorb knowledge and to contribute by research through questions and answers. And if some questions had no ready answers, why didn't they?

The days of moving students up through grades automatically, with or without learning, were gone. There were no grades. There were, instead, levels of absorption and contribution. Children no longer were required to attend a given course in a particular building, for every home had a schooling room and a computer. The student

Independence

was identified by a handprint or fingerprint on the computer.

Worldwide libraries in every language were networked to the schooling computers housed in cubicles six feet by six feet equipped with a scanning module to assure that the student was studying alone. Poor families were provided with the schooling modules. Students were required to spend, according to their ages, a stated number of hours each day in learning and contributing.

The decisions of supervision in learning were placed in the hands of those responsible for the child; one or both parents or appointed guardians. No set hours were required as long as the mandatory requirement was filled every twenty four hours. More time could be utilized if the student so desired. This was the basic function of home schooling computers.

Parents could also register palm or fingerprints for access to information; thus, parents and teachers shared equally in the education of children. Many adults refreshed their memories and the degree of social and individual discipline increased by leaps and bounds. Emergencies were the one over-riding factor for all communications were put on hold until the situation was resolved, then the schooling continued.

There was no emphasis on schooling, but rather, a need to know in order to survive in a highly technical society. Curiosity was encouraged to question and to understand new worlds opening for human exploration that would bring change. The prime directive was to create change in a positive way, without harm or damage either physically or culturally to the new worlds.

****

Earth - Mars

The symbol that had appeared in the Star Cave photos taken by Dr. Hardwick was later transcibed by George to read A.D.1000. It baffled Dr. Bontor and George. How could the civilizaion of another planet in another time know the letters and of what significanse were they?

The scientists could not present any reasonable hypotheses, nor could Dr. Grousham, eminent Historian that he was, who had reviewed Earth's year 1000 at least ten times. There were no doubts about George's translation.

Kenneth Rackner, deep in thought, staring through the crystal window into space, was startled by the sudden extraordinary presence of the rough clothed man with the calloused hands and heavy work shoes.

"I wish you wouldn't do that!" he exclaimed. "Why don't you ring a bell or something so I don't almost jump out of my skin."

"I'll try to alert you," the Angel laughed. "But you have more important things on your mind."

"We are trying to solve a mystery. You know what it is. You know everything else!"

"Yes, I do and I have a message for you. Humans get hung up on solving a problem before it is in its proper place. I shall leave you with a quotation made by one of your eminent servants of the Most High, the Cardinal Newman in his *Dream of Gerontius*.

> For spirits and men by different standards mete
> The less and greater in the flow of time.
> By sun and moon, primeval ordinances -
> By stars which rise and set harmoniously -
> By the recurring seasons, and the swing,
> This way and that, of the suspended rod
> Precise and punctual, men divide the hours,
> Equal and continuous, for their common use.

Independence

> Not so with us in the immaterial world;
> But intervals in their succession
> Are measured by the living thought alone,
> and grow or wane with its intensity.
> And time is not a common property;
> But what is long is short, and swift is slow,
> And near is distant, as received and grasped
> By this mind and by that, and every one
> Is standard by his own chronology.
> And memory lacks it's natural resting-points
> Of years, and centuries, and periods.

Think on those words. The Most High created the Cosmos, He created human beings. He gave them a place to begin, but not a place to end in this dimension. Here, everything has a time and a place and man is confused and disrupted when he forgets his logical chronology of time and events." The Angel vanished.

The hum of his tape recorder disturbed Kenneth. He rewound it and played it back. The words spoken by the Angel were recorded. He played it several times. He shut it off and remained seated, confused, staring at the stars.

He thought about the disks that had started the Martian scientific community to reconsider the Tenth Century. He thought about the disks and the infinity symbol. Only one half of the infinity symbol had been investigated for they had been so excited over the discovery they had not gone into the second half. They had assumed that what they had found was all there was to find!

Kenneth hurried to the Communications Room. "Call Dr. Hardwick," he told the operator. When he was on the screen, Kenneth asked,

"Dr. Hardwick, when you were poking about Noctus

Earth - Mars

Labyrinthus did you ever investigate the second half of the infinity symbol?"

For a second, Hardwick looked puzzled, then he sheepishly said,

"I was so excited and trying to be so careful with the disks, I never gave the second half of the symbol a thought! I'll look over the area, but it's large, so it may take some time."

""Take your time. I just want to cover all bets. Tell your staff to forget about the 1000 A.D. and get them back on their regular projects. You and I and Grousham will work on it later. Agreed?"

"Yes. If I find anything, I'll send it directly to you and to Grouse without going through the computer. By the way, the green lichen is changing into a large leaf plant. One of the staff who lived in the Okefinokee Swamp in Florida said they dump waste products, even toxic ones, into the swamp and the swamp plants neutralize them. It's worth looking into. We should try it on that toxic stuff at the South Pole. Some of it is floating in Clavius Lake, which by the way, is now thirty feet deep! The oxygen, nitrogen and carbon dioxide levels just above the surface are Earth normal."

Ken smiled. The Doctor had a tendency to ramble lately. Ken found his mind wandering at times, too. Old age, he thought.

"What do you think about trying it on that South Pole toxic stuff," the Doctor repeated.

"Sure, go ahead and try it," Kenneth replied. He signed off and returned to his studies of the atmospheres of each of the planets, using Earth's envelope as a control. The computer made comparisons of composition and quantities, then displayed the statistics as numbers, then line graphs, then bar graphs. At this point, Kenneth

214

Independence

was seeking information. Solutions would come later after a series of conferences with the scientific staff.

****

Dr. Hardwick had recruited the scientist who had offered the idea of using green lichen on Lake Clavius to neutralize waste products. They had tried it on the deadly chemical deposits at the South Pole, but it had made no difference at all. The plants had died.

The scientists next experimented with a very small amount of the toxic material, mixing it with a measured amount of water. The mixture worked at one hundred parts water to one part toxic waste. Measured by human Earth standards, it would take a long time to neutralize the South Pole area, but at least it was a start. Dr. Hardwick smiled. That problem was on its way to being solved.

Mars began to resemble Earth. Human populations settled in small villages and towns. Corporate commercial operations mining the Asteroid Belt and Mars needed working crews to run the numerous robot diggers, draggers, loaders, transporters, transmission towers and platforms. These people needed support services of food, shelter, clothing and recreation. One of the large chains of grocery stores opened a multi-service unit as an experiment. It proved to be a huge success.

World residents looked outward and became restless on Earth as travel accomodations became convenient and reasonably affordable.

Old Grousham saw the years pass with a swiftness beyond comprehension. He had become the world's lone sentinel on the development of human accomplishments measured against the health and development of the environment. Old Grouse's computer, and his refusal to

215

Earth - Mars

deviate from the necessity to deter humans from repeating a disastrous circle of destruction, caused many organizations to call for his dismissal from his post, but there always was an equally vocal number who approved of his work.

He did not move around too much and sometimes he could not recall what problem he was working on. But given a moment's time, his photographic memory would come through and with a contented sigh, he would summon his new assistant. Selected for her sharpness of mind, her photographic memory and her high proficiency in advanced mathematics, Grouse could give her the problem, turn his back to his computer and doze.

Hardwick was content to wander through the maze of Noctus Labyrinthus looking for signs of undiscovered disks. In ten years, he had covered about one eigth of the area. He refused to permit anyone to accompany him for it was his project and he wished to see it through. His legs gave out often and he would sit and rest, sometimes doze, then stumble to his feet, look at his map and go on.

Mars was humming with industry. Plans were being made to send probes, then probably an expedition, to Venus, then to Jupiter. The Martian atmosphere was, at best, tenuous. It extended from the surface, at any given point, only one half mile into space. There was still a great deal to be accomplished before Mars could be totally independent of Earth.

The Earth's environmental problem, including toxic wastes, that had worried Grousham for so many years after studying the disks, had been solved. Waste was daily transformed into usable products which was a giant step forward at its initiation, but that had done nothing to rectify the damage that had already been done to the environment.

Independence

Nature had healed some of the wounds for they had not reached a point of no return. Man injected newly discovered chemicals into the worse places and that had helped toward a gradual return to normalcy. Barring any laxity, the Earth would bloom again.

Northern Maine had one small problem. An insidious desert of sand was slowly enlarging and nothing seemed able to stop it.

****

The blond haired young man worked tirelessly to undermine Old Grousham's efforts, but his every move had been thwarted. Sitting a half mile from Kenneth Rackner's Space Station, he stared moodily at it. He should have destroyed all the disks when they were found; he was considering destroying them now, and all the computer data along with them. He could create a neutron storm, divert the Asteroid Belt, something. He was in trouble and he did not wish to face the Old One without a successful attempt at stopping the humans.

The stranger in rough clothes appeared ten feet before him. The blond haired young man smiled at him but his eyes were cold.

"We cannot have a confrontation in this dimension," he reminded the Angel. "What do you want?"

"Do not do what you are thinking of doing! You have been warned twice earlier that you cannot interfere with the natural order. I have been sent to tell you not to do it again."

"I'll do as I please! This is my territory. You do not belong here." The blond young man disappeared.

The Angel raised his eyes. "I tried," he sighed and remained still, listening, then he too vanished.

Earth - Mars

The blond haired young man and his legion formed a large circle around the Space Station one mile from it. They had assumed their true atomic profiles and were red and purple. They began to whirl, faster and faster, until they seemed to be dual colored.

"NOW!" screamed the part of the circle that was the blond haired young man. From every part of the arc of the circle, bolts of alternately red and purple laser lights streaked toward the Space Station. In a fraction of a second before they struck the Space Station, concave mirrors enclosed the structure. The laser rays reflected from the mirrors and returned to their source, resulting in soundless explosions reminiscent of Earth's northern lights, but one hundred times brighter.

A bright, shimmering red and purple streak flared across space toward the Antares Solar System. Half way between Mars and the System, it burst into a bright new sun, never to change; too hot for habitation, too cold to light anything but itself. Through eternity, it was to serve as a warning.

The Space Station occupants observed nothing for the event had occured in the wink of an eye. Looking directly at the point where they appeared and disappeared, Kenneth and his staff would have seen a slight flicker.

The ancient Old One appeared off the rim of the dying red star. "Come out and face me!" he roared from the thin, cruel lips in the wrinkled face. He called his workers to come out of the mass, but with no success. A voice whispered a reply.

"Thy mischief hath run over the bounds I set for ye! Go ye to thy dwelling place and come not out therefrom, until I bid ye so!"

The ancient Old One, for the first time since he was driven from the Most High, was exiled to a place of no

Independence

dimension; the place of nothing except that which dwells within the ancient Old One. He became a twisted, raging creation, living within himself, for nothing else existed for him.

****

Old Grousham was tired. He turned off the gravity in his office and floated in null gravity, but his bones still ached as they had for a long time. He was weary of the constant battle to keep the environment and the entropy balanced. Humans didn't help. They kept forgetting the lessons of the disks and their greed overshadowed their responsibilities. Little by little, he pushed his work to his young, capable assistant.

Sitting in his office one afternoon, Mars time, he got the urge to contact Hardwick. The Com officer patched him through to Mars Central and as luck would have it, Hardwick answered.

"Hello, Grouse! How did you know I was going to call you? I think I've found the set of caves in the other half of the infinity symbol."

"Good," Grouse replied with little enthusiasm. "Be sure to record accurately where it is. I have the urge to see your face again. How about coming for a visit? I need someone I can talk to who understands my language. The youngsters here are alright, but they speak a strange language when they aren't being scientific."

"Sure," Hardwick readily responded. "I don't understand them either. It'll be good to sip a little brandy and talk. I'll be right down."

When Grouse opened the door, they stood looking at each other. It had been five years since they last met and time had made some differences.

Earth - Mars

"Dr. Grousham Havenshaker, is that you behind all those wrinkles?" Hardwick laughed, but there was a tinge of sadness.

"Come on in, Hardhead. I wouldn't talk about wrinkles. You look like a prune. I'm glad to see you."

They shook hands, almost formally, then embraced as old friends. A little embarrassed, they separated and Grouse motioned Hardwick to his favorite chair, alongside a table that held a bottle of brandy and two snifters. Hardwick settled himself and said,

"A fireplace?" They faced an electric fireplace with imitation logs.

"I had it installed when I knew you were coming. I thought you might like it; I know I do. I've been getting a little homesick lately."

"I like it," Hardwick smiled, stretching his long legs toward it, resting his space boots on the hearth. They discussed the early days when they had come into space, the good times, the bad times, and they agreed that man had made some progress. After the third brandy, their eyes began to droop and their talk became desultory, when a voice startled them.

"Gentlemen, you have done a good job; fought a good battle. You deserve a rest."

Grousham dropped his glass, spilling the brandy. Hardwick jerked his legs from the hearth almost overturning his chair. They both recognized the stranger with work-worn hands in the rough clothes. Hardwick gasped.

"I do wish you wouldn't do that. Why can't some celestial music announce you before you speak?"

You mean like this?" A celestial choir filled the room with the most beautiful singing they had ever heard. Grouse mopped at the brandy and grumbled,

Independence

"Yes, that would be more like it."

The stranger sat on the hearth between the two old men. "You believe," he said, "that once man has changed the direction of humanity through his efforts to improve, it will remain so forever or be replaced by something even better.

That is erroneous thinking. Man has free will to make choices, both good and bad. Bad choices are against the natural order established by the Most High. A single positive human being, or a group of positive human beings, cannot establish an unchangeable trend for all humanity. Each generation does that for its peers.

The overlap of generations can cause some confusion. Some will consider the fate of future generations as you have done, and others will live only for themselves in their existence. A prime example is your recycling of waste materials as opposed to piling up refuse.

Each generation is responsible for its actions and those actions must be of a positive nature. The Earth is recovering from the carelessness of past generations for nothing is destroyed. It can only be changed into something else. Mankind can repeat the cycle recorded on the disks, history does repeat itself, if man is careless and selfish.

But, gentlemen, I wish to take you on a little trip to see a place that is special to me." The stranger changed into the form of an Angel traditional to humanity.

They found themselves seated on a fence between two white clouds from which they viewed the panorama of the Solar System.

"Do not be afraid. You cannot fall. A generation ago, I sat here with a farmer. Look, with your eyes, into the past."

The vision of man's first efforts to travel into space

Earth - Mars

filled the panorama, then advanced through the years showing the successes, the failures, until it remained in the present.

"That, gentlemen, is what you helped to accomplish. Mankind is out of the cradle and is now exploring the rest of the house. I explained to that farmer a generation ago about the transition of a chrysalis to a butterfly, but he was afraid and thought there was death. What the Most High created never dies. It goes through a transition."

Hardwick and Grouse were no longer weary. They looked at each other and realized they were clothed in snow white robes and wearing wings. They spoke simultaneously,

"Butterflies!"

The Angel smiled and the three disappeared.

* * * * * * * * * * * * *

There is a distinction between the cycle of human nature and the cycle of human history. They are, in a small way, interconnected, but not so much as to forego the manipulation of the former by the latter. To a point, human beings are predictable. If they were not, we would not have successful politicians.

Unpredictability in most instances, on the global scale, is due to small conditions; the health of an individual, conditions of a living environment, and an ability to react, or to initiate action, within a range of reasonableness and logic.

Even with the elimination of hunger and the broad provision of affordable shelter, there are no guarantees that humans will react to a given set of circumstances with reason and logic. There are always mavericks and rebels. The removal of concern for the basics of human

Independence

comfort leaves mankind in a state of boredom.

In the beginning there was a sense of well-being, almost contentment, but that was replaced by unrest and boredom. It was natural that a sense of challenge would develop, which formed the basis for action. The ancient proverb, *Idle hands and idle minds are the devil's workshop*, became apparent in the actions of many, but there were those who turned their minds to consider the Solar System (looking into the future) and the study of history (looking into the past.)

Psychologists and psychiatrists recorded the trends of humanity. Special attention was paid to a comparative analysis of the reaction of humanity after the construction of domes as opposed to earlier psychological profiles. Mankind previously found basic survival a demanding effort. With the construction of domes, survival was easily accomplished, but it created a void. Into this void, stepped the Old Man and his Legions, not with thunder and lightning, but with the insidiousness of a warped genius.

Little things turned people away from logic and reason. The appeal of I, Me and Mine, that had lain dormant was suddenly redefined as the right to satisfy every whim, urge and emotion that appealed to man. In some, it was strong enough to defy love, compassion or understanding. The subjective was twisted into an unrecognizable mess of the physical and the objective. Marriage, Truth, Love, Family; all became terms of derisive humor.

The trend alarmed reasonable citizens and they tried, within existing laws, to do everything possible to halt or to change the trend. The establishment of a governed people, all being equal under the law, was the basis of humanity's existence not only within the law itself, but in

Earth - Mars

the spirit of the law, that which the law was made to serve. But, when justice was completely forgotten, man's behavior deteriorated into hypocracy.

The legion was winning. Nothing completely satisfied the people of Earth and their search for happiness and contentment through articifial means led to more and more destructive behavior. Drug and alcohol abuse led to a lack of morality that in turn led to self-destruction. From the tiniest atom to the largest sea, the creations of the Most High conformed to a pattern. Disruption of that pattern led to greater problems for humanity.

****

Kenneth Rackner was saddened by the loss of two friends, but he recalled their accomplishments and felt pride in having known them. He remembered the farmer who had initiated the program to feed the world and who had led to the elimination of the farm subsidy program. Each had contributed much in their own styles and in their own places.

"I suppose James will take Professor Hardwick's place on Mars," George remarked. "He is a good scientist."

"Yes, he is," Ken agreed, "but he must also be an able administrator to coordinate the scientific projects. This effort demands teamwork, not individuality."

"I know the young man very well," Bontor interjected. "He was one of my students at the university and I am confident he can handle the job."

"Then have him appointed," Ken said, "and let's get on with our work." He had little inclination to debate issues. His equations to increase the height of the atmosphere on Mars were not working out, and he was grumpy. He was just past ninety, but his mind was sharp

Independence

and his thoughts clear.

"And you, Professor Bontor, shall go to Earth's Moon to fill in for Grousham. I realize that computers are not your specialty, but do the best you can. Send that lady assistant to me. She's sharp in mathematics and might find a miscalculation in my equations." Rackner turned. "And you, George," he said, will run the laboratory as your permanent assignment. Set it up as you see fit, as long as the work is done. Now, both of you, get out of here and go to work."

George knew that the many tests he would make fell into three classes: liquids, gases and solids. He had often dreamed of setting up a lab with three sections designed to handle these areas and before long, he had a completely automated three-section lab that would become the envy of any earthside group.

Bontor landed on Earth's Moon and was met by Grousham's assistant, Zelda Chambers. "Welcome," she said, "to Moon Central. Would you like to go to my office or to your quarters?"

"Let's go to your office. I'd like to have a cup of coffee."

Settled in the office and with his coffee in hand, Bontor said,

"Kenneth Rackner asked me to tell you that you have been transferred to Space Coordination Center as his assistant. The old boy needs help. I believe that he won't be with us much longer and he needs someone to carry on his work. Your particular mathematical skills are needed to work out the formula for correcting the atmosphere on Mars.

I am also authorized to permit you to remain here if you wish. The choice is yours, but I must say again that he needs you. What do you say?"

"It is an honor to be asked to work with Mr.Rackner."

Earth - Mars

Zelda was delighted at the thought of working with the originator of the Dome Formula. "I feel badly about leaving Dr. Grousham's work. You know, we are inputting the total history of mankind with the idea that we can avoid future mistakes that might repeat previous cycles."

"I understand," Bontor replied. "I'll do my best to keep on the right historical track, but you are needed at Space Central more than you are needed here."

"I can leave within an hour," Zelda told him. "I have little to pack. If there is anything you can't find in the files, just call me."

George greeted her at Space Central. "Welcome," he said and smiled. "Just drop your things here. You can stow them later when you have the time. Right now, I'll take you to the Lounge."

Kenneth Rackner rose to meet her. "It's been a long time since we have had a woman here. Feel free to order anything you need from Earth Central. I must say, you have an impressive record. Maybe now I can make some headway on this problem."

Zelda caught sight of a pad with notes and computations. "I'll be all the help I can," she replied, distracted by the written figures. Kenneth smiled at George and signaled him to leave. He was pleased at Zelda's quick attraction to his notes. "There's nothing frivolous about this young lady," he thought. Zelda sat beside him and checked the types and proportions of various gases, finding only one minor mistake. She asked questions which Ken patiently answered, then she sat back and studied the list beside the crystal window of the gases that comprised Earth's atmosphere.

    Nitrogen   78.084
    Oxygen   20.946

Independence

Carbon Dioxide	0.033
Argon	0.934
Neon	0.00182
Helium	0.00052
Krypton	0.00011
Xenon	0.0000087
Hydrogen	0.00005
Methane	0.0002
Nitrous Oxide	0.00005

Water vapor a necessity.

"Mankind can only survive in an atmosphere of these gases in these proportions?" she asked.

"That's what I have been taught," Ken replied.

"Nitrogen and oxygen are 99% of the gases and carbon dioxide is the result of human breathing. People exhale carbon dioxide. Green plants absorb carbon dioxide to manufacture oxygen for growth. That's what I was taught." Zelda told Ken.

"Perhaps we should be concerned with only the first three," Ken mused. "We have on Mars small green plants, just a start, I admit. What do we have to add to create a continuous reaction?"

"We can imitate the condition on Mars on a small scale and adjust the model as conditions change. We could also introduce changes ourselves in small amounts and then study the results."

"That's a good idea! If it works then we can make models of all the planets. It might just be possible to take a gas from one planet and use it to create a change on another planet. We might even be able to interchange parts of each atmosphere." Ken's voice softened. "We must be very careful, though, to monitor results because the removal of a gas from a planet will effect a change in that

Earth - Mars

particular atmosphere.

They grinned at each other with excitement at the thought that all nine planets could become habitable. Kenneth touched the inter-com button.

"George," he commanded. "Come in here. We have to have a conference."

George was not happy at being disturbed and his face betrayed his feelings. Kenneth explained what he and Zelda had in mind and as he talked, George's attitude changed. He listened with concentrated attention, then dropped his gaze and stared at the floor. There was a dead silence until he glanced up.

"It's a good idea as far as you have taken it. We can create the physical model in the laboratory, but then, we can use the halogram equipment to project the model to the center of the room to study it on a large scale. That saves transporting it and the chemicals around the space station. It's not easy to move a vacuum and it will have to be placed in one to duplicate conditions.

George paused, then added thoughtfully, "I am a little afraid of this idea. We may start a chain reaction in any one of the planets either by removing or by adding gases. But I am willing to try it, with great care."

"Zelda will help you in the lab. When I need her I will call," Ken told him. When they left, Ken stared at space through the crystal window. "Ah! These young minds are so sharp," he thought, "they get right into the heart of things. I'm getting tired, too old maybe. If this approach solves a long standing problem, the boys on Mars will be happy."

His eyes closed and he dozed.

✷✷✷✷✷✷✷✷✷✷✷✷✷

Independence

There was a change on Earth first noticed by the off-worlders when food supplies and materials necessary to maintain the colonies were found to be poor in quality, and in some cases, defective. Off-worlders were repairing and adjusting equipment before they could use it and their complaints were ignored or shelved. They brought no results.

Corporations, whose home offices were on Earth, registered complaints that were also ignored. To make matters worse, more people were going off-world and the influx of colonists added to the problems.

On Moon Computer Central, Bontor was entering all the information he could gather. He included protest marches, new critical organizations, personal habits that became public, attitudes of those living in the United States. He included any subject imaginable from civil disobedience to senseless crimes; costs of manufactured goods and prices the consumers paid. He added a comparison of foreign prices and the prices paid by off-worlders for the Earth governments no longer subsidized off-world exploration.

Bontor found that governments had been paying for the research to support life in the planetary system, but the government scientists were selling the results of their research to the corporations who profited from the information.

The system was breaking down to where it had been before the advent of the domes and the new mathematics of Kenneth Rackner, but there was a small core of scientists and historians who would not be swayed from the goal of opening space for human habitation. It was a new frontier that challenged man to greater heights. To be what the Most High wanted them to be, Children of the Cosmos.

Off-worlders watched the change and knew that it

Earth - Mars

would be necessary to become self-sufficient and fully independent of Earth. They were saddened, but helpless to control the attitudes, nor could they initiate any action to stem the practices. Quietly, they planned for their independence.

    Kenneth, George and Zelda enclosed an extra two square miles of open space to propagate green plants and large-leafed trees for the conversion of carbon dioxide into oxygen. Voltaic batteries converted the sun's radiation into light. Dehumidifiers gathered and maintained water levels. A store of dehydrated foodstuffs was housed, enough to last for a century.

    Bontor on Earth's Moon did essentially the same thing. There was more room to expand and there were larger numbers of personnel assigned to Moon Station. The Base soon covered fifty square miles of enclosed space. They analysed the soil composition and added chemicals to make it fertile.

    During off hours, staff members spent time exploring the surface of the Moon. One scientist crossed Mare Tranquillitatis (The Sea of Tranquility) and as he approached the Apenine Mountains, he discovered a deep fissure. He descended one half mile into it and found that the walls of the fissure were moist. He returned to the surface and radioed five other scientists who joined him. The group followed the fissure to its end, and there, they found a large body of underground water.

    After testing, they conditioned the water for human consumption with the addition of chemicals. Overjoyed at the find, the scientists estimated that at the present rate of consumption, the supply would last for decades. Pumps and insulated pipes were installed leading directly to the main water storage tanks.

    Following the example set by the Space Station,

Independence

dehydrated food supplies were stored, but these did not satisfy everyone. Experiments began in setting fruit trees with grassy lanes between them. One small test area was planted with wheat and oats. The crops were not entirely successful, but they devised techniques in farming that produced smaller amounts of fruits and grains which were twice the size in bulk of any on Earth.

The scientists next imported pairs of cattle and sheep which grazed on the grassy lanes between the fruit trees. In a few years, the basic supplies of food, water and shelter made them independent in their limited environment.

A Select Committee began to consider the future development of industry which would lessen further their dependence on Earth.

Scant attention was paid to the off-worlders, as the people on Earth were concerned only with their individual well-being. Most ignored the vast banks of data available to them for general improvements, taking from the society those conveniences that suited their immediate pleasures.

Before the Dome Culture era, the census put Earth's population at three billion. Professor Bontor's statistical records logged three million people occupying Mars, the Moon and a few outposts on the moons of Jupiter and the Asteroids, but approximately only two billion people on Earth.

When the President reviewed the demographics, he was astounded.

"Where have they *gone?*" he asked Bontor, who checked all his computations and was shocked by the results. He provided a truthful report.

"Mr. President," he began, "in the past fifty years the population has been reduced by revolutions and a few local wars, but the greatest decimation has been the resurgence of the abortion syndrome.

Earth - Mars

At the time when space exploration had begun, all abortion was made illegal with an exception of a doctor's order in certain circumstances. This law still stands and technically, it is not being violated. A birth control substance has been widely distributed that successfully aborts a fetus at any time from the moment of conception to the last day of pregnancy.

Demographic statistics in the United States now report only one birth for every one hundred deaths.

Sociologists have termed this 'pleasure syndrome'a part of the American culture, pleasure in any manner under any circumstances that excludes responsibility for an indiviual action.

I have researched trends through the past fifty years and have found only one condition that pinpoints a vast popular movement. The introduction of addictive drugs led to promiscuous behavior that became publicly acceptable, and it inevitably was introduced to children.

There was some outcry at the time, but the insidious concept of the birth control as only a pill with no side effects and almost immediate healing, overrode the moral objections to drug use and promiscuous behavior.

The use of the abortion pill is decimating the population. There is also the development of a virus that is as dangerous as the Black Plague in the MIddle Ages. It's origin has not been determined and there is, as yet, no cure. Somewhere we have confounded the natural order and the results are catching up with us.

The analogy in the past fifty years would be the toxic waste disposal problem in which we almost destroyed the fragile ecological balance which would have, in turn, destroyed the human race. All but a few people lacked a sense of integrity, and those directly involved decried their responsibility, until it was shown how the Earth

Independence

would be destroyed by their actions.

Earth has been restored to a beautiful planet, but humanity is unaware of it, psychologically insane and unaware of anything but their personal pleasures. Dr. Grousham's work solved the problem by finding a break in physical history; we must find a breakthrough in human psychological behavior. For the pleasures they enjoy will become unbearable burdens.

The information from the disks, and all the work based on their discovery, is available to you. There is much work to be done."

Shaken by the report, the President sent his reply.

"Dr. Bontor, I appreciate your response and perhaps we can change the psychological profile that you have presented. I know that off-worlders have massive problems of survival and development, but if there is anything to suggest, your asistance would be appreciated.

"You on Earth," Bontor stated, "are the anchor for our efforts here. You can depend upon our cooperation."

Copies of the report and the President's remarks were sent to the Space Station, Mars, all the outposts, and the few tiny settlements on the moons of Jupiter.

Kenneth, George and Zelda shared an identical immediate response to the report. Atmospherics! What could be done to the atmosphere to make any kind of smoking uncomfortable? Marijuana, the Indian hemp plant dried and smoked, was basically a poison. Tobacco was proved to be carcinogenous.

They turned their attention to fashioning a duplicate model of Mars, which unlike Earth, was almost circular. They made a plastic ball and covered it with clay and the scaled down model, with the clay the thickness of Mars' highest peak, was carefully placed in the computer access compartment with a single pin stuck through the bottom to

Earth - Mars

hold it in place. The computer was linked to the satellite that was in orbit circling Mars.

The access compartment was designed to carve the topography as it moved slowly around the surface. The topographical mapping took forty-four hours and produced a beautiful replica.

****

James Carpenter, accepting the post after Doctor Hardwick's death, decided to continue the Doctor's quest of the meaning of the infinity symbol. He reviewed all the information translated from the disks, and following a reference to a particular program, he punched in all the numbers, letters and symbols. The computer screen showed a map of Noctus Labyrinthus with one eighth of it's area shaded in black. One red dot, outside the shaded area, appeared to be at the entrance to the valley. James then activated the printer and reproduced the map of the area.

"At least," he thought, "I have a place to start."

He stuffed the map into his space suit pocket and turned back to the computer seeking information concerning the map. To his surprise, he received the following message:

"To whomever may be my successor in the search for the disks, I believe that I have found the entrance to the other half of the infinity symbol. It is indicated on the map.

I am very tired, and after I rest a few days, I shall return to further explore the valley. There are traces of the crystalline matter lining the sides of the valley. Approach this area with extreme caution. The area is not as stable as the first circular deposit and it may collapse. Take care and good luck."

Independence

James donned his face mask which was still required for protection against the cold, as well as the lack of conclusions about micro-organisms which might be in the atmosphere. He headed toward the Noctus Labyrinthus range and was half-way to the foothills when he saw a large hump in the plain that he had not seen before.

"Strange," he thought. "I haven't heard about quakes in this area recently." He slowly approached the mound, his thumb on the button of his Instant Dome instrument. (Off-worlders found it more practical to defend themselves with impenetrable domes rather than with defense weapons.) It became apparent there was nothing to fear in the form of man or animal. The hump was a plant growth of small, tree-like plants with many trunks, small, green and very long. The leaves were similar to what James called elephant-ears, heart shaped with pointed ends.

James marked the site on his map, then radioed Mars Central. "Tell the ecologists we have something new here." He gave a brief description and the location, then continued his trek to the mountains.

"Perhaps," he thought, "this dog-gone planet will make it back to normal, whatever normal is!"

He threaded his way through the valleys, cliffs and peaks, gingerly walking under overhanging rocks that all looked like they should be falling, rather than jutting out in rust-colored ledges. He was getting tired, and he recalled with amazement the strength and perseverence of Dr. Hardwick who had trod these places throughout the years.

He stopped and consulted his map; he had about one mile to go. As he passed through the gap in the peaks, he saw a change in the rock formation. Most of the past terrain was covered with lichen and the reddish brown dust, but here, the lichen was a few inches taller and the rock formations were rounded and smooth, flowing from

Earth - Mars

one to another.

    James noted comments on his voice monitor and ran his color camera as he walked down the slope of the gap to the flat area at the bottom. There were no signs of a passage or an entrance to a cave. He spread his map open upon a smooth stone and looked at the red dot that had indicated where the opening should have been. Perhaps he was in the wrong position to see it.

    He back-tracked to the edge of the flat field and side-stepped around the circular area, taking photos all the while. Two thirds of the distance around the flat space, he saw it! The three corners to the entrance were rounded. Two were placed evenly, pointing toward the center of the flat place, and the third was set in with a tongue and groove effect. The outermost piece was off-set at the bottom and could have been easily overlooked unless one was concentrating on finding it.

    James thought once again of Hardwick, whose eyes must have been sharp as old as he was. He marveled at the ingenuity of the placement of the entrance pillars, then he realized that they were manufactured, so closely resembling the natural structures it was difficult to discern the difference. James felt a cold chill. What would he find? He was most fearful of making a mistake that would destroy the usefullness of the disks.

    He recalled the details of Hardwick's entrance into the previous cave complex. As he rounded the first pillar, the entrance was narrow. He turned, first, to his left, took three steps, turned to his right, took three steps, then to the left again.

    At the final three steps, he switched on his flood light and was almost blinded by the reflected light that flared back at him from the crystalline walls. He dimmed his beam, his eyes adjusted and he stood there in wonder.

Independence

    The walls were the most beautiful he had ever seen. In a reflex action, he started the second camera which had no film in it. Photographic experts had found that changing film and focussing, along with the lesser amounts of radiation, was too cumbersome and time-consuming when things happened quickly. These cameras tied directly into the main computer where the imaging was recorded in its banks. Practically everyone on Mars carried one and when they left the shelter domes, they automatically switched it on.
    James made a detailed inspection of the entrance, looking for any type of automatic trip beams, but he found nothing. There were twelve hours of half-dark and half-light before the sun would make its next appearance, so James sat with his back leaning against a crystalline wall, recalling the conditions that Hardwick had observed in the previous cave. James could see nothing but walls; no beam or statues, so he dozed while he waited for the sun.
    After two hours, he had a sudden thought; one of those things that occur when one is half awake and half asleep. He got to his feet, removed a small tripod from his pack and set the camera, pointing it into the cave from the entrance. He made himself comfortable and when the time had passed, he was awakened by the reflected light in the entrance that signalled the arrival of the sun.
    He glanced down into the cave, but nothing appeared to be different than before. His muscles were stiff and his back was sore, but he retrieved the camera and the floodlight, stretched and shook off the soreness, then walked slowly into the depths of the cave.
    The cavern floor sloped gently downward and he noted this fact on the voice monitor. After one hundred feet, it became level, and ahead, reflecting in the light, was a barrier of some kind made of the crystalline material.

Earth - Mars

There were crystal lines about two inches apart forming a barrier from the ceiling to the floor. Dare he break the barrier? For almost one hour, James stood ten feet from the barrier, watching for some change and trying to decide what was the best thing to do.

He approached the barrier and slowly stretched his arm toward it to feel the surface with his fingertips, to test its density, its strength. Before his fingers made contact, the barrier crumbled and disappeared from view without even a trace of litter on the cavern floor.

Startled, he stepped back, then he walked slowly forward to pass through the place where the barrier had been. The type of beam found by Hardwick was activated, but now there were ten beams, and they focussed to form a hologram of the unexplored cave ahead.

James pointed both cameras at the hologram while he recorded on the voice monitor a detailed description so that Mars Central would have all the data. Rays that streaked from the cavern walls were golden until they formed a shifting rainbow effect around the hologram, which was a deep blue color. Tunnels were shown in white and at the end of each tunnel, there was a white square. The image remained in his memory for the rest of his life and he felt he had been in the presence of something greater than the entire universe.

There was no sign of any disks, so James decided not to explore the cave at this time, but to return later with others to help. He made his way back to Mars Central.

Later, drinking coffee with Mike and Joe in the Mars Central lounge, James discussed a return trip to the cave. He believed that more disks would be found in its recesses, but Joe petulantly objected to the trek on foot.

"I don't see why we can't use a flitter craft," he

Independence

said. "I have a lot of work to do at the South Pole and this trip is going to take a lot of time."

"We can't take any chances," James explained. "The disks might have a reaction to an ion drive and I would hate to have them disappear as they did in the water."

"Yes," Mike agreed with James. "The stuff you're working on has been there thousands of years, so a few days more won't make any difference in your research. This disk exploration is really important."

"Alright," Joe grumbled. He was a small-framed man, brilliant and scholarly. "There had better be disks there or there will be hell raised and I'm the one that's going to raise it!"

The two laughed in mock fright as it was the last thing anyone would expect from Joe. They donned their helmets, and as they left the lounge, stepping into the Martian air, they checked each other's equipment. With James in the lead, they set off toward the Labyrinth mountains, carrying with their gear a special case to hold any disks that they might find.

They were expert mountain climbers, able to pace themselves and to make the trip in good time. At the cave entrance, James removed his back packs. He instructed the others.

"Mike, take off your pack and stand opposite the second pillar. The entrance is too narrow to enter wearing your packs. Joe, you hand the packs to Mike and Mike will hand them to me. I'll go on in and stack them."

Inside the cave, they retrieved their packs and waited for James.

"There are three caves, or tunnels," James explained. "Should we each take a tunnel? Or should all three of us explore one at a time?"

"In the tunnels Hardwick explored, there was a

Earth - Mars

hologram that encircled the walls and showed the history of people from age to age," Joe recalled. " I think we should all go into the same tunnel. We will be in a better position with three cameras to record anything that happens."

"For someone in a hurry, you've picked the slow way of doing this job," Mike chided Joe. "But I do agree with you. I think we should stick together and record all the information that we can."

"Agreed. We'll take the first tunnel on the right," James said and took the lead down the main tunnel to the right hand entrance, with Mike in the middle and Joe bringing up the rear.

The brightness of their three flood lights showed each detail in sharp relief, the crystalline sparkling like billions of multi-colored sequins. They slid filters on their camera lens to photograph the five hundred yards they walked into the tunnel, recording details too bright for visual examination. At the arch, marking the entrance to the square room, they crowed closely together, then the trio stepped into the room.

A glow eminated from every surface and there was no need for their flood lights. A soft sliding sound was heard from an undetermined origin, and a line appeared on the wall beginning at the entrance and running completely around the room. Opposite the entrance where they stood, the wall moved upward and then, a crystal platform arose bearing disks, similar but smaller, than those found in the other half of the infinity symbol. They were neatly stacked in rows.

The three stood silently, remaining in place with cameras working, for there was a slight movement on both sides of the platform. On the lower half of the lined walls a pictorial history was shown of a race, far superior to

Independence

the present humans on Earth.

The heighth and the facial features appeared similar to those on Earth, and the bodies neither obese or thin, were clothed in close fitting seamless silvery garments. Their hands and fingers were long and thin.

James focussed the wide-lens camera on the area of the crystalline platform. Mike focussed his camera on the area beside the platform and Joe, on the left side where the images progressed around the walls, disappearing behind the stack of disks.

The pictures expanded into the top half of the lines and the three had to widen their lenses. The colorful images not only portrayed a people, but their machinery and vehicles, none of which were recognized by the scientists. Then, the schematics and the details of their construction was shown.

The graphic exhibition ended with the sight of a beautiful city, all spires and platforms, that seemed to float above the Earth. The panorama was breath-taking. The three stood silently, in awe, without words to express what they had seen. They felt like children, unable to comprehend the sciences in which they were all experts.

James cleared his throat. "Joe," he said in hushed tones, "gather the disks from this tunnel. Mike and I shall wait for you at the entrance."

Joe walked forward and knelt by the platform. Then carefully, he picked up the disks and placed them in the spare pack. As the last disk was stowed away, the bright crystalline platform began to crumble and the walls began to crack.

"Run!" James shouted. "Run back to the main corridor!"

As they stumbled hurriedly along the corridor, the walls were cracking and crumbling behind them. When they reached the entrance, the walls of the tunnel they had

Earth - Mars

just left collapsed completely. The hole disappeared, as if it had never existed. Mike walked over and touched the facade.

"I have never seen anything like this!" he exclaimed, touching the smooth crystalline surface, devoid of cracks and perfectly smooth.

"Hardwick knew and told us the other tunnels had crumbled. Now this one. I imagine," James said," that the other two will repeat this same close-down operation. We don't have time to stand around. Let's get into the next tunnel. We'll leave the main one until last."

With the lights on flood, walking slowly, they followed the same procedure and approached the entrance arch to the room at the tunnel's end. They crowded closely together and stepped into the room. Immediately, they heard the sliding noise, the platform rose with disks upon it, and a line ran around the walls of the room.

They could not be sure, but the pictorial display seemed to take up where the other had left off. The images were foreign to them and they were unsure of what they were photographing.

Mike picked up the stack of disks when the display ended and they quickly made their way out of the room, down the tunnel to the main entrance. The second tunnel collapsed exactly as they first tunnel had collapsed.

Fatigued, the three sat in the entrance to the cave system.

"Did you notice something different about the second string of pictures?" James asked.

"Yes," MIke responded. "There were less people and something peculiar about the open areas that were shown."

"I saw it, too," Joe added. "Something was wrong with the equipment and the machinery. There weren't as many new developments as in the first show."

Independence

Well," James sighed, "Professor Bontor has the time to interpret the films. He'll get the historians together and they will tell us what we have seen. Let's get back to the main tunnel."

They all groaned as they arose. Even in the light gravity, their muscles were stiff and sore. They had travelled a long distance and the stress they had all experienced in the collapsing tunnels added to the fatigue.

They left the two packs of disks behind and made their way with lights and cameras into the main tunnel. The walls were rougher than the other tunnel walls, as if fashioned with less preciseness. They walked for an hour and entered the room whose walls were as rough as the tunnel.

They stepped, closely together, into the room and as before, the sliding sound was heard, the platform appeared and the line travelled around the walls. The three had the cameras set and started filming. They were dumbfounded at what they saw in the appearing images.

Slightly out-of-focus pictures showed a civilization on the verge of extinction! Partially erect, dull buildings were uninhabited; equipment was broken and rusted and dust was everywhere, a reddish brown dust.

Some twenty space ships landed, one after another, and the people who disembarked were of all races, yellow, black, white, and some a reddish brown, like the color of the Martian dust. The last scene depicted all of the people boarding another space ship.

The three scientists stood quietly for a few minutes as the images faded and then James approached the platform holding the disks. He paused before reaching for the stack of disks and told the others to leave.

"I don't like the looks of the walls in this room and the tunnels," he cautioned. "They may collapse faster than

Earth - Mars

the others. You both go ahead, so I can leave quickly when I pick up the disks."

Joe and Mike agreed and stepped out of the room, hurrying through the rough-walled tunnel back to the entrance. James picked up the disks, turned quickly and ran from the room. As he ran into the tunnel, the room collapsed behind him. He ran with all his strength through the tunnel, barely ahead of the collapsing walls.

Joe and Mike had already taken the packs and moved out. Halfway past the three pillars, James heard them cracking. He was flung into the flat area as the tunnel complex disappeared.

"I hope these things were worth the risk. You okay, James?" Mike asked. James shook his head. "Yes," he said.

"You know they are worth it, "Joe told Mike. "Let's get home and send the news to Kenneth Rackner."

They ate meager, dry rations, rested for a short spell, then walked to Mars Central. After a film check against what had been transmitted, they loaded the disks to be shipped. The transport contained a shielded section for items that might be damaged by the ion drive. It was there they placed the disk package and sent it to Kenneth Rackner and George at Space Coordination Center.

* * * * * * * * * * * * *

George was caught between a rock and a hard place. He wanted desperately to work on the new disks, but he had been told to work on the models of the planets. He read, several times, the report James had sent about the tunnels and the pictorial displays. James had added his personal opinion concerning the differences in the tunnels, as well as his interpretation of the events portrayed in the display. George read the report again with trepidation.

Independence

If he were to translate the disks, it was imperative that he have no preconceived notions of their meaning. In the laboratory, he placed them in the order marked by James, and carefully stored them. Then he took the report to the lounge.

Kenneth and Zelda were working on the percentage of gases necessary to sustain life, coupled with a biological study of the effect of gaseous combinations over given periods of time on human metabolism. They logged changes which they thought had a high probability of occuring in the future.

"We have received the new batch of disks from James," George announced. "Here is his report with his notes and some comments." Kenneth looked up at him. "What do you want me to do about the disks?" George continued. "I can't do both the disks and the models. They both demand concentration. I have looked at the disks with my other sight and their molecular structure is the same as the ones from the first half of the infinity symbol."

"There is no emergency as far as the models are concerned," Kenneth replied. "In fact, the disks might help us in relation to the atmospherics. Translate the disks and give us a report which we can compare with James' assessment. Zelda can take over the work on the models."

"Good," George said. "C'mon, Zel. Let's get busy."

"My name is Zelda," she snapped. "I can see this is going to be a difficult period in my life!"

"No, it isn't," George laughed. "I'm sorry. I was trying to be funny. The model project is yours. I'll be too busy with the disks to interfere, but if you need anything, just ask."

They left the lounge, snapping good-humoredly at each other, George to the computer and Zelda to the model.

Earth - Mars

They became an efficient, valuable team.

****

Mike and Joe communicated frequently with each other for James had assigned the field work to them concerning the mechanical operation of the atmospheric project and they cooperated closely. Joe took the South Pole area where the black, toxic material had been found.

Joe measured the blackened area and the ice cap. He found that the ice cap was melting more quickly than the black area was enlarging. That raised the question, "Where was the water going?" Joe recalled a trick used in the olden days called Slant Drilling. Wild Cat oil drillers would purchase land lying next to an oil discovery, then they would drill on an angle into the deposit.

Joe instructed his crew to drill at the one hundred foot level, then he raised the bit head and found that he had just touched the edge of the tar-like black field.

Joe changed the order to drill at the two hunderd foot level. Two thirds down, the drill broke through and was drilling nothing. He stopped the rig.

The last length of drill pipe was drawn out and the bit end appeared. There was a line across it; one-half was the black toxic material and the other half was dry. Was there a void under the black tar-like substance?

Joe inspected the bit head and found it dry. This was unnatural since they were using water to drill through the surface. He reached with his gloved hand and touched the bit head. His glove burst into glowing embers as there wasn't enough oxygen to flame. He flung the glove away from him.

"There must be the fires of Hell down there!" he exclaimed. "Continue to drill at half mile levels to the two hundred foot level. I'm going to report this."

Joe contacted James on the radio and told him of the happening. Then he added,

"James, can we lower a small vision camera when we drill? The crew is drilling every half mile around the perimeter of the toxic field. We might get a picture of the conditions below."

"I'll send the camera right out. Tie it into the computer so we have a permanent record in case something happens to you and the crew."

"You sure are encouraging. Thanks a lot!" Joe growled. James laughed.

"I do all I can to help," he said."

Drilling on the perimeter lasted one week and when the last hole was drilled, the camera arrived. It took an entire day to set it up and to connect it to the transmission gear and computer. It was lowered slowly and carefully into the two hundred foot hole.

The strata was photographed and the analysis was surprising. There were many layers of precious metals and other metals that scientists could not identify. As the list grew, so did excitement about the find.

The small-vision camera slid down into the last fifty feet and the heat was becoming intolerable. Joe let the camera drop the last ten feet quickly and as it passed the end of the tube, the camera exploded.

The last few pictures showed the toxic material in liquid form floating above what appeared to be the melted core of the planet. Joe radioed the results to Mike at the North Pole.

"Odd," Mike mused. "I drilled and found a giant aquifer and a water table. The core of the planet seems to have shifted from the center of the planet to the southern end. Let's talk to James before we go any further."

Earth - Mars

"Agreed," Joe replied. "I'll meet you at Mars Central. I don't like the idea that I'm sitting on something that could blow the place up or cause some inverse reaction."

Joe signed off and instructed his crew to stop drilling, but to keep taking and recording measurements of the toxic field and the polar ice cap. He stepped aboard his Sand Crawler and sped toward Mars Central.

Mike and Joe met at the Center. "Looks like you are having some excitement," Mike commented.

"Yeah," Joe smiled. "And I'm not too sure that I like it. Let's see what James has to say about it."

In his office, James was studying the last pictures transmitted by the small-vision camera. "Hi," he said. "Sit down. Looks like we might have a problem, but then, you might have inadvertently solved a problem."

"I don't see how anything could be solved," Joe said. "If that stuff explodes, there might be a chain reaction."

"That's right," Mike added. "One of the reports says that toxic stuff is highly volatile."

"Listen to this," James said. "The heat and the bottom of that toxic material must have been here for a long, long time. When it is winter on Mars, there is a balance between both materials, the toxic stuff and whatever is in the core. The heat keeps a thermal pressure on the bottom of the toxic material and the material is so dense, it's mass is so great, that the heat cannot penetrate to the surface. The ice cap is formed when the little bit of moisture left in the atmosphere condenses.

Now, summer comes to the South Pole and the balance of heat is no longer maintained. The heat from the sun is added to the heat from the core and the Ice Cap begins to melt at the edges. When the toxic material meets the normal surface material, it slowly turns to

248

Independence

liquid and as it spreads, more of the ice cap disappears to form atmospheric moisture.

This cycle is repeated season after season as long as nothing disturbs the system."

"That's where I come in," Joe interrupted. "In effect, I punctured the cycle balloon. What will happen now?"

"How many holes did you drill?" James asked.

"Twenty, all told," Joe replied.

"Go back and test the air escaping from the drill holes for toxicity. Take cameras with you, more than one, just in case. Be sure the computer link is firm and keep me informed." James sat back. "There is one thing for sure. We have either solved a problem or created a catastrophy."

Joe and Mike left James' office, collected all the necessary equipment and sped back to the Southern Ice Cap. Joe's crew was crouched over one of the drill holes, closely watching the instrument used to measure various gases in the atmosphere.

"What have you found?" Joe cried out.

One of the scientists turned to Joe and said in a puzzled tone of voice,

"We have checked every one of the drill holes. This is the last one. According to this instrument, all of the holes are emitting the purest Earth-type air imaginable. Don't ask me how or why. That Hell fire below is now converting this black toxic mass into an Earth-type atmosphere!"

Joe and Mike sighed with relief. "Get this camera down as far as we can. It's the shielded one, with a thermometer on one side and an atmosphere tester on the other."

At the one hundred foot level the temperature was nearly two thousand degrees and the atmosphere was Earth-type. At the one hundred fifty foot level, the temperature

Earth - Mars

read five thousand degrees and the thermometer exploded. They lowered the camera quickly to the bottom of the tube, then rapidly raised it.

The shielding had begun to melt and the tester was destroyed, but they did have a photographic record of the thermal gas content. The pictures showed the black mass melting and running down the sides of a cavern. As the black streams of toxic material entered the planet's core, giant clouds of gases were formed. The last notation on the atmospheric tester, before it was destroyed, showed the gas content almost exactly that of the Earth's atmosphere.

"By all that's Holy!" Joe exclaimed. "We inadvertently did the right thing! I'll notify the labs and tell them to stop trying to neutralize this mass." The word spread from Mars Central to Earth-Moon Central.

The winds of Mars and the sudden dust storms had not abated during exploration at the North and South Poles. There had been a lessening of the dust content and the growth of lichen made the winds less damaging, but they blew just as hard.

These winds caused the moisture from Sea Clavis to circulate and to mix with the Earth-like atmosphere emanating from the South. The winds picked up the heat that arose from the drill tubes surrounding the southern ice cap. The entire process added to the richness of the atmosphere, although it would take decades to stabilize, if indeed, it ever did.

The scientific community was not prepared for the accidental discovery at the South Pole. It had interjected an unpredictable variable, but they were happy with the results. Monitoring stations were set up that covered the planet like a fish net, in the lowest levels of the surface and on the highest mountains.

Independence

Mining of ores and minerals continued and there was no waste material, no slag heaps. Unused materials were converted by chemical means to an original state and were stockpiled. Fertilizers were manufactured by one small company and experiments were undertaken to increase the quality and size of the ground cover.

An agreement had been reached by the Space Consortium on Earth that there would be no attempted settlement of any other planet until all countries and people were involved on Mars. Mars was to become habitable and stable, and would serve as a platform from which further exploration could be made. There were a few outposts on the moons of Jupiter, but they were far from self-sufficient and served only as observation posts for the scientists seeking to stabilize Mars.

****

Professor Bontor was puzzled. He had taken a few hours off from his usual duties of inputting data from every scientist and colonist on Mars in proper catagories. All was recorded, even ordinary geological formations which they traversed.

He was reviewing Grausham's notes concerning the social strata of Earth which dealt mostly with trends and the development of technology. Dr. Grousham had been intensely interested in breaking the self-destructive cycles that evolved with humanity over thousands of years, but there was one fascinating file dealing with natural disasters, those not caused by human negligence or meanness. The 14th Century was listed as the worst century for those disasters until the present 24th Century.

From approximately 1330 until 1351, an estimated 88,000,000 people died from starvation and the plague.

Earth - Mars

Grousham did not totally exclude humanity from the causes, but the deaths could not be attributed to anything manufactured by this society. It might have been something they failed to do, through ignorance or greed, that planted the seeds of the catastrophy.

The next terrible period was the last twenty-five years of the Twentieth Century. The cause of the disaster was the same, and yet, not the same, for it was a virus called the Acquired Immune Deficiency Syndrome. It was dormant until the body developed an infection of any kind, then, the virus lodged in the white subcells would be activated when the white cells attacked the infection. The virus would destroy the white cell and rapidly reproduce itself, in turn destroying other white cells, until the body had no defense against infection. The virus called AIDS was active five, to perhaps twenty-five years, before the public fear and panic emphasized the need for a cure.

Newspapers interviewed doctors of renown and reported on the few institutions that had begun research. At first treated like the common cold, the virus later produced a panic when it was seen that there were no survivors. Where did this deadly thing come from? Who were common carriers?

It was traced back to Haitian people, to Central Africa and then to the monkeys who populated the area. In the contemporary society, the virus was most prevalent in homosexuals and addicted people who injected drugs with needles. The rush was on to find a cure and a chemical preventative. There were very few measures taken to teach abstinence from sexual or drug activities.

A young doctor, infected with the disease in 1990 through a blood transfusion during surgery, awoke one morning in the throes of despair. He pondered on the situation and began to think of the disease in his scientific terms. A virus is composed of protein and nucleic acid. In the beginning, it was thought the virus was highly contagious and that isolation was the only precaution to be taken. But that was disproven. Many AIDS patients had not passed on the virus by casual contact. The majority of cases involved sexual contact or needle injection into the blood stream.

He ran statistics through his office computer on AIDS patients in categories; homosexual, lesbian, bisexual, drug addicts and victims through transfusions. He also ran a profile of comparison of societal norms of five year periods through the history of the Twentieth Century.

Divorce rates, prostitution and promiscuity had increased dramatically as an abhorance grew for the words propriety, decorum and morality. Free will for the individual replaced the ties to family. The doctor could see in the printout, man defying natural law and nature striking back.

He went to a friend who worked in a laboratory and explained an experiment he wished to run. His friend laughed at him, but went along with it to please the doctor. They did not find a cure for the AIDS virus, nor did they find a preventative vaccine. They did find the origin of the virus.

The human digestive system begins in the mouth, progresses to the stomach, proceeds to the colon system and waste is expelled from the body. During the hydrolytic process that occurs in the alimentary tract, the virus can pass into the blood stream at any part of it, from the oral cavity to the anus. Abnormal sexual activity lends itself to the absorption in the blood, of an abnormal virus which is stronger than the white cells because of its excessive protein content.

The doctor died shortly after and the lab assistant was promoted.

Earth - Mars

Dr. Bontor started a new analytical program into which he added all the known facts concerning Earth from 1960 through 1970. He had lived through those years and he remembered the protests, at one point, vitually a prisoner in his parents' house.

By the end of the 20th Century, when the AIDS virus died out, it had killed sixty million people, ninety per cent of which were practicing homosexuals. When the program produced the finished data, Bontor sat back and sighed,

"Grouse, this was one thing you could do nothing about."

Kenneth Rackner's discovery of the ion drive came at a turning point of attitudes towards institutional protest. It seemed that the world's population began to consider reasonable causes, and instead of taking to the streets in marches and sit-ins, the people began to look into themselves for solutions to their problems.

Humans had confounded the natural order and nature had fought back.

Natural disasters and unheard-of diseases became fewer and fewer. In time, some like AIDS, disappeared altogether. It was during this period that the waste problem was solved chemically by converting it to a product that was useful. Man found himself helpless, shaken once again by the fact that he could not solve every problem in nature.

At the end of the 20th Century, the people had fought and won a battle in a war they didn't even know they were fighting. Within them, the little bit of the Most High that had all but been forgotten, came to the fore. Compassion, understanding, and logic prevailed. They grew mentally and physically, becoming the second man in the old saying of the philosophers:

Independence

*There were two men in jail.
The first, looked through the bars,
And saw mud.
The second looked
And saw stars.*

Humanity looked seriously at the stars, and it swept, like a tide, over every country. Before long, the exodus had to be limited. It was proposed that colonization be controlled by the birth rate and the world population approved.

"That old fox, Grousham," Bontor smiled. "He knew what that would do."

Family Planning Centers closed; Abortion Clinics closed. Those who wanted to venture off-Earth could not depopulate the world.

Dedicated to interrupting the destructive cycle of human history, Old Grouse was smart in another way. He had some of the diamonds and precious metals converted into stock in the largest computer news chain (there were few newspapers left) and an enormous advertising corporation. He made sure that Space Exploration was constantly before the public.

Now there were clusters of golden domes all over the surface of Mars and of Earth's Moon, but the population of Earth remained constant.

While Bontor relaxed in Grousham's leather easy chair, George had just completed the disk translations. The last group from the center cave had been most difficult as there was no semblance of order. It was as if they had been done in a great hurry.

Coordinating the disks with the pictures had been done through the computer. Now he sat back and stared at the wall of the laboratory. He had witnessed the fall of

Earth - Mars

an entire civilization!

Apprehensive and confused, the little he knew and understood about his own civilization looked suspiciously like that which he had just viewed. He began to punch buttons on the computer to make a transcription for Dr. Bontor, then he repeated it and produced a copy for Kenneth, who spent most of his time in the lounge trying to solve the atmospheric problems of the nine planets.

Kenneth had the model of Mars set in a plastic ball on the low work table before him when George entered with Zelda. George said,

"You might want to see this before you go any further."

"It's amazing how little things can mean so much!" Zelda added. "It's hard to describe. You will have to see for yourself."

Here was a summary of how a civilization had grown from the cradle of ignorance to a highly developed society, all that the people who had occupied the planet had been. The disks found in the Infinity Symbol had been placed there before the small group had emigrated to Earth.

The scientist who had made the first disks and laid them in the intersection of the Infinity Symbol, had carried some of the material with him to Earth. He continued to inscribe the history, not of the experience on the new planet, but only the history of the past.

The first set of disks described humans left on a planet with nothing but their bare hands to work out their survival, growing intellectually and building a new technology into a powerful force in the Solar System.

The second set of disks exhibited the perfecting of machines and the development of human attitudes and, to the close observer, the self-centered egotism that these possessions set in motion. All thought was for the "now"

Independence

and little thought was for the "future", no further than a few years from the moment.

Developing technology was not confined to a constructive vein, without forethought that it could, and probably would, be used destructively. It would have been simple to develop it in such a manner as to preclude destructiveness.

The most horrible thing was the way they suffered the distruction of their environment, doing it themselves in little stages. Not with great wars, nor the loosing of deadly bacterial strains, not with great mistakes; it was done with little mistakes in common sense and reasonableness.

A little thing, like throwing a bag of trash from a vehicle, multiplied by many and the carelessness of a people that became common, but still was not so overwhelming to the environment.

A little thing like discharging or burying oils, waxes and soaps from washing vehicles, multiplied by thousands, coupled with industrial waste materials surrepticiously dumped and buried, and the arrival of dumping grounds where a throw-away society unloaded its trash in the hopes it would disappear by deterioration.

Much of it did not deteriorate, but it mixed with other elements in the trash and became a toxic mixture which the rain washed into the ground water and the water tables.

The trash that did not deteriorate soon broke apart and with normal rains, washed into lakes and seas. Before long, waste materials were dumped directly into the waters where bacteria multiplied quickly and affected sea life forms.

Everything manufactured by man was done so with chemicals. In the normal environment, all chemical composition is balanced so delicately that nothing can

Earth - Mars

exist without this balance. Man's ignorant interference created a chemical imbalance that was dumped into the environment.

This entire scenario was displayed in retrospect as the first set of transcriptions portrayed a greatly advanced civilization, engaged in space travel, studying other planets from a distance of a mere five thousand miles.

Engrossed in the pictorial display, Kenneth, George and Zelda were startled to see ten, not nine, planets in the imaged Solar System! The tenth was not a familiar type. It was rather dark and, situated between Mars and Venus, it reflected little of the sun's radiation although in that particular position, it should have reflected an enormous amount of the sun's rays.

There were three pictures of the odd planet; one as it enntered the camera's range, one centered, and one as it left the camera's view.

"There goes another indisputable fact concerning our Solar System," Kenneth said. George looked at him and asked,

"How many more can there be?"

"We'll find out when we get there," Ken replied.

The transcriptions depicted a technological society with automated housing complexes, robots performing industrial labors, transportation based on coordinates of particular places controlled by robots to be accident-proof. It appeared to be a Utopian society with a well-balanced population.

The last disk of the first set marked the beginning of a change. George brought to their attention that less people were in the market places and the recreation areas.

The second set of disks showed even fewer people, a dynamic technology and greater use of robotics. In one Space Port, it was obvious that two long lines of parked

Independence

Space ships had not been used in a long time.

The disks told the entire story. Vast areas became slowly-increasing deserts. Waste products overcame nature's ability to heal itself. The planet was dying, and as it died, medical scientists could not cope with the strains of virus that appeared.

Governments became desperate. Space crafts were sent to the third planet where humanoid beings had developed an intelligent, although antiquated, civilization. The Martians sent four space ships of scientists to study, without making their presence known, the terrain and the environment. They reported four continents, although for their own purposes, they classified them as two.

In a desire to replace some of the population that had been destroyed by the viruses, they sought a sturdy, independent people and they found the race they needed on one continent, close to the equator, who called themselves the Maya. Examined from afar, these Mayan were free from disease, living in a relatively primitive society. The scientists found it amusing that they never counted days, weeks, months, or years. The passage of time to them was "It was, It is, It will Be."

The Space Ships landed during the annual Earth time called 1000 A.D. One entire area of Mayan residents were anesthetized, loaded into the Space Ships and delivered to Mars. No one was left within fifty miles to record the event.

There was grave consternation among the kidnapped Mayan people, but as no harm was done to them, they learned to work and they were bred with Martian women to increase the population.

But, the planet was doomed. It was shown that decades later, nothing could stop the sands and the deterioration grew rapidly. The second set of disks

Earth - Mars

transcribed the message of a lost civilization.

"The historians," George remarked, "will have a field day with this."

"I almost hate to go to the last batch," Zelda said. "Those poor Mayans! I remember studying about them in school. No one could have guessed they were kidnapped by aliens."

"They might not have been as alien as you think," Ken said thoughtfully. "I have a feeling they were our ancestors. Remember what was written in the first disks. They were about to take off for the third planet."

George put together the last reel of the transcription with a peculiar feeling there was something he had not done. Then it came to him. The very last disk was not included in this reel. He focussed the machine and asked Kenneth to excuse him as he had forgotten something.

"Does it concern the disks?" Ken asked.

"Very much so," George replied.

"Then go, and return quickly." While the display on the screen and the metallic voice of the computer tolled the death of a civilization, George retrieved the last of the disks transcribed to a small reel.

The importation of the Mayans had not been at all successful. They were more susceptible to the killer viruses than the Martians. Within a decade most had died, and the destruction of the planet continued. It had started at the Equator, progressing in both directions, toward the north and south poles.

Soil, once fertile, became a reddish-brown sand containing no organic matter. Soil is a combination of organic and mineral compounds, but these were now disappearing rapidly.

The decline in population was followed by the neglect of buildings and equipment. Great sections of the

Independence

cities needed repair, others had crumbled. The atrophying of nature caused a change in the atmosphere which in turn caused a deterioration of the cities.

The vicious cycle progressed with alarming speed. Humans died from virus infections, from earthquakes, from starvation, from the carbon dioxide in the atmosphere.

The last scene showed a small group of people boarding a space ship. The camera man walked toward the hatch of the ship and as the hatch-way was photographed, the reel went blank.

George handed Kenneth the reel he had retrieved from the laboratory.

"What's this?" Ken asked. "I thought we had just seen the last one."

"See for yourself," George said quietly. He reset the projector and turned on the switch. The image leaped at them.

It was the face of a neanderthal human, and as he moved away from the camera, it showed him, barefooted, clothed in animal skins. The metallic computer voice spoke.

"We begin again," he said, "for when we arrived here fifty years ago, our space ship crashed killing five of the women, although all the men survived. We are alien to this planet, just as we were alien when we landed on the fourth planet.

We have retrogressed. We have lost the ability to speak. I am the last to remember. The others communicate with grunts and growls. They wish only to survive.

I hope, beyond all hope, that the disks shall be found or this effort shall be a waste. The camera is set on a stump, running automatically. They don't know that I have it."

A figure appeared behind him, a bare arm raised a club over his shoulder that made a horrible thud as it

Earth - Mars

was brought down on his head. The film went blank.

Dumbfounded, Kenneth and Zelda sat rigidly in their chairs. George knew how they felt. He had the same experience when he had transcribed the last disk.

"How? How?" Kenneth and Zelda posed the same questions. "How did the film get from Earth back to Mars?"

Fifty years later, a second space ship?

****

Notification had been received by the residents of Mars and the Moon of Earth that a special program would be televised. Ken Rackner had two film experts transported to the Space Station to cut and splice the film presenting explicit messages left by the Martians. Kenneth was not sure why he had not included Earth in this first showing of the disk materials, but he had an intuitive hunch that he should, at this time, confine the showing to the off-world population.

Kenneth also excluded from the public showing, all of the technical diagrams of Martian equipment that had been in the originals. He could not justify this exclusion, only that he felt he should not show too much.

It was the first time in his lengthy career as the administrator of Space Control Central that he had withheld information from Computer Control Center on the Moon. He had instructed George to set aside the original disks which he eventually locked in his personal safe.

The film began at 2000 hours (Mars time) and ran for two hours until ten o'clock. The first call came from Professor Bontor on Earth's Moon.

"Ken," he asked apprehensively, "do you realize what you have done?"

"I certainly do," Ken replied. "I have shown all the

Independence

off-earth people what will happen once again if we don't stop Earth from following this path to self-destruction. Have you taken a good hard look at Earth lately?"

"Yes, I have. The Earth culture is proceeding exactly as Grousham predicted."

"Yes, doing exactly what the good doctor predicted, which means that if we can't change the direction, it will soon be too late. Old Grouse made those predictions to give us an opportunity to turn it around, to stop the cycle from repeating itself. Come to my office and we'll rerun the film. You'll see what I mean."

"I'll come tomorrow," Bontor promised and signed off.

Comments were arriving from all parts of Mars, even from the Asteroids. Ken instructed the Communications Officer to record them then run them off on the printer so he could review them later at leisure. Ken returned to the Lounge where George and Zelda were waiting.

"I don't see how we can change a people's culture or their way of thinking," George commented. "If they *want to do* the things they are doing, we can't force them to do otherwise."

"I agree with George," Zelda said. "I don't know of any method we can use to change their direction, unless we use guns on them."

"That is the point," Ken explained. "They cannot be forced, so that leaves out physical force. We must find a psychological answer from the best scientists on the Moon and on Mars."

He sent a memorandum from his office to all of the professional staff members asking for suggestions and methods to help solve Earth's problems. The replies were many and varied, but most said to show the film to Earth people because any other type of psy interference would not be taken kindly. Earth people were unpredictable and

Earth - Mars

it would be better to play it safe.

The best recommendations were that the film be made a part of every college and university curriculum in mandatory courses for all degrees. The film should become the center-piece of all educational efforts regardless of grades and ages and that once a year, it should be presented during prime-time television.

These recommendations were accepted by Rackner and he called the President who asked how things were going with the atmosphere project on Mars. Ken assured it was going as well as could be expected, although slowly. But then he asked,

"Have you been keeping up with the translation of the disks found on Mars? "

"No." the President said, "Things have been so busy here, I'm afraid I've let that slip. Can you fill me in?"

"I can give you a thumb-nail sketch, but I'm sending you a complete report by messenger. Please do not publicize this report until you have read it and can tell me whether or not you agree with the recommendations."

"You've raised my interest."

Ken related how the disks were found, then briefly the translations and the infinity symbolism, the discovery of two deposits of disks in each circle of the symbol, the presentation of the film and its meaning. He omitted his final decision and the details of the recommendations, noting merely that they would be included in his report.

One month later, Kenneth received a formal message from the President stating that the Secretary of Education had implemented the recommendations and that the major networks had agreed to show the film. A series was prepared to keep the facts before the public. Earth scientists had begun work on preventative programs, but they had to proceed carefully for the Constitution could

Independence

not be abrogated. In addition, an effort was raised to study the planets with a view toward colonizing Venus and Jupiter.

Kenneth sent a copy of the message to Bontor at Moon Computer Central and he, in turn, placed it in the official file then notified all interested parties.

Bontor set up a comparison chart to log the results as a matter of personal interest, as well as an official record. "At least," he thought, "the record will not depend upon someone's memory."

As interest grew, probes were sent to the Scorpio Constellation and as close to the Antares Solar System as possible. Although it would take several years for the information to return, everyone thought it was worth it.

The greatest subject of interest was Mars itself. Concentration on statistics became intense and resident scientists were deluged with suggestions on how to change it to an Earth-like planet.

They smiled and gave the suggestions the attention they deserved, ranging from good to ridiculous, but they did not stop accepting them. They held the philosophy that an active interest should not be discouraged.

****

The ice caps at both poles of Mars were shrinking and a green belt was forming, particularly in the area called Lake Clavius. The oxygen-nitrogen atmosphere now surrounded the entire planet. Some of the lichen plants were growing into something other than plain lichen, but they reached a certain point in their development and would grow no further.

The scientists knew that something was missing and most of them had reviewed the statistics of Earth's

Earth - Mars

atmosphere until they were as familiar to them as their hands, but their minds were actually on their own jobs and projects and they were only half-thinking about an outside problem.

Kenneth, at Space Computer Central, was bent over his table in the lounge when he realized the air was stuffy and the room considerably warmer. He checked the thermostat setting and found it set as usual. Alongside the thermostat, the instrument that registered various gases needed to maintain life in the Station, showed a higher carbon dioxide reading. Ken buzzed George.

"Please adjust the Carbon Dioxide level in the instrument room and see if the plant room has enough water vapor, if the plants are alright."

"Sure,"George replied, "but I'm no agronomist."

"I know. There's a chart on the wall that will tell you if everything is alright. Compare it with the instrument readings.

Ken returned to the table. "Blast it!" he shouted. "That's it! Carbon Dioxide. Venus has too much and Mars doesn't have any. I wonder..." He fumbled through the charts and calculations on his desk and finally found the atmospheric comparison chart that he wanted that showed opinions by various scientists for the balance of Earth's atmosphere.

Ken looked at Plate Tectonics and Volcanism. There is no PLate Tectonics on Mars as the crust is too thin and the planet is essentially waterless. Since there was nothing to balance the gases, CO_2 escaped into space and the planet's heat disappated.

Ken concluded that it would be necessary to rebuild the atmosphere of the planet using plant, animal and sea life. Mars would have to be seeded. His opinion was disseminated to other scientists, asking in return, for any

Independence

ideas to utilize excess gases on neighboring planets.

Ken's postscript included the current report on the atmosphere of Mars after their efforts over the years. It showed an improvement as far as the total amount of atmosphere was concerned, but that the gases they now generated were leaking off into space. A large amount of CO_2 would have to be added before Mar's could maintain a balance.

****

Bontor was uneasy. His study of the analysis of Earth's social system showed no signs of deterioration in the basic structure, but he was uneasy. He felt he was watching a two-dimensional display of human behavior bent on breaking the cycle of history, but the acting was shallow. Bontor liked to relate his studies to the theater in an allegorical manner.

The three billion people on Earth were taking action to preserve the environment, to assure peace between nations, to care for the poor , the ill and the elderly, but Bontor was uneasy because human nature does not give in so easily. Everything seemed to be following the fundamental premise of Dr. Grousham. Perhaps the disk translations made an impact, he thought, but it would not have lasted this long.

He left the tapes running. They would repeat themselves as he sat in his easy chair and watched the scenes unfold before his eyes. Finally, in disgust, he turned them off and returned to the main computer.

Information arrived from Mars in bits and pieces; geological reports, scientific observations, film of unusual topography. In the background of some photos, he saw the golden domes that signified the start of a scientific

Earth - Mars

colony. One scene flashed by as the scientists recorded mineral formations that resembled gold.

"Wait a minute," he muttered. "Let's see that segment again." He thought he had seen a tower where he had not expected to see one. He replayed the segment slowly, stopping the run when the scene of the settlement appeared. He looked closely, touched the enlargement key, printed the results. With a magnifying glass, he studied the print.

There was a tower. It was a transmission tower and platform, and resting on the platform were two racks of missiles. Using a scale, Bontor determined they were twelve feet long, and from the markings, they contained nuclear warheads.

"Oh, no," he groaned. "They wouldn't! Not here, too!" He sat back in his chair. There was a law against unauthorized transmission towers, as registry was necessary with the Central Earth government with strict penalties for illicit use after the destruction of the system by underground scientists some decades ago.

Bontor called Kenneth at Space Coordination Station orbiting Earth. Zelda came on the tele-transmission tube.

"Dr. Rackner is ill," she told him. "Can I help you?"

Bontor expressed his concern. "I didn't know he was ill. Is it serious?"

"Three doctors are attending him," Zelda said, "but they are not sure what it is."

"I need a conference, but in the light of Ken's condition, I'll gather my information and I'll come there."

"Yes, I wouldn't want to leave right now. I don't think Dr. Rackner will be able to help much. He doesn't get around as well as he did."

"I'll be in tomorrow," Bontor answered and closed the circuit. He decided to have James, Mike and Joe meet

Independence

him at Space Coordination Center as soon as possible and left a message that it was of the highest priority. Two hours later, they responded that they would join him in two days.

Bontor gathered his data, ran some computer searches and found more than enough to prove he was on the right track.

****

Every bone in Kenneth Rackner's withered body ached. He felt as if he had been beaten with a baseball bat. Flat on his back, he stared at the steel overhead, letting his mind roam to the early days of space travel, back to his adopted father's library and the books he had sneaked in to read.

Superimposed on all his memories was the sight of Mars, just far enough away to capture the full-blown beauty of the red planet. To him, it was not red; it was a multi-colored sphere whose resurrection had begun. He had often flown alone in the flitter craft close enough to appreciate its beauty.

He thought of the times he had stood before his crystal window and looked at the stars, turning out all the lounge lights behind him, while his mind flew through the fabric of space as if it were all that existed.

In his mind, he could see every star and all the planets in the universe, the colored reflections of their light on the dust and gases of space. He lay there in his old, wrinkled skin and his heart was young again and his mind as sharp as it ever was. His eyes shone with an unearthly light as his mind transported him throughout creation.

Zelda quietly came in, bringing coffee and a food

Earth - Mars

bulb, but when she saw his eyes, she retreated just as quietly so as not to disturb him.

During the night, or the dark side of the orbit around Earth, Kenneth awakened from his dream fantasy. He lay for awhile trying to recapture the sensation of travelling through the universe, but it was of no use. His muscles, cramped from lying in one position so long, and his aching bones would not let sleep return with its soft velvety forgetfulness of pain.

"It's no use," he thought. "If I could make it to the window, I would like to see the stars once again."

"Why don't you try?" a voice asked from the corner of the room. The voice had become familiar and no longer startled him. Ken smiled and said,

"I wondered when you would show up again."

"Here I am." The man wearing work clothes and work shoes, with his roughened hands, approached the bed. "I'll give you a hand if you want to see the stars." He reached out to Ken.

"I know you mean well and that you can do anything," Ken replied, "but, let me try this on my own."

"Ever the indominable spirit," the stranger smiled.

Kenneth gritted his teeth, slowly swung his feet over the bed, then sat for a minute gathering his strength. The Angel stood silently, watching him. Kenneth stood. His head was spinning and his feet didn't know what to do. The Angel gestured with his hand, a small gesture. Ken's feet carried him out the door, down the hall and into the lounge. He sat in his chair which was no longer behind his table, but placed before the large crystal window.

The lounge lights went out and the panorama of space blazed sharply into focus. The Milky Way Galaxy in all its splendor shone with added intensity and color. The stars glittered with changing hues, their gases spewing

Independence

with added efforts to make themselves more beautiful than usual.

Kenneth was awed by the sight, speechless and staring. The Angel spoke.

"Why sit and stare? Would you like to visit them?"

"You mean..?" Ken began, then stopped.

"Yes," answered the Angel. "You can go anywhere you wish."

Kenneth found himself drifting outside the Space Station with the Angel, through the Solar System, the Galaxy, then the Universe. He saw the known stars and then some unknown stars, and planets waiting to be discovered. They drifted through gases that changed into all the colors of the rainbow, plus some colors Kene could not identify.

Ken turned to the Angel and saw it had changed into its proper shape, that of an atom, the most beautiful atom Ken had ever seen. It spoke.

"I am your escort, Kenneth, to the dimension into which you are destined. Do not be afraid. Your work is finished here and the Most High has greater work for you. Close your eyes and rest. When you awake you shall be there. I must return for my work is not yet completed.

Kenneth Rackner felt at peace, rested. He closed his eyes and drifted out of time and space.

****

Professor Bontor arrived at Space Coordination Center the morning after he had called James and his aides. He arrived just after George and Zelda had found Ken sitting in his chair before the crystal window, his head resting on the back cushion, smiling. He was dead.

Zelda was shocked. She knew he was very ill and was expecting it to happen, but the fact of it was so final

Earth - Mars

it was hard to accept. She and George carried Ken to his bed and at that time, the chimes announced the arrival of Bontor. He knew by their faces that something was wrong and exclaimed with sadness when they told him,

"Oh, no! Such a good friend! I will miss him so!"

"We all will," Zelda answered, her eyes filling with tears. Later, Bontor presented a piece of paper with some numbers written on it explaining,

"This is the combination to Kenneth's personal safe. He gave it to me years ago, told me to open it and follow his instructions if something ever happened to him. Perhaps we should go to his quarters and find the safe before the others arrive. I feel we should not put this off."

Zelda and George agreed. When they found the safe, Bontor opened it and removed a large envelope. They sat around the table and Bontor removed a single sheet of paper. He read it quickly himself, then read it aloud and the three were dumbfounded. It contained his funeral preparations.

"He gave me this several years ago," Bontor stated. "How could he know?"

"He must have had an in with that Angel we all kept seeing," Zelda offered.

"That's the best answer I can come up with," George agreed. They read the note once again.

Upon my transition (death), I wish to be firmly fixed in my easy chair and launched toward the Antares Constellation. Space is now my home and I would not like to leave it.
Kenneth Rackner

In the presence of a chosen few, George rigged a rocket under each arm of the easy chair with a remote igniter. Zelda and Bontor dressed Kenneth in his space

Independence

suit without his helmet and placed him in the easy chair, using a fine nylon cord to fasten him in his seat. They all donned space suits, evacuated the air from the cargo bay and opened the doors.

"What direction is the Antares Constellation?" George asked.

"I've already entered the coordinates into the main computer so that the cargo doors face directly towards the Constellation," Zelda told him.

"Okay, then," Bontor said. "Let's push him off towards his destination."

The three gave the chair a gentle shove and when it drifted straight out 500 yards, toward Antares, George ignited the rockets. Kenneth, in his chair, became a memory.

"That was quick!" whispered George.

"I think we had some extra help," Zelda remarked quietly.

"This has been difficult." Bontor rose and spoke to them all. "Your sorrow is great, but in reality we did expect Kenneth's death. He lived almost a century and was responsible for providing solutions to many of Earth's problems. He was always available for advice to anyone in the off-world colonies and his achievements will never be forgotten. Although we will all greatly miss him, we must carry on with our tasks. It is what he would have wanted us to do.

It is what the Most High would want us to do. There are many depending upon us at these centers to keep a steady track. So, let's get to work."

The Professor turned away with tears in his eyes and he hurried to the Communications Room.

The arrival of James, Mike and Joe brought a sense of normalcy to the Space Station, although the sense of

Earth - Mars

loss to the Space Program was deeply felt. Bontor greeted them and seated them around the large table in the lounge. He assumed the role vacated by Kenneth and pushed a button on the small board located on his right, just below the top of the table.

The tabletop became transparent and a model of Mars appeared, rotating slowly, until the area under discussion centered itself. Bontor stopped the rotation and pointed to the spot that marked the site of the illegal transmission tower.

Do any of you know anything about this cluster of domes?"

"I've been by it a few times, but I never stopped to visit," James said. "Come to think of it, I've never seen anyone outside, and I can't recall any signs of activity. The area around the domes did not seem to be disturbed."

Mike and Joe had traveled past it also, but neither of them had noticed anything out of the ordinary. But now that James mentioned it, they had never seen any people about.

Zelda and George had been to Mars a few times, but not in that particular area.

"Do you want me to take a crew to the settlement?" James asked. "I can bring my equipment from the poles and make short work of that tower."

"No," Bontor said, "not yet. We must first run some tests over the area. James, you can run some radiation tests. There is a range of low hills a quarter of a mile away where I want you to take some seismic readings. Do it in a hurry and get back to me. Take pictures! Wait around and see if anyone comes out and take lots of pictures, before and after the tests."

"Sure enough. Keep the radio open in case we run into any trouble."

Independence

As they started to leave, they suddenly found themselves seated in their chairs. The room shimmered a second and the Angel in work clothes appeared. His face was impassive.

"The adversary awaits," he said flatly. "Be careful from this time on. The Hounds of Hell are snapping at your heels."

The Angel became transparent and slowly dissolved from sight.

They all sighed with release from the tension.

"I have never seen the Angel so implacable before," remarked Bontor. "Are we doing something we shouldn't be doing? Or is something going on between the Adversary and the Angels?"

"It must concern the tower," Zelda said. "He came after we spoke of the tower. and he said we should be careful."

"I think you have it," James offered. "We might be tinkering around with something that isn't human. But we must have a go at it."

George was deep in thought, but finally addressed Bontor.

"You caught the tower from data recorded from Mars. Do you remember anything else that didn't look right? Say, from the Earth? Or the Asteroids? It could be that something slipped by into the computer banks that the crew didn't pay any attention to. Could we review the past month or so? Something might turn up that doesn't fit into the normal progression."

"It is possible," Bontor replied, " although we try to keep a close check on everything. It is also possible that somehting is going on that *isn't* being fed to the main computer."

James spoke up. "I think we should proceed with our

Earth - Mars

original plan."

"Right. Go ahead with the tests while we review the past month's input."

"What about us?" George asked. "What about Zelda and me? What shall we do?"

George," Bontor ordered, "you will take charge of the laboratory. With your ability to see the structure of the material world, it would not profit the Space effort to have you any place else.. With Ken gone, you, Zelda, will take command of Space Central. Your expertise in mathematics and analysis will aid in creating a sizeable atmosphere on Mars.

Whatever we accomplish on Mars will have an enormous effect on future space exploration. Any questions?"

"Shall I continue to work on the models of the planets?" George asked.

"You can both work on every aspect of planetary atmosphere, globes or anything else. Work together. You are a team." Bontor rose from his chair. "I'm heading back to Moon Central. If you have a need for help, call the best person in that discipline to answer your questions. I am not your boss.

The President of the United States Assembly is, so, when in doubt, ask him."

Bontor laughed and went to his flitter craft.

George was not pleased that Zelda was in charge of Space Central as he had hoped to be chosen. Zelda's appointment was confirmed by the Assembly of Nations, which also appointed George as the Director of all Space Laboratories.

This pleased George as he now was provided with unlimited funds for research. He could now acquire new equipment and move forward his plans for greater efficiency in all the labs.

Independence

His memos went to all field laboratories informing them of a new administrative structure. He issued as well an order that all unknown or unidentifiable physical material, organic or mineral, was to be delivered directly to his lab. The primary function of the field labs, in these cases, was to insure safe packaging and transport of the materials. Labs were required to make pictorial recordings and to provide written physical descriptions which were copies and sent to the Computer Central on Moon Central.

Zelda had crated and transported all of Kenneth Rackner's personal possessions to a large warehouse maintained by Space Command on Earth for storage while off-Earth people worked or settled off-world. She moved into Ken's quarters and gave them the woman's touch.

In the lounge, she arranged her set of official files. On calling the Communications Room, she was told there had been no reply from James and his crew to the queries sent by the Communications Officer and that they were a little worried about this.

Zelda reminded them that it was probably too soon for any productive tests to have been made, or that James might not want to risk communication at this point. They all waited.

At the testing place on the tower site, James turned down the receiver system on his radio so that they could not be heard any further than ten feet away. Mars atmosphere was very thin, but it did carry sound and he didn't want to take any chances on being overheard. James, as well as Mike and Joe, were nervous as they approached the dome cluster.

Mike put together a small series of charges for geological soundings while Joe removed the geiger counters from the packs and adjusted them to offset the local

277

Earth - Mars

radiation. James connected the powerful binoculars to the camera which hung about an inch and a half below and as the binoculars were focussed, the camera was automatically in focus.

James crawled up the small hill top to a point where he could just see the domes and the tower. He focussed the glasses on the top of the tower and slowly lowered them as the camera whirred taking pictures. He then began at the base of the tower and platform, working left around the cluster of domes.

When he had finished, he set the camera at a wider setting and repeated the procedure using, this time, the domes themselves as a guide to the right. Thus, he got shots of the surrounding terrain.

James shut down the camera and continued to view the dome village through the glasses. There was no human activity between the domes and he could not see inside the domes. The longer he looked, the more uneasy he felt.

There were no footprints around the domes; there were no tracks leading to or from the tower or the transmission platform. It looked like a ghost town. He watched for half an hour and there was no movement of any kind.

Joe crawled up beside James and, relieving him for half an hour, then Mike crawled up and relieved Joe. For nine hours, they relieved each other at half hour intervals.

Mike and James felt a handful of sand strike them. They scrambled up to Joe who motioned for silence. They didn't need glasses to see that several large boxes were on the platform. They waited to see who would come for them.

The three were taken completely by surprise when the center of the platform was lowered and the cargo disappeared underground. The square space remained open

278

Independence

for about two minutes, then the rising platform filled the space, fitting perfectly, leaving them unable to discern the edges.

"They are underground," Mike said. "I know the domes are real, but are they used?"

"Let's go down and see," Joe said eagerly. "I bet they are for appearances only."

"No, wait," James told them. "Let's think this thing through. They may be using one of them for a watch tower. Look at the one in the center. It has a small object rotating on the top."

They took turns looking through binoculars and agreed that the center dome was some sort of observation structure. James told Mike,

"Get your charges placed. Form a straight line to cover the dome area and a quarter of a mile to either side. Joe and I will have the flitters ready for an immediate take-off after we set the oscilliscope and the computer to record the readings. Don't trigger the charges until you get back to the flitters. As soon as we are ready, I'll contact Mars Central to contunue recording the readings and we'll get out of here as fast as we can. When we take off, follow me. Leave the equipment where we put it. Got it?"

They set about their tasks. When Mike was ready to activate the charges, he returned to James and Joe at the flitters. He climbed aboard.

"Let her go," James ordered as they took off, and he watched the oscilliscope screen. There was a muffled roar. A perfect profile of the area's terrain appeared on the oscilliscope, including that part lying under the domes.

They saw a flash of a structure, but it was enough to show its considerable size, then it was gone. But it had been registered on the main computer at Mars Central.

Earth - Mars

The two flitters rode low behind the hills as they sped toward the Center. James first spotted a low-flying small space ship as it came around the end of a low cliff. He signalled the craft behind him and the two flitters separated, weaving back and forth, like broken field runners.

With disbelief at what they were seeing, blue streaks from the space ship's laser fired at them and missed, striking the ground, raising puffs of dust and the acrid smell of burnt sand.

"Play dead!" James whispered into the intercom. A blue flash barely missed his flitter. He dropped his low-flying flitter and flipped it over. Minutes later, Joe and Mike did the same. James hung in his seat, hunched over with a small laser gripped in his right hand.

The space ship circled deliberately for nearly thirty minutes, then slowed descended and landed about fifty yards from James' craft. A side hatch opened and a space-suited figure emerged. James calculated from the size of the pilot, that only one person could fit in the small space ship. With his eyes closed to mere slits, he watched the approach and when the figure was three feet away from the flitter, James flung out his arm and opened fire. The laser blast caught the faceplate and passed through the back of the helmet. The figure crumpled slowly and dropped onto the rust-colored Martian sand.

James was raging with anger at the unexpected violence. There was no need to attempt to kill them, but he had been thrust into a defensive situation where violence had been forced upon him! Mike and Joe slid out of their flitter and met James as he snatched a laser pistol from the hand of the dead pilot.

Mike reached down removed the helmet cautiously and they stared in amazement. James had destroyed, not a human, but a robot!

"Check out the ship," James told Mike. "Look for recording equipment or transmitters. Joe, help me with this thing."

They stripped the space suit from the robot, exposing its shining metallic exterior. Joe commented,

"That is one sophisticated piece of equipment!"

"I've never seen anything like it. It has got to belong to those people in the underground building." James looked at Mike, who returned and was staring at the robot. "What did you find in the space ship?"

"Nothing. Absolutely nothing. The ship is a completely stripped down model. Doesn't even have a radio in it; only the drive mechanism and the laser equipment."

They loaded the broken robot into the flitter with James, then both flitters sped back to the Center where James contacted Zelda and George.

"Wait 'til you see what I have for you!" he teased. "I'm sending it on the next shuttle with a full report. We've got something here that may be beyond our own micro-technological development. Also, get a full report from Main Central Computer on the Moon. They have a full photographic record of the underground structure. I caught a brief impression when the blast went off and I think it is a large one."

"Get your men together and we'll meet here as early as possible tomorrow," Zelda told James.

"I'm going down to meet the shuttle," George told Zelda. She laughed and signed off.

James, as head of Mars Central, believed that time was a grave factor in the consideration when he arranged the conference. He notified other scientists and then proceeded to Space Coordination Center alone.

281

Earth - Mars

Zelda, who had replaced Rackner as head of Space Coordination Center (in orbit around Earth), Bontor, who had succeeded Grousham at Moon Central, and James met in the lounge after the full conference of engineers and space scientists had agreed that James should make the decision concerning the disposal of the illegal Tower Village.

But the discussion focussed, not on that issue, but on a puzzling force that was affecting their computers systems. It was first noticed and reported when the main computer on Moon Central ran through all the data in its banks and would not accept new data until it emptied itself completely of the stored information. Then, suddenly, the data flowed back into the system leaving it as it had been before the run-out. Exactly the same thing happened at Mars Central and the Space Coordination Center.

"What has occurred since?" Bontor asked.

"Nothing that I can discover," Zelda replied.

"One small thing," James interjected. "I have noticed a slight drop in power in the Solar batteries that we use on Mars. The graph showed a distinctive drop when the run-out occurred, and now it has returned, but is slightly below normal."

"I never thought to check that," Zelda and Bontor said simultaneously. They laughed and the Professor said, "Let's check it now."

Zelda asked George via the intercom to bring the Solar Battery output graph for the past month. Bontor, in the Com Room contacted Moon Central and them to transmit the same information. Within ten minutes, the printer delivered the figures.

"Well, what do you know," Bontor said aloud and returned to the lounge. George had brought the Center's graphs. Both graphs showed identical drops in output.

Independence

Bontor suggested he take the graphs to his office so he could run a computer search for related information. They could do nothing more at that moment, so they all agreed.

James voiced the same opinion about the disposal of the tower. He needed time for careful consideration and a study of the possibilities before he could recommend a course of action. With that, talk turned to the robot.

Zelda was concerned, but she believed that George was capable of analyzing and reporting fully to them about its mechanism. After the conference, she went to his laboratory and gasped when she entered.

"You've got the thing standing! Are you sure it's safe?" she asked. "Remember, this machine tried to kill three people while it was piloting a space craft!"

"Don't worry, Zel," George replied confidently. "I've disconnected the brain from the motor-driven parts." He had removed the back plate from the robot's head and was photographing the internal works. He would do the same with its arms, legs, hands and feet. "I'll tell you one thing, Zel. We've got to bring in an electronics expert. I can remember reading a long time ago about psionic brains, and I think this robot has one."

"I'll notify the Commission and get the best," she told him. Leaving the Com Room, she thought, "I hope that nut doesn't get it working. He knows ions and molecular structures, but he doesn't know a thing about robotics and psionic brains." She stood before the crystal window and a thought came to her suddenly. Zelda ran back to the Com Room and called James.

"Can you come back here with Mike and Joe?" she asked with tense excitement. "I've had a brainstorm and I think we can solve the atmpsheric problem if we work it right!"

Earth - Mars

"Okay! Okay! Don't get excited," James told her. "I'll round up the guys and we'll come as soon as we can. Just stay calm or you'll bust something."

"Alright," she laughed. "I'll take a deep breath and look into a couple of things until you get here. If I don't have the answers, I will at least have some more deep questions." She signed off and walked slowly back to the lab.

"George," she asked, "have you ever heard of dome structures being used for anything but houses, storage rooms or greenhouses? And is it true that that air inside them cannot escape, but that gases can enter from the outside?"

"You're talking about the old ones," George told her. "The new domes can be adjusted either way; to let air and gases escape and enter, or not to let anything through at all." He was busy adjusting lights and focussing the camera lens, so his reply was a bit peremptory.

"This is important, George," she said impatiently. "Stop that and listen to me."

"Alright! Alright! What can I help you with?"

"Tell me," she said seriously, "what is the largest dome you have ever seen? How large can they be made?"

George stared at the floor, scratched his ears, then he said,

"The largest dome I have ever seen covered a football stadium and that made a lot of people mad."

"Why would they get angry?" she asked in a puzzled voice.

"The domes were round and the stadium was oval, so the dome covered some houses near the stadium. People that were in, couldn't get out; people that were out, couldn't get in. There was a big fuss."

"Has a dome ever been formed in the air?

Independence

Completely round and enclosed?"

George scratched his other ear. "Can't say that I ever did. Why do you ask?" He looked sharply at Zelda. "Oh! You're thinking about the Mars atmosphere! Say! That's an idea, if it can be done."

"James and his crew are coming in to talk about it. Would you join us? We need all the brains we can get."

George looked pensively at the camera equipment and the robot, but agreed to come as soon as he could. They all met in the lounge.

"I don't know much about the domes that were a result of Mr. Rackner's mathematics," Zelda began, "so my proposal might sound far-fetched. As I see it, it's the only answer as we have tried everything else.

We must attempt to construct domes formed in a completely round structure, like a huge ball. If we can do that successfully, we will have a vehicle to fill with gaseous combinations.

The size is the problem. Could one be constructed that would encircle Mars? If we can do that, then we can establish a controlled atmosphere."

There was a long silence as the idea was absorbed and pondered. George spoke.

"Mr. Rackner spent most of his life trying to solve the atmospheric problem on Mars and here she comes up with a possible solution based on his very own work!" He shook his head and looked at Zelda with admiration.

"This problem won't be solved until we try it," James commented. "Remember, the Solar batteries and the projector are *inside* the dome structure. Someone will have to activate it and when they do, if it forms an enclosing circle, how will they get out? How do we get the gas in? How do we transport it to Mars?"

"Wait a minute," Mike interrupted. "I still want to

Earth - Mars

know if the dome strcuture can be made like a balloon. That is the first hurdle. Can't we make a very small structure, install a timer switch to turn it on, and place it about a mile in orbit from this station? If it works, then we can pursue Zelda's idea further."

"Sure," Zelda answered. "George can help you with anything you may need from the laboratory."

Converting the half dome to a full dome was not difficult mathematically in the main computer, while George and James rigged a timing device. When the parts had been assembled, George and James donned space suits, picked up a small dome activator, then loaded all the equipment into a flitter craft. Just opposite the crystal window, approximately one mile off the surface, James activated the timing device, attached it to the dome switch and returned to the station.

They entered the lounge when the timer switched on the activator. A round orange ball came into view and hovered where before, there had been nothing at all. Zelda glanced at the clock to establish the time in case the dome could not sustain itself. It floated, one mile off-station.

"At least we know it can be done," Joe said as they all smiled with satisfaction. At that moment, a bell sounded and they all jumped. "What the heck is that?"

Laughter released their tension as Zelda explained,

"We've got company. I think it's the elctronic engineer I requested to help us with work on the robot."

She left the lounge and went to greet the newcomer at the inner door of the entrance lock. Glancing through the window, she saw no one. The inner door activated and in stepped the shortest man she had ever seen. He was four feet tall with bowed legs, and a head with bushy hair sticking out of his jump suit.

Independence

"You must be Zelda," he said. "I am Manfred Ballinski, electronics engineer. Here are my credentials."

Zelda started to smile, but the look in his eyes was challenging, so she extended her hand and seriously greeted him.

"Welcome aboard," she said gravely. "We are in great need of your expertise. Follow me to the lounge and I shall introduce you to our team."

Zelda graciously towered over him as she introduced him. "And this is George," she said, "with whom you shall be working."

George shook hands. "I'll have to get some taller work stools," he remarked and anger flooded Manfred's face. But he looked at George and said easily,

"You take care of the high stuff and I'll handle the short."

Laughter released the moment and Zelda related Manfred's inpressive credentials. His thesis was *The interaction of forces that control molecular structures and their impact on electronic currents*. They all clapped and made mock bows. The little man snorted,

"That is all gobble-de-gook. Where is the laboratory and when can I get started ... what in blue blazes is that thing outside your window?"

Zelda briefly described the placement and purpose of the orange ball floating off-station. Manfred rubbed his chin.

"Sounds interesting," he said, "but right now you want me to work on a robot. Is that right?"

"Those two are our most pressing problems," Zelda said diplomatically, "although you may work on whatever you wish."

Schedules were set, programs rearranged, then goodbyes were said as James, Mike and Joe prepared to

Earth - Mars

return to Mars Central.

Manfred's mouth dropped open when he first saw the robot. "I didn't realize that we had developed technology to this high state," he gasped.

"We haven't," George told him grimly, then explained how it had been acquired and the urgency with which they were working. "There may be more of these robots," he concluded, " and that Tower Village might constitute a threat to everyone."

Manfred examined the robot thoughtfully. "The first thing we should do is to remove the head. The rest is merely mechanical. We must discover how the psionic brain functions."

"Agreed!" George replied.

They began to dismantle the robot.

****

James was worried. Since the crew's violent experience with the robot, James did not have sufficient time to consider a neutralizing action against the transmission tower and what they thought to be nuclear missiles below ground. Bontor had not turned up anything remotely connected to the domes, tower or platform. James finally decided to call the President and ask for advice.

"I must take this," the President told him, "before the General Commission. Do nothing to antagonize the situation, but maintain a vigilant observation of the site."

"Thank you, sir. I shall wait to hear from you."

Mike and Joe set up photographic observation posts discreetly that were manned around the clock. Within twenty-four hours he had a reply from the President and instructions.

"Until you hear from me again," the President told

288

Independence

James, "do not permit anyone within ten miles of the Tower Village. We shall take care of the problem from here. Is there anything within the area besides the tower, platform and domes?"

"Nothing, sir. The area is clear."

"Good. Keep it that way until further notice."

The President maintained a select, well-trained, non-military force of battalion size. These citizens served their country when needed, meeting twice monthly for instruction in a specialty. They held positions in industry, but performed services as criminologists, investigators, some adept in military arts, not in formal, but in unorthodox techniques. The spectrum of modern arts and sciences was represented, although few were aware of their existence.

Jim had an inkling that something was happening when he looked at the computer monitor and did not see the tower standing in its usual place. It was lying horizontally across the top of the small mound behind the domes. He called Mike and Joe and they watched the monitor together.

A brilliant light appeared along the length of the fallen tower. It glowed brighter than the sun and as quickly disappeared. Joe said,

"That was a powerful laser."

"Look," said James, "look at the size of that ship!"

A huge space ship landed beside the group of domes. A continuous line of men and women streamed from the dome entrances and entered a hatch that had opened on the space ship. When the last person entered, the hatch closed, the ship rose above the domes, then streaked out of sight.

Thirty seconds later, the ground rumbled and the entire dome village sank about twenty feet. There was

Earth - Mars

little dust and no disturbance to the surrounding area. The radio call bell sounded and James answered it.

"James, this is the President. As far as we are concerned, the Tower Village never existed. The people who occupied that area are now in quarters on Phobos, their new home. Thank you for your cooperation."

"Thank *you*, Mr. President. Now we can get on with our work." James signed off.

****

James, as head of Mars Central, made occasional trips to Noctis Labyrinthus, but he also visited the Space Central Station. Zelda, Manfred and he worked to enlarge the dome system to cover Mars. Manfred suggested that they construct a large one to set on Olympus Mons, the tallest mountain on Mars.

"I don't think size will have much to do with it," James commented. "We know we have to make one larger than the largest one now being manufactured. I think we should concentrate on how to increase the power."

"I don't see how we can do that," Zelda said. "But wait a minute. I recall reading about some fellow in a science quarterly who had invented a motor that multiplied the input of a motor generator thirty-five times. If one volt of electriciry was needed to run the motor, the generator output was thirty five volts. I think it was in some of the stuff we stored when Mr. Rackner died."

"Your the only one who would know where to look for it, Zelda. Can you try to find it?"

"Thanks, James," Zelda laughed. "I should have kept my big mouth shut. I'll change and take a flitter right away. By the way," she turned to George. "If anything

Independence

happens to me, you are next in line."

"Hurry back," George told her.

Zelda had a strange feeling when she approached the Storage Shed, then spoke to the clerk at the entrance who demanded to see her identification explaining that access to storage from space was restricted. Zelda was passed through and led to a black-marked bin.

"All who died in space have their belongings marked in black," the clerk said. Zelda made no comment, but went through looking for the magazine she wanted. She reported to the clerk that she wished to take it back with her, but the answer was negative.

"I cannot let you do that, Miss," the clerk said. "Those bins are legally sealed. You can take it to the copy office and ask them to help you."

The entire article was copied for Zelda and the clerk returned the magazine to the bin. Zelda paused a moment, looking at the bin that contained the physical posessions of Kenneth Rackner and the strange feeling flooded her. Very softly, she said,

"Thank you, Ken." Zelda returned to her flitter, blinking back tears.

During Zelda's absence, Manfred began work composing a mathematical formula to neutralize a section of a large dome that would permit access and egress from the interior. James measured the size of the orange orbiting dome and the output of a generator. He reported to Manfred,

"In their present condition, the voltage level drops slightly when the dome is turned on and the generator labors a little, but the voltaic batteries soon catch up with the demand."

"I thought that would be so," Manfred said, "but I hope we can make a new generator with voltage control

Earth - Mars

that will provide more than enough power."

When Zelda gave Manfred the magazine article, he exhaled explosively.

"I know this man!" he exclaimed. "I talked with him and I was one of those who didn't believe in his theory! I must go to Earth to find him. He might have the answer we need."

Manfred abruptly turned on his heel and left them.

"Well!" James laughed. "You set him off. That is the fastest I have seen him move since he came here."

"I guess the article touched a nerve," Zelda replied. "There isn't much we can do until he returns. Do you think we could help with the robot?"

"Not really," George told them. "We have the brains of this thing scattered all over the bench and only Manfred knows what goes where. The rest of the robot is easy to figure out. We could make as many as you like. It's the brain that has us stopped."

"It looks like Dr. Manfred Ballinski is becoming the center of this operation," Zelda laughed. "As small as he is, he has the right intelligence at the right time."

"That is no small man," James said. "Right now, he is Atlas holding up the world. If he finds a solution, do you realize what it will mean in the long run? Mars will be economically independent of Earth. We can set our own prices on some things like the new minerals and the new methods for producing industrial goods in one third gravity.

Scientists have been talking about Mars as an independent world and if they get a taste of prosperity, they won't want to give it up. Once an atmosphere is established, nothing will stem the tide."

Five days later, Manfred returned to the Space Station and burst into the lounge waving a handful of papers.

Independence

"I've got it!" he shouted. "I've got the formula and some plans. We can build a generator and make it a part of the dome activator and projector. I have designed a gadget that will allow a space craft to pass through the dome with an immediate closing and very little leakage of atmosphere." He called George. "Get the engineers together. We must get these things operational."

James set Mike and Joe on the project, who often retrieved from Mars materials and parts from old electronic equipment. Zelda and James spent countless hours in the laboratory with Manfred and George, supervising, suggesting, experimenting with a horde of scientists and engineers.

In an incredibly short time, all was ready for a shake-down run. Bontor on Moon Central had monitored the project through the Moon Central computer and he asked if he could join them at the test site on Olympus Mons.

As the equipment was flown to the test site, James took one last precaution. From his headquarters, he made a general broadcast requesting all residents on Mars to don space suits, then explained the possible results of the test to take place.

They grouped on the crest of Olympus Mons, then activated the generator and projector.

Within minutes, they were enclosed in a giant dome.

In earlier experiments, James and his crew had generated oxygen with electrolytic converters in the Sea of Clavius where they had managed to create an acceptable atmpsohere up to ten thousand feet. They had planted, at one mile intervals, atmospheric testers with automatic transmitters reporting to Computer Central on Mars.

Manfred had to determine if the dome was higher than ten thousand feet so he told teams to board flitters, each of which was equipped with a little dome neutralizer.

293

Earth - Mars

"Measure the height of the dome," Manfred instructed. "Do not go through it. Go in opposite directions and be sure that our calculations are correct. We wish to know if the entire planet is enclosed."

"We will keep in touch through our transceivers," Zelda said. The flitters rose slowly, cautiously. In his flitter, Manfred read the altimeter at 20,000. He alone touched the button to activate the dome neutralizer. Nothing happened. At 30,000 feet, his little flitter touched the dome.

Manfred pushed the activater for the dome neutralizer and it slid through the barrier like a hot knife through butter. He looked below him. The dome was intact. He could not tell where he had passed through it.

With a great sigh of relief, he landed gently on the exterior of the dome. "If it didn't work," he thought," we would have been prisoners permanently in the dome."

He touched the activater once again and the flitter sank through the dome, which sealed itself above him. As he flew back to Olympus Mons, he radioed his success and asked if the planet was completely enclosed.

"I set the altimeter at zero on the peak of Olympus Mons which is 87,000 feet above the mean surface. That means the top of the dome should be 117,000 feet high. I hope we got this thing completely around the planet!"

"It is completely around Mars!" Zelda reported. "The dome forms a perfect circle. We should be getting atmosphere readings from the instruments."

"Manfred," James called. "Let's put atmosphere gas testers on all the high peaks as well as the mean surface levels. The computer will then determine when the atmosphere is safe and the amount of each gas that is present."

"As far as that goes," Mike cut in, "we might just

Independence

stir up a bacteria or a life form not known to us. Let's put a complete package of testing equipment at those locations and tie them into the computer along with the cameras."

"Excellent ideas" Manfred agreed. "James, that falls into your camp. Zelda! George! Let's get back to the space station. I want to have another try at that psionic brain."

Everyone burst into laughter. James remarked,

"The good doctor has developed the proper space attitude: problem solved, forget it, go on to the next. I'll bet he will solve that one too."

The flitters sped apart; George, Zelda and Manfred to the Space Station, James to Mars Central, Mike and Joe to the North and South Poles.

****

Zelda notified the President that an atmosphere was being established on Mars, information he was greatly relieved to hear.

"Zelda," he began, "this is difficult to say. As far as the Commission Eleven is concerned, support is turning away from space exploration. Some of the people are interested in it, but the majority show a disinterested apathy and funding is less available. Many feel that the costs have been too high."

"I'm sorry to hear that and I don't pretend to understand it, Mr. President, but I shall pass the word along to James at Mars Central. I hope that we can maintain trading privileges. The corporations will not like it a bit. What about the Moon and this Station? What will happen to us?"

"We will keep the Moon under our protection and will provide supplies. I suggest that you acquire enough

Earth - Mars

fuel to establish your orbit around Mars. I shall ship it during the next two weeks, before the Commission meets." Good luck to all of you," he said and he signed off.

Zelda arranged a conference connection and warned them of the impending bad news from the President.

"Good!" James said sharply. "Most of us have been talking about severing Earth connections. We have an atmosphere and it is working. Trade levels are greater from us to them. We have minerals, metals and a developing agriculture. Let them go."

"I share your feelings," Bontor said on Moon Central, "but I guess I'm stuck here. Always remember I will be available whenever I can help."

"I'll keep you informed of things here," Zelda offered and with mixed feelings, they signed off.

They gathered from every place on Mars; executives from corporate field offices, explorers from Phobos and Deimos, miners from the mountains and valleys. They activated portable dome homes around Mars Computer Central, close to 50,000 people. They all wanted a part in the formation of a Mars government and they all had transceivers to hear and to contribute when the opportunity arose.

James was the moderator, a spokesman who had thought and talked and considered all possibilities for a long time. He opened the all channel transmission switch.

"We propose," he began, "the adoption of the same Constitution and the Bill of Rights that form the basis of the government of the United States. We believe that law is a necessity if accepted by the majority of the people and if the spirit of the law is considered, and the circumstance of an individual instance. The spirit and the letter of the law to carry equal weight.

The original ten commandments given to Moses,

Independence

which we acknowledge, cannot be considered in the spirit of evolution, social change or circumstance. We will form no government until you, the people, feel the need for one, and that will be kept at a minimum.

In the interval existing until nominations are made to represent us to off-worlders, and to settle disputes on-world, we ask you now to name two people to temporarily give guidance.

Your transceiver will record your indiviual vote for two temporary representatives and the count shall be made in the main computer during the next ten minutes. Thank you."

The tally produced two names, James and Zelda.

James opened his switch and thanked them.

"We will keep you informed of all actions taken by us in your behalf. Keep your printers and your display units on permanently. If you need assistance, use the emrgency button on your transceiver.

Think carefully how you wish to be governed, what laws you want to initiate. We can expect no aid from Earth unless we pay for it. The impact on our industry will be great, for you are, at this moment, your own corporation.

I shall inform the President that we have seceded from the United States and the Earth.

We are on our own."

※※※※※※※※※※※※※※

The Obsidian Planet turned slowly on its axis in orbit around the sun. The library, with no human caretakers, accumulated data from all transmissions. The primary system was backed up by a secondary system, but only minor gltches had occurred. The system was working perfectly.

Earth - Mars

The independence of the Martian Colony was duly registered in the historical and technological progress of humanity and the library hummed along, unnoticed by off-world or world communities.